GOOD INTENTIONS

JAMES P. SUMNER

GOOD INTENTIONS

Fifth Edition published in 2021 by Both Barrels Publishing

Copyright © James P. Sumner 2016

Editing and Cover Design by: bothbarrelsauthorservices.com

ISBNs:
978-1-914191-20-6 (Paperback)

Visit the author's website: jamespsumner.com

My own new chapter...

GOOD INTENTIONS

ADRIAN HELL: BOOK 6

1

I snap my eyes open and gasp in a desperate breath. I bolt upright.

What the fuck just happened?

I glance around, but nothing looks familiar. I check my arms. There aren't any tubes or needles. There's no window in front of me. No audience. The floors, the walls, and the ceiling are pure white. There's a faint buzzing of lights somewhere overhead.

I put a hand to my chest, searching for the reassurance of my heartbeat.

Wait...

Oh, *there* it is!

Okay, so I'm not dead.

First of all—yes! I'm *not* dead!

Second of all—not to sound ungrateful, but *how* am I not dead, exactly? The last thing I remember was getting the lethal injection. I'm pretty sure that was meant to kill me. The clue is in the name, right?

I sigh. One thing at a time, Adrian.

I lie back down. It feels comfortable and soft. I move my hands and legs. I'm not tied to anything. I lift up the sheets. I'm wearing light green scrubs.

So, is this a hospital?

It doesn't look like one. I can't even see a door... just plain, white walls all around me. No equipment beeping, no clipboards, no doctors or nurses. Just me in a room, slightly confused.

I stay still for a few moments, breathing in and out, relishing the air entering my body. It's weird, doing something I'd already come to terms with giving up. I had prepared myself for the inevitable. I felt ready to die. I wasn't thrilled about it, obviously, but I figured I had it coming after everything that's happened. And I don't just mean in the Oval Office. I mean over the last fifteen years of killing people for a living. You don't get your own cloud, a halo, and a set of wings for that shit. You get fire, brimstone, and a pitchfork straight up the ass.

Which brings me back to my original question. How am I not dead? Was I spared by some miraculous, inexplicable twist of fate? Or am I *actually* dead, and this is just some crazy, vivid afterlife hallucination?

Oh, God, I'm not in the final season of *Lost*, am I? Fuck...

Okay, focus.

I examine my extremities. Everything seems okay.

I look around the bed. I'm definitely not plugged into anything.

I put my hand to my chest again, feeling the steady thump of my heart.

Definitely breathing. Just making sure...

I throw the covers back. I swing my legs over the side and place my feet on the clean, tiled floor.

"Ah, shit, that's cold!"

I stand slowly and pace around in a small circle, making sure I don't fall over or throw up.

Yeah, I'm fine.

I close my eyes, take in a slow, almost meditative breath, and then re-open them. I look around the room once more but this time with a composed, expert eye. There *must* be a door somewhere, even if it's well hidden. I make my way along the walls, all around the room. I move my hands carefully across the surface, feeling for anything camouflaged by the layout, like a door or window or switch. Anything.

It takes me a few minutes, but I eventually arrive back where I started. No luck.

What the hell? How did I get in here if there's no door?

Okay, that's... strange. But I'm not too concerned. End of the day, if I can't easily get *out*, chances are no one can easily get *in*. At least not without me noticing. No, I'm more bothered about who put me in here. Who's watching me? I mean, come on—there's no way whoever did this isn't keeping tabs on me, right? So, where is it? Where's the camera?

I check the room again—the ceiling, in the corners. I check the walls for any security panels I might have missed the first time around. I check the bed, the floor, myself...

Nothing. No sign of anything.

Huh. That's fucking weird. Why would anyone imprison me somewhere like *this* and not keep an eye on me?

I sigh.

Whatever. I'll just add it to the list of shit that doesn't make sense at the moment.

I have an overwhelming urge to call out, but I stop

myself. I physically bite my tongue to stop words escaping. That would be the worst thing I could do. Just because no one's watching doesn't mean they're not listening. If they can't see me, they might not know I'm awake yet, which means I could still have some element of surprise. Besides, crying out is a sign of weakness and fear. I'm neither weak nor afraid, but I don't mind admitting that I'm starting to get a little worried. I've gone from being dead to being alive to essentially being a prisoner, all in the space of about five minutes. Something isn't right...

I continue to gaze around in search of any clue as to what's going on. The walls are clean. There's nothing on the floor. There's nothing on the—

Wait a minute.

I stretch up and touch the ceiling with my fingertips.

Jesus, that's a bit low, isn't it?

And it's not the same as the other surfaces. The walls are solid and sturdy, made from thick white paneling, and the ceramic-tiled floor is cold and harsh. But this feels fragile, temporary, like plywood painted a glossy white to blend in.

Hmmm...

I stand on the bed, hunching low, pressed against the ceiling. I slam my fist against it a couple of times. It sounds hollow and weak. I reckon one good knock and...

I slam my hand a third time. A thin panel flies up and away to the side, revealing a network of metal beams forming a grid a few feet above me.

Jackpot!

I reckon these beams will take my weight. They look sturdy enough. I stand straight and reach up. I'm just a bit too short. I compose myself, then jump up on the spot. I manage to grab one, and I try hoisting myself up, but I struggle to find the necessary strength. I hang down for a moment and catch my breath, then I swing my body back and forth slightly to generate some momentum before trying again.

This time, I manage to climb up onto it.

The beam's narrow but strong. The thick metal girder is colder than the tiles were. Carefully, slowly, I stand, balancing sideways with my feet at ten and two and my arms out to the side. I look around. The beams seem to cover the same area as the room, but beyond that is spacious and mostly empty in every direction, like a massive warehouse or an aircraft hangar, shrouded in darkness.

Okay, now what, smartass?

I shuffle along toward the middle, where there's a cross-junction of beams. It'll be easier to stand on that while I'm working out my next move. I crouch, place a hand down next to me for stability, and look around. Despite the surrounding gloom, I can see faint traces of light ahead of me. I can't make it out from here, but it could be an EXIT sign above a door, maybe? Any light is better than none though, so that's where I'm heading.

Now I just need to get down...

I stand cautiously and shuffle along, minding my step and making my way to the nearest edge. I peer over at the floor below. It's about ten feet, I reckon, which could be worse. I crouch again, place both hands to my right, and drop down, twisting and hanging from the side. I glance down again.

Ah, piece of cake!

I let go and drop the last couple of feet, landing quietly on the cold floor of what definitely looks like an aircraft hangar.

CLICK-CLICK.

I know that sound...

I feel the barrel of a gun press gently against the base of my skull.

Shit.

I hold my hands out to the sides, palms open.

"Don't move," says a male voice I don't recognize. "Turn around slowly."

I sigh. I start turning my body clockwise and get maybe halfway around before making my move. It's an instinctive reaction. I didn't consciously choose to do it, but when someone puts a gun on me from behind, there's only one thing I'm ever going to do.

I whip around, fast and sudden, and bring my hands up. I grab the guy's wrists, forcing him away from me. As I complete my turn and face him, I slam my palm up against the underside of his fist, knocking the gun loose from his grip and into the air. I catch it with my right as I jab his nose with my left. Not hard enough to break it but enough to distract him and maybe make his eyes water a little, ultimately giving him something to think about other than me. I level the gun at his forehead, ensuring the safety is off and my finger is resting against the trigger guard.

I smile. "I moved. Sorry."

I've never seen the guy before. He's a little shorter than me, lean, and toned. He's wearing jeans and a jacket with fashionable sneakers. He's holding his nose and looks pissed.

Well, it serves him right. Sneaking up on me like—

CLICK-CLICK.

CLICK-CLICK.

Oh, come on!

I glance left and right. Two more men have appeared, and they're aiming guns unwaveringly at my head.

The guy in front of me flashes a cocky smile. "You shouldn't have moved."

I flick my eyebrows in agreement. "Yeah, fair point."

I put the safety on with my thumb, hook my finger in the trigger guard, spin it in my hand, and present him with the butt of his gun. He takes it calmly, and I hold my hands out to the sides again. "Sorry about that. Can't blame a guy for trying, though, right?"

He promptly knocks the safety off again and places the barrel against my forehead. "Have you got the silliness out of your system now?"

I shrug. "Honestly? I'm not sure. I was contemplating taking *this* guy's gun..." I nod to my left. "...and shooting you in the knee as I elbow *this* guy..." I nod to my right. "...in the throat. Then, seeing as you all have the same model Sig Sauer, I figured I would take the mags from two of them and head for the exit, armed with the third... see what happens."

He raises an eyebrow and exchanges a look with his friends. I take it as uncertainty over whether I'm joking.

I'm not.

I smile. "But that's an awful lot of effort, isn't it? How about *I* promise to behave if *you* all promise not to shoot me until I speak to the man in charge."

He raises an eyebrow. "What makes you think you're not?"

I smile again. "I'm sorry, friend. Don't take this the wrong way, but you're not management material. Forgetting how quickly I took your gun off you just then, people in charge don't get sent in first. So, come on. Who's calling the shots around here? I figure I owe them a drink."

Footsteps echo in the darkness to my right. They're slow, patient. Whoever it is, they're in no hurry. This could be them now...

No one moves or speaks as the sound grows louder. A figure steps into the faint glow of the overhead lights. He's wearing black leather shoes and a brilliant white suit. He stops a few feet in front of me, just behind the guy with the sore nose, and regards me silently, expressionless.

Huh...

My eyes go a little wide with surprise. "Fuck me... Colonel Sanders? What the hell are *you* doing here? I thought you said your offer had expired on account of me taking too long to think about it?"

He takes a deep breath, stroking the loose skin under his chin. "We're not completely without heart. I was perhaps a little unfair pressuring you like that, under the circumstances. You have potential, so I thought I'd take a chance on you. How are you feeling?"

I shrug. "I'm not dead, which is nice. Have I got you to thank for that?"

He nods. "You have, and you're welcome. We replaced some of the guards and the doctors in that facility with our own men. I have to say, it all went better than I had hoped. Your execution made for good viewing."

"Glad I could entertain. So, how *exactly* did you..."

He smiles politely, without humor, as if he was expecting the question. "We switched the chemicals usually found in the lethal injection with a neuro-inhibitor known as TTX."

I frown. "Isn't that... oh, what's it called? Tetro-something?"

He nods. "That's right. Tetrodotoxin. It's extracted from the pufferfish, and with just the right dosage, it can essentially simulate death. You were officially pronounced dead in front of President Schultz a little over forty-eight hours ago. You were then given an antitoxin shortly afterward to counter the effects. We brought you here to recover."

"Right. Well... thanks for not killing me. Sort of." I glance around. "And where's *here*, exactly?"

"That's not important. What's important is *this*."

He nods subtly. The guy on my left grabs the back of my head, forcing me to look down. I feel something cold press against—

"Ow! Hey!"

I spin around and push him away, then clasp my neck. That piece of shit just injected me with something!

"Calm down, Adrian," says the man in white.

I turn back to face him, frowning. "What did you just do?"

"We simply implanted a small tracking device into you. It's accurate to about three feet. It's nothing to worry about. It's for your protection, more than anything. Everyone who works for The Order have them. It allows us to monitor your progress while on a mission and assist you, should things go wrong."

"Uh-huh. You forget, I used to work for the CIA. When people inject you with shit and say it's for your own good, it usually means it's not."

He nods, as if he understood my point of view but ultimately could care less about it. "I appreciate this must be... overwhelming for you, Adrian. I know it's a lot, asking you to trust me, but you're a member of The Order of Sabbah now. From this moment on, this is the only life you have, and you need to come to terms with that."

"Yeah, yeah—fine. Just next time, if you need to stick anything in me, can you just ask? Or at least buy me a drink first..."

He nods, smiling humorlessly. "Of course. Now I have to be honest—getting out of that room and giving you the tracking device were just the first part of a test. An initiation, if you will. There's no doubting your skills, Adrian, but we haven't existed for so long by letting just anyone join our ranks."

I raise an eyebrow. "First part?"

"Yes. The second part will begin shortly." He nods to the man on my left.

"Wait, what do you mean? Can someone just tell me what the f—"

2

I open my eyes slowly. It takes a moment for my vision to focus. I put a hand to the back of my neck and scratch where I was injected.

Ow!

My head's throbbing from where I was hit. I'm definitely shooting the bastard who was standing behind me next time I see him! Piece of shit, thinking he can—

Hang on...

What's that noise? It took a minute to register, but now that it has, it's deafening! It sounds mechanical, like an engine. A really big engine...

I look around. I'm in a large, empty space, sitting on a bench that runs along the full length of one side. I glance down and see I'm dressed in unmarked khaki coveralls. Sitting opposite me are two men. I haven't seen either of them before. They're dressed in similar outfits, and they're both holding automatic rifles. Carbines, I think—hard to tell from over here.

I close my eyes and sigh. I'm fairly certain I'm in the back of a cargo plane, and judging by the noise, I would say there's a good chance I'm not on the ground.

I look over at the men facing me. "Hey, where are we?"

They exchange a glance and smile but don't answer.

I frown. "Hey! *Assholes!* I said, where are we?"

The one on the left stands, adjusts his grip on the rifle, and walks steadily toward me. He stops a few feet away.

Oh, yeah. *Definitely* a carbine...

He smiles. "You're in a plane!"

I roll my eyes. "No shit. Wanna tell me why?"

He reaches behind him and produces a brown envelope, which he throws unceremoniously into my lap. He nods at it and walks back over to sit next to his friend.

I open it and take out a black and white eight-by-ten. Looks like an image taken via satellite. It's a little grainy but otherwise good quality. It shows two men standing side-by-side, seemingly deep in conversation, in a clearing surrounded by trees and undergrowth.

I look across at them and shrug. "Who are these guys?"

The man on the right leans forward. "The short one on the left is who we want you to kill. The one on the right is his head of security. You'll probably need to go through him to get to your target."

I look down at the picture again. The guy on the right is probably twice as tall and twice as wide as the guy on the left. And the difference is all muscle. It's practically bursting through his shirt.

Great.

They both glance to the side and place a hand to their ear. I'm guessing they're receiving a message over comms. A moment or two later, they stand and walk over to me. "On your feet," says the first guy. "Turn around."

I fold the picture up and stuff it inside my pocket. Then I stand—not because they told me to but because my options for rebellion are vastly limited when I'm on a plane, in the air. A stray bullet would kill us all, and I don't know how many other men are on board. It's not worth the risk.

"Arms to the side," says the second guy.

I move them and feel a backpack slide over my shoulders. It's bulky. Actually, it feels more like a...

I sigh.

Ah, shit.

It's a parachute, isn't it?

I sense this isn't going to end well.

"Turn around," says the first guy again.

I do, and one of them lets his gun hang loose on its strap as he reaches over and secures the backpack around my waist. He then moves over to the rear of the plane and grabs a lever on the side. He throws it down, and a mechanical whirring sounds out, loud enough to be heard over the roar of the engines. The floor of the tail lowers slowly to reveal a mostly clear sky rushing by outside. A scattering of light cloud surrounds us, but there's still a good level of visibility. He holds onto a handle next to him, fighting against the pull of the wind.

I take a small step forward and peer over the edge.

Fuck me sideways! We must be twenty thousand feet up, easily!

I look over my shoulder at the guy still standing with me. "What the hell's going on? If this is a contract, where's my briefing? And my weapon?"

He smiles and shakes his head. Without warning, he

grabs me with both hands and shoves me backward. I'm not prepared for it and lose my footing, stumbling down and...

Shit!

The plane rushes up, away from me. The cold wind bites at my face, forcing me to squint against the sheer speed of it.

Sonofa*bitch*!

??:??

I landed in a fucking tree! Seriously!

A wind picked up and blew me off course, and I came down over some forest. The parachute caught on the branches of a big-ass tree, so I'm now hanging maybe twenty feet above the ground, suspended by the straps. I have no weapons of any kind, no immediately obvious way down from here that won't sting like a bitch, and all I have to go on is a picture of some guy and his beefed-up bodyguard. They could be anywhere in the hundreds of miles of forest I'm dangling above...

I'm starting to think the lethal injection maybe wasn't so bad after all.

Okay, let's think about this for a—

Whoa!

One of the branches just snapped! I've dropped a couple of feet. Must have snagged on one lower down. Think I jolted my shoulder too. I'm trying to rotate it as best I can and loosen it up, but it hurts like hell.

I close my eyes for a moment and take in a few deep breaths while trying to remain still. I don't want to fall from this height. The risk of injury would be high, and I'm in the middle of nowhere. The last thing I want is to have my movement impeded in any way.

I reopen them, breathing slowly. I'm calm. I'm a professional, after all. I've been in much shittier situations than this. I just need to—

Whoa!

Shit!

Ow!

Fuck!

Ugh!

I'm lying flat on my back, staring up at the treetops and the clear blue skies beyond. The ground feels soft. I move my hands around next to me. Yeah... twigs, leaves, and damp earth.

Oh, man, that sucked.

I raise my head slightly and look down my front. Both straps broke. My back is sore and I'm a little winded, but thankfully, I don't feel too bad. Hell of a fall, though.

I prop myself up on an elbow and twist my body, slowly rising to my feet. I stretch everything, take a breath, and turn in a slow circle. I hear birds tweeting above me. Aside from the occasional noise of whatever wildlife is nearby, it's unnervingly quiet.

Where the hell am I?

Okay, think. It's humid. My first thought is that I'm in a jungle, but there's no sound of water, and the trees look too... green. It's hot, but it's not tropical. These trees see their fair share of rain, I reckon.

I glance at the ground, searching for any signs of tracks. It doesn't look as if any animals or people have passed through here in a while, either. I'm nowhere wild... so I'm going with forest. It's a dense tree line, so it makes sense. If that's the case, I reckon that puts me somewhere in the region of twenty miles from civilization. And that's a rough guess. I'm far from an expert on the great outdoors. The Discovery Channel was always Josh's thing, not mine.

Shit! Josh!

I haven't had time to stop and think about much of anything since waking up after my fake execution. It sounds awful, but I completely forgot about him. I can't imagine how he must be feeling right about now. He thinks I'm dead...

I'm such a prick for putting him through that. I should have told him. I should have found some way to let him know that—

You know what? Now probably isn't the time.

I look up, find the sun, and set off walking toward it. I don't know what time it is or where I am, so I'm either heading north or south. I guess it doesn't really matter which one. Everywhere leads somewhere, right?

??:??

My body clock isn't what it used to be, but I think I've been walking for about an hour. I've kept a steady pace, only pausing for a few moments occasionally to make sure I'm still traveling in a straight line. I'm following a faint path through the trees and plants. In the last ten minutes or so, I've been able to hear the gentle sound of running water in the distance. I've covered maybe three miles now, so I'm hopefully closing in on somewhere.

I tread carefully, trying to minimize the noise of my foot-steps. I'm always glancing left and right ahead of me, alert for any sign of a threat. Bottom line is, The Order sent me here to kill someone, and no matter how far off course I was blown, I can't be too far away from where they intended for me to land.

With a bit of luck, I haven't been walking in the opposite direction to my target for the last hour...

CRACK.

What was that?

I drop to a crouch, placing a hand on the ground for balance as I hold my breath.

I heard rustling over to my right.

I wait patiently.

CRACK.

There it is again.

Might be an animal? No idea. I don't know where I am. Could be anything from a squirrel to a grizzly.

Too quiet for anything bigger than me, though, which is a small comfort.

I shuffle toward the nearest tree trunk, rest against it, and peer around. The sound of water is more prominent now. There might be—

There!

Through the gaps in the trees, I can see a figure moving confidently across my line of sight. It's hard to see, but... yeah, it's a woman. Small. Can't see her features.

Where are you going, lady?

I stand, staying low, and make my way quietly toward her. I pause behind each trunk that's big enough to cover me.

I don't want to scare her and definitely don't want to hurt her—she's no threat to me—but she's the first sign of life I've seen since I was pushed out of the airplane. I have to take this opportunity to find out where I am.

I slowly circle away from her to my left. I need to see if

she's alone, and I need to be able to approach her openly, so she can see I mean her no harm.

She stops and crouches on the spot, looking at something. I make my way farther round and draw level, directly ahead of her—maybe a hundred feet. I'm low, hidden behind another tree. I have a better view of her now. She's carrying a basket and picking fruit. She's wearing a long dress, which is fitted tight to her legs. She turns her head as she puts something in the basket, which she then places beside her on the ground. Her skin is tanned, a light brown. I can see from her eyes that she's Asian. She has a headscarf around her and a garment covering her top half, like a poncho.

I let out a short breath. I have to play this right.

I wait until she's picking fruit again and stand. I hold my arms out to the sides and walk slowly toward her. I smile and try to appear as friendly as I can.

She looks up at me. Our eyes meet for a brief moment. I stop no more than thirty feet from her. She frowns for a second and then her eyes go wide. Her mouth opens and I see her body tense. She takes a deep breath.

She's going to scream, isn't she?

Shit.

I don't think. I just run, lunging as I stretch out to her. I reach her at the exact moment the sound passes her lips. I clasp my hand over her mouth as I dive forward, and we both hit the ground, landing awkwardly next to one another. My shoulder takes the brunt of my weight, but I ignore the pain. She's on her back and doesn't try to fight me off. She's probably paralyzed with fear, the poor thing.

I feel really bad about this.

I kneel next to her and look down. Her dark, unblinking eyes are accentuated by her tanned skin. Despite her ethnicity, I still have no clue where I am, besides somewhere East of India.

I take a deep breath. "It's okay. It's okay... I'm not going to hurt you."

She screams into my hand. Her breath is hot on my palm.

"I'm sorry about this, but I really need your help, okay?"

I try to keep my tone calm and mellow. I'm not sure if she can even understand me, but communication isn't always about words. If the sound of your voice isn't threatening, it doesn't matter what you're saying. People will be less inclined to perceive you as a danger.

Her breathing slows and her face relaxes.

I nod. "That's it. It's okay, I promise. I'm not going to hurt you. I just need your help. Can you understand me?"

She's still for a moment, her eyes darting around in all directions, still panicking. Finally, she nods.

Phew!

"Good. Now I'm going to move my hand. Please don't scream. I'm lost and I need your help. That's all. You have my word I won't hurt you."

She nods again.

"Promise you won't scream?"

Another nod.

"Okay, here goes..."

I gradually lift my hand from her mouth. She takes some quick, shallow breaths. For a moment, it looks as if she's going to shout out, but she doesn't. She uses her hands to scramble backward and put a little distance between us. I don't move to follow her. I want her to feel safe. She pushes herself up, brings her knees to her chest, and hugs them.

I sit down in front of her and do the same. "I'm sorry about that. I'm just not sure where I am. I didn't want you to make any noise in case there was anyone around who might be dangerous. I hope I haven't hurt you?"

She shakes her head.

"Good. What's your name?"

She goes to speak but stops herself. It's as if something inside her caught the words before they could escape.

"It's okay. I'm a friend. My name's Adrian."

I extend my hand, not thinking for a moment that she would accept it. But much to my surprise, she does. She shakes it gently. "I... am... H-Hong Yun."

I smile. "That's a lovely name. It's nice to meet you."

She nods but says nothing.

"Tell me, Hong Yun, where are we?"

She frowns. "You not know?"

I shake my head. "Not a clue."

"This is Vietnam."

I raise my eyebrows, unable to hide the surprise. A forest in Vietnam, eh?

"Where do you live? Is it nearby?"

She nods and points to her right. "Not far."

"Can you take me there?"

She shakes her head. It's a rapid movement this time, and I see the look in her eyes change. I see fear. "No! You no come with me!"

I hold my hands up. "Okay, okay—I'm sorry. I won't come with you." I slowly reach inside my pocket and take out the picture I was given on the plane. "I'm looking for somebody. Maybe you've seen him?"

I open it up and hand it to her. She takes it and looks down. I see that same fear in her eyes again. She says nothing but desperately claws her way to her feet and sets off running away from me.

Shit!

I jump up and run after her. I quickly catch up to her and place my hand over her mouth again, just in time to muffle the scream she lets out. I stand behind her, holding her close to me with my arm, allowing her to calm down.

"Please, I'm *not* going to hurt you. I need your help." I let her go and spin her around to face me. "Do you know the man in that picture?"

She nods.

"Who is he?"

"H-he is... Mr. Way."

"Mr. Way? Okay. And what does Mr. Way do, exactly?"

She looks away from me and stares at the ground. Her eyes well with tears, and she begins to shake as the unrestrained emotion spills out of her.

Oh, for fuck's sake. As if I don't have enough on my plate, I now have a crying woman to deal with! I'm not trained for this shit.

I rub my eyes and forehead, then put an arm tentatively around her. "It's okay... you don't have to say anything."

And I mean it. She doesn't need to. Her tears say it all. A young, attractive woman in the middle of nowhere, in Vietnam, near where a man I've been sent to kill is supposedly based. Whatever he does, I suspect it's not good, and she's clearly not happy about being a part of it.

After a few moments, she looks up at me. She stares right into my eyes, as if searching them for something. "What is it you want Mr. Way for?"

I purse my lips together and tense my jaw. I take a deep breath. I wouldn't normally be this honest—I don't want to scare her any more than I already have—but seeing how she reacted when she saw the picture of him, I'm going to take a chance.

"Hong Yun... I'm here to kill him."

She goes through a whole catalogue of emotions. She frowns, as if trying to hold back tears. She looks concerned, surprised, afraid... perhaps even happy, at one point. But then the tears start to flow again. This time, however, she buries her head into my chest and throws her arms around me. She shakes uncontrollably as she sobs.

That reaction speaks for itself, I guess.

I stand, my arms out to the side, with a woman I've just met crying on me. I stare ahead until my vision blurs. The last forty-eight hours fade away, and I'm left with a familiar and comforting sense of purpose.

I don't know who this Mr. Way is, but I know all I need to about him.

That piece of shit is a dead man.

3

??:??

My God, it's hot! The tree line has thinned, and there's less cover than before. The sun is beating down relentlessly, and it feels as if it's sucking the air out of the forest. I've rolled the sleeves of my coveralls up over my forearms in a futile attempt to cool down, but it still feels like I'm walking through the Amazon!

I've managed to convince Hong Yun to show me where she lives—where Mr. Way is based. If I can get a good look at the place, I'll be able to plan my attack.

I absently scratch the back of my neck, where that asshole injected the tracking device into me earlier. I'm guessing Colonel Sanders is looking on, sat behind a fancy desk, watching a satellite feed where they had me when I first woke up.

I never thought they would have me jumping through hoops—or out of planes—and taking all these tests. I figured the fact they approached me to join The Order meant I was already in. But *no*... I have to prove myself. *Prove myself?* I've been doing this shit for nearly fifteen years! Everyone knows I'm the best in the business. Hell, they wouldn't have come to me in the first place if they didn't think that, surely? Having to audition for them is almost insulting. I know they saved my life, but even so...

Hong Yun is walking a few paces in front of me. She hasn't said much since we set off. I tried to find out whereabouts in Vietnam we are, but other than *north of Ho Chi Minh City*, I didn't get much out of her.

I offered to carry her basket for her, which she reluctantly agreed to. After the first five minutes, she said I could help myself to a piece of fruit. I graciously accepted with no hesitation. I'm so hungry! I haven't eaten since I died...

It feels weird saying that.

A handful of berries later, I'm craving a steak and a Bud like you wouldn't believe, but I have to block thoughts like that out for now. I have more important things to worry about.

We've been walking for maybe twenty minutes. I see a clearing up ahead, and Hong Yun slows down.

I draw level with her. "Is this it? Are we here?"

She glances at me and nods. "I... I can't—"

I hold a hand up and smile. "It's okay... I know you can't take me in yourself." I hand the basket back to her. "You've been a great help. Thank you. And I'm sorry again for scaring you back there."

A smile flashes across her face, and she looks at the ground. "No apologize, Adrian. You... a... kind man."

I shrug and try to hide how uncomfortable I feel receiving a compliment. She looks as if she wants to say something else, but she's stopping herself.

"Hong Yun, what is it?"

She sighs. "Are you really here to kill Mr. Way?"

I clench my jaw muscles and nod curtly. "Yes."

"W-why?"

Huh...

Well, I didn't expect that. I had the impression earlier that she would be glad when this guy's dead, but now she's questioning my motives? And you know the worst part? I don't really have an answer. How bad is that? I mean, what can I say? *Because someone told me to?*

I stroke my chin. There's nearly three days' worth of stubble there, and it grates against my hand as I contemplate my answer. But as soon as I start thinking, my mind rushes off on a tangent...

What the fuck am I doing here? I've never carried out a contract I didn't research beforehand. And by me, I mean Josh, obviously. But in all my life, going back to the Army, to the CIA, to D.E.A.D... I can't remember a time when I've ever fired a bullet I wasn't completely certain needed to be fired. And now here I am, blindly following the instructions of a guy I don't even know, who runs an organization I didn't even believe existed until a few days ago. Granted, the guy saved my life, but what has he done since then? Imprisoned me and thrown me out of a plane? I'm angry with myself for neglecting to notice how much of a prick this guy actually is.

Hong Yun is staring at me expectantly. Her brown eyes are wide and innocent.

I sigh. "Tell me... is he a bad man?"

She nods slowly.

I shrug. "What other reason do I need?"

She smiles momentarily and stares at the ground again.

Well, at least *she* believes me, even if *I* don't.

I place a hand on her shoulder. "Look, you'd better head back before you raise any suspicions."

She nods again. "The camp is not far." She points ahead. "Just past clearing."

"Thank you."

"Be careful. There are... many men and... many... guns."

Oh.

I chuckle and wave my hand dismissively. "It'll be *fine*..."

With basket in hand, she turns and scurries off through the clearing, bearing left. I watch her until she's out of sight.

So... many men and many guns, eh?

Sounds like fun!

??:??

I decided to head left before the clearing and make my way clockwise around the perimeter in a wide arc. I reckoned the place where the path opened out would serve as the main entrance to the camp, so I would essentially be walking up to the front door and knocking if I followed Hong Yun. I wouldn't normally worry about that, but I have no weapons, so I figured discretion is the better part of valor.

It took me over ten minutes of careful maneuvering through thick bushes and tree lines before I was able to locate the camp's borders. A tall fence, shrouded in forest, runs along the left side and, presumably, all the way around. I can't get too close, but I've found a spot a few hundred yards farther on that gives me a good view. I'm crouching behind a small mound of broken trunk and trampled shrubbery, looking through the fence at the camp within.

It's not what I expected, if I'm honest. The place looks more like a military base. There are guard towers... a vehicle pool... barracks... lots of men with guns patrolling the compound... look-outs—the works!

Who the hell *is* this guy? And more importantly, how the hell am I meant to—

Oh, shit!

I hold my breath. A guy's stopped right in front of me! He's maybe six feet away, stood with his back to me. He's dressed casually, wearing jeans, boots, and a thin sweater underneath a thick, sleeveless hunting jacket. Christ, he must be melting wearing that out here!

He turns slightly, and I catch a glimpse of his gun. It looks like a variation of the old Vector SMG, but I've never seen this particular model before. The barrel is long and thin, with a disproportionately large suppressor attached to the end. It has a magazine sticking out of either side on a forty-five-degree angle.

I frown. It kind of looks like...

I squint and lean forward as much as I dare to get a closer look.

The guard turns again, momentarily stepping out of the shade of the trees and into the glare of the sun. The metallic weapon glimmers, and I can just about see a logo engraved on the side.

GlobaTech Industries.

Fuck! I *knew* I recognized the design. It's just like the AX-19 Oscar gave me a few days back. I wonder if Josh knows people like Mr. Way are using his weapons...

I shake my head to re-focus. That's a problem for another day. Well, it's not, actually. Not for me, anyway. I'm dead, remember?

Okay, so there are lots of guys, and they're all well-equipped with top of the range hardware...

Piece of cake!

First thing's first—how do I get in the damn place?

I slowly back away, dissolving silently into the forest. I continue left, keeping the fence visible. It takes me a good half-hour to make my way around the perimeter of the compound. I find a spot and crouch low behind a cluster of trees, almost directly opposite where I was before. On my left is the clearing that leads inside.

I hope Hong Yun is okay. No reason she wouldn't be, I guess, but my spider sense is tingling, and it's making me paranoid.

As I made my way around, I was looking for any gaps in the fence or any easy ways over it, but there was nothing. This place is locked down tight, which leaves me with few options. I have to hand it to The Order—if you want to be a member, you have to work for it!

Okay, think, Adrian. I need to get inside. I'm unarmed, so I can't exactly mount a frontal assault. I need a weapon, but the only place I'm going to find one is in there. I can't scale the fence because, as best I can tell, wherever I come out on the other side is in full view of someone...

Dammit! Think, Adrian... c'mon!

Wait...

No, that's just stupid.

I could always...

No, I couldn't. Shit.

Oh, hang on...

I could always...

Hmm...

Light bulb!

I search the ground around me and soon find what I'm looking for—a broken twig with a sharp edge. Without thinking, I run the splintered end over my palm and my cheek, hard and fast.

I wince. Shit, that stings!

I feel the warmth from the trickle of blood running out of each wound. Next, I get two handfuls of dirt from the ground and squeeze them in my fists. I rub them over my forearms and face. I dust off the excess, stand, and then take a few paces back and forth to practice my fake limp.

Okay, that should do it. I reckon I look suitably messed up.

If this works, I'm a genius.

If it doesn't, I'm dead.

I make my way slowly over to the clearing, trying my best to look out of breath and sore. I follow the path I saw Hong Yun take. It veers left slightly, and after a few moments, a guard post appears up ahead. A makeshift gate made from wire mesh between two metal poles on wheels blocks the way. There's an armed man standing on either side.

I approach them slowly, running through every possible outcome in my mind as I slip into character. They see me and exchange the briefest of glances, then raise their guns, aiming at me with an unnerving steadiness.

Showtime.

I thrust my arms into the air, then lower one immediately, as if forgetting a pain. "Oh my God, please help me! I'm..." I stand still for a moment, then drop heavily to one knee. "...I don't know... where..."

I fall flat on my face, eyes closed. It's a risk, but I think I did all right. Josh was always better at this than I was, but I can play a part well enough when I need to. As I lie here, listening to the hurried footsteps of the guards as they make their way over, it occurs to me that there weren't many things Josh *wasn't* better at than I was. He was smarter than me, better with computers, more organized, a better actor, more levelheaded... arguably the same taste in music... I'm *definitely* better at killing people, but that's hardly something to shout about, I guess.

Oh—here we go.

I feel them hook my arms and hoist me unceremoniously to my feet. I fight the urge to support my own weight, instead hanging loose in their grip. They're pretty strong, and they drag me easily over to the post, shouting to one another in a language I don't recognize. Strangely, it's not Vietnamese. At least, I don't think it is. They don't sound like Hong Yun did, anyway. But I can tell from their tone that they're concerned... maybe even a little afraid. That gives me something to go on. All these people, all these weapons, yet they're on edge when one beaten up, unarmed man collapses on their doorstep. Why so touchy?

I hear the gate roll open, and I'm dragged through. As it closes again, I notice another set of footsteps coming toward me.

More voices.

I think these two ass-hats holding me up are explaining to the new arrival what's happened. That might mean whoever's in front of me is in charge. Mr. Way? Nah, I doubt it. If he's the big cheese around here, he won't bother himself with shit like this.

I feel a hand grab my jaw and squeeze, making my face pucker. They lift my head and shake it back and forth.

Okay, okay—I'm up...

I slowly open my eyes.

Holy shit!

There's a guy's face inches from mine. And he's an ugly sonofabitch!

I twitch, startled. It isn't part of the act. "Wha-what's happening? Where am I?"

I watch as the guy in front of me narrows his eyes and stands straight. Jesus, he's a big bastard! He must be damn near seven feet tall!

I act drowsy and allow my head to droop, mainly because I'm not sure I can hide the frustration from my eyes. It's Way's head of security. I recognize him from the picture. And he's...

Shit!

The picture!

It's in my pocket! If they search me, I'm screwed!

The guards on either side of me let go of my arms. I drop to the ground and land on all fours. I tense, bracing for a kick to the ribs, but nothing comes. The head of security utters something and walks away. The two men standing with me start arguing.

I look up at one of them. "Where... am I?"

He turns to me and smiles. "You in *Hell*!"

Oh, man—that's disgusting! The teeth that aren't missing are yellow and black...

I sigh. "Oh, good. Glad I asked..."

They heave me back to my feet and march me across the open yard. This is my first real look inside the compound. I move only my eyes, keeping my head still, so I don't make it obvious that I'm scoping the place out.

It's big. There's a row of small, temporary housing units over on the right—maybe seven of them side by side. Each one could easily accommodate thirty people. They look like the ones GlobaTech have been shipping all over the world to help out after 4/17. In fact... yeah... they *are* the ones GlobaTech have been shipping out!

Whatever else Mr. Way is, he's a fucking thief! Wait 'til I tell Josh!

Oh, wait... I can't.

Damn it.

Lining both sides, probably every three or four hundred yards, is a guard tower. Crude wooden structures stand maybe fifteen feet high. There's a platform at the top, protected on all sides except the one that has a ladder leading down from it. I count seven of them on the left and nine on the right.

Directly across from me are a half-dozen 4×4s, parked at random angles in between a fuel dump and a small workshop.

Ahead of me, at the far end of the camp, is a large tent. The kind military generals used back in Roman times. To the side of it is a fenced-off area, maybe twenty feet square, full of grass and plants. I can see four women crouching as they tend to it, all of them dressed similar to Hong Yun.

I see movement on my right and glance over as the door to one of the housing units swings open. A woman steps out. Well, I say *a woman*, but she can't be older than twenty. If that.

I can't help it. I turn my head and body to get a proper look, intrigued, thinking the worst and reacting accordingly. I take slightly more of my own weight than before, so I'm not being dragged as much by Tweedledum and Tweedledee here. The young woman is wearing a bikini. She doesn't have much of a figure to speak of. She's slim, almost skinny. As we draw level, I see she actually looks borderline malnourished.

She doesn't look happy, either.

As we pass, the door opens again, and a man dressed the same as my escorts steps out. He's fastening his pants and has a satisfied, yet annoyingly arrogant smile on his face.

Oh. That doesn't—

"Hey!" I look at the guard to my right, eyebrows raised. He slaps me, forcing me to look forward. "Eyes down."

His English is passable, but it's definitely not his first language. He's not Vietnamese, but he has the same complexion and similar features. Chinese? No... they're still struggling after the attacks. Thai? Could be... but I don't think that's what they're speaking because I'd recognize the dialect. Korean? Hmm, probably not. The South is in the same position as China, and the North are unlikely to get involved in shit like this while they're still trying to take over the world. Or are they? I should probably ask about that. I wonder if Josh has managed to kick their asses yet?

Ah, forget it. I'm sure I'll find out soon enough. We're heading for the tent at the end, which must be where Mr. Way is. I guess I should get my story straight...

We stop outside the dusty gray tarpaulin structure. Each guard pulls a section back to reveal the interior, then they shove me through. I stumble inside. The sections drop back into place behind me, shutting out the natural light. There are plenty of standing lamps lighting up the place in here, though. There's a low humming coming from somewhere too—presumably from a generator.

There's a bed in one corner, a couple of tables in the middle serving as a desk, and a seating area to the other side, with a computer station in front of it. Behind one of the tables is Mr. Way. I recognize him immediately from his photo. He looks much older in person. The picture I was given was flattering. In reality, he looks as if he belongs in a care home. His skin is loose and mottled, and he looks frail, despite the liveliness in his eyes. He's wearing a baseball cap backward, which looks ridiculous. He's far too old to get away with dressing like that!

Standing beside him is the monster head of security.

He's wearing a T-shirt that looks three sizes too small—except it probably isn't. It's just that his arms are that big. His pants stretch over his legs in a similar way. He's leaning over, resting his palms flat on the desk. They appear deep in conversation, but they fall silent and look over as I step cautiously toward them. They exchange a nod, and Way shifts in his seat to look at me properly.

He looks me up and down, curiously. "Who are you?"

His accent is different again, but his grasp of the English language is far better than anyone else's around here. There might even be a hint of American in his tone. I'm not sure.

I take a deep breath. "I'm... I was out camping with a group of friends. We got separated when I fell. I stumbled on the ground and dropped down a small hill. I... I landed pretty bad. I lost my way, and now I don't know where they are, or even where *I* am. Thank God, I found this place. I really need your help getting back to—"

He holds up a hand, so I stop talking.

"I'm a businessman. A wealthy one. I didn't achieve that by trusting many people. I'm sure you understand..."

His bodyguard moves fast. He draws the gun he has holstered to his hip and aims it at me in a flash. He moves over to where I'm standing and places the barrel against my head.

I hold my hands up, feigning panic. "Oh my God! Please! No! I just want to find my friends, please! Don't kill me!"

I hate myself.

Way is smiling at me the way people do when they're confident that they know something you don't. He's sitting comfortably with his hands clasped in front of him, resting on the surface of the table. "No one camps in these woods, Mr. Mystery Man. I know that for a fact. It's why I built this operation here. We're all alone. For miles and miles. Which means *you're* all alone. So, you can either tell me the truth, or my associate here will put a bullet through your brain. Who are you? Really."

I stand tall and let out a heavy sigh. I glance sideways at the gun and the tall, horrible bastard holding it. Then I look across at Mr. Way—the smug little shit who thinks he's in charge, smiling at me as if I'm beneath him.

I lower my arms, pausing only to rub my eyes.

Here we go...

4

Mr. Way gestures to me with his hands. "I'm waiting, Mr. Mystery Man..."

I'm running everything through my head. Every move, every possible counter, every potential ending...

In most scenarios, I get shot. Which sucks.

I need to buy myself some time.

I keep my body still to make sure I do nothing that might provoke a pre-emptive bullet. I forget the act that got me this far and fix him with a cold, fearless stare. "What is this place?"

He laughs. "No, no, no—that's not how this works. *You* tell *me* what *I* want to know, not the other way around. You seem a little reluctant to tell me who you are, so let's try something else. Who sent you?"

I let out a small chuckle. "Heh... that's what I'd like to know! Listen, I'm gonna be straight with you, okay? I honestly don't know why I'm here or really who sent me. All

I know is someone, somewhere, thinks you're a piece of shit, and they've asked me to come down here and kill you."

A palpable silence falls. The tension is immediate and obvious. I feel as if my own heartbeat is audible. No one speaks, moves, or even blinks. Seconds tick by like hours. The gun pressed against my head remains steady. Way's eyes narrow.

Then he smiles.

Then he laughs.

"You a funny man, whoever you are!"

I shrug, a little confused. "Thanks?"

"Okay, Mr. Funny Man. I'll play along... out of curiosity." He gestures around him with his arms. "This is my home. It's where I run my business from."

I glance around. "It's a nice place. And what *is* your business, exactly?"

"I... work with people, shall we say? People—mostly men—from all over the world contact me, wanting other people—mostly women—who will provide a service. And for a modest price, I supply one to the other."

"Lemme guess... by *service*, you don't mean cooking or cleaning?"

He shakes his head.

"And when you say *women*, you actually mean girls?"

He pauses for a moment and then nods.

"Well, you're a sick fuck. I'll give you that. But what I don't understand is how you are making any money. Companion clubs are legal now. Why pay black market prices for something you can buy over the counter? Figuratively speaking."

Way stands. He's maybe half my height. He looks like a hobbit—all hairy and unclean.

Not to be disrespectful to hobbits or anything.

He shakes a finger at me and smiles. "Ah, yes, but it's only legal in *America*. Not here. Not every country jumped on your president's bandwagon. Besides, you would be surprised what some rich men like, my friend."

I shrug. "I dunno... I'm a rich man. Or at least, I used to be, I guess. But that doesn't mean I'm interested in young girls. Money don't mean a thing. Fucked up is fucked up."

"I am not here to pass judgment. I simply supply to meet demand. And I've been doing well from it for quite a while." He nods at his head of security next to me, who hasn't moved an inch this entire time. "And no one—certainly not a stupid little American asshole like you—is going to change that. Now, if there's nothing else, I'll leave you to die."

"Well, there's one thing, actually..."

He raises an eyebrow. "Hmm?"

I knock the gun up with my arm and shove the big bastard who's holding it with as much strength as I can muster, using both hands. He staggers back a few paces but doesn't go down, which is okay. I just wanted a bit of space...

I run toward him and jump, crashing into him with my elbow and knee raised. They both connect at the same time, hitting him in the jaw and chest respectively. He staggers back again but remains stubbornly upright.

I move toward him once more, walking quickly and with purpose. I don't want to let up for a second. I can't afford for him to recover and aim his gun at me again. I swing my back leg around, low and hard, catching him flush on the outside of his knee. His leg buckles under his weight. For the first time since I started, he falters and looks as if he's going to drop, but he doesn't.

This guy is just ridiculous! If I'd kicked Way like that, it would've snapped his leg in half...

He raises his weapon, but I'm close enough to him to make the gesture ineffective. I brush his arm away and throw three punches in quick succession to his sternum and gut. He takes another step back, stunned. He drops his gun, and I push it away with my foot, making sure it's nowhere near anyone.

I step forward and throw another hard combination— one more to the gut, followed by a shot to his kidney. He wavers, but this time, he plants his feet. I see his body tense, and he shakes his head, clearing the cobwebs.

Oh... shit...

He lunges forward and—

Whoa!

—wraps his... colossal... hands... around my... throat!

He lifts me clean off the floor and throws me backward. I land heavily, maybe ten feet away from where I started. I blink hard, trying to clear my head and refocus.

Fuck me, this guy's strong!

I glance over at Way, who's standing behind his desk, looking amused.

Oh, I'm going to smash that smile off your face, you pompous little—

"Holy crap!"

I'm hoisted into the air again and thrown out of the tent. I land awkwardly on the ground outside. The soft earth does little to cushion the impact. I scramble to my feet. I can't afford to lie still, even for a second. If Goliath grabs a hold of me again, I'm—

Ugh!

A fist that felt like a brick just buried itself into my side. I'm back on the ground, struggling to breathe and trying not to throw up.

Fuck me! How did he move *that* fast? It feels as if a train just hit me!

I move my head and look over just in time to see him charging toward me again. He raises his arms and leans forward to grab me.

Not again!

My instincts take over. Without thinking, I thrust my foot out and kick his knee—the same one I went for before. It stops him in his tracks but does little else. I risk one more, which thankfully finds its mark, then roll to the side as his leg finally gives out. He lands face-first next to me with a loud thud, like a tree falling in the forest.

I'm straight up to my feet, ignoring both the pain shooting around every inch of my upper body and my apparent inability to take a deep breath. I take a quick look around, aware I'm out in the open and exposed.

Yeah... that's what I was afraid of...

A large group of men has formed a loose circle around us. There must be twenty of them, easily. They all have weapons hanging from their shoulders by straps, and they're shouting and cheering as they look on. Behind them, in the fenced corner where crops are growing, the women are watching too. Over to my right, Way has appeared in the entrance of his tent, his arms folded across his chest. He surveys the scene like an emperor watching his gladiators. I look back at head of security.

Whoa!

Instinctively, I lean back and narrowly avoid a big right hand that would have taken my head clean off, had it landed. He stands and drops into a loose fighting stance, smiling at me with menace in his eyes.

I notice he's favoring his left leg, though, which is good. Shows he can be hurt. Plus, now that the fight has slowed down a bit, I can think clearly. Yes, he has almost a foot in height on me. That's fine. He's built like a tank, and that's okay too. He's strong, but he's slow, and his leg isn't a hundred percent, which gives me the advantage. Maybe. I just need to play it smart, pick my shots, keep moving, and wait for the mistake. Time to antagonize...

I love this part!

I stand casually, my arms by my side. "So, tell me... how are you so fucking ugly with only one head?"

His eyes go wide, and he snarls at me, baring his teeth like a wild animal.

At least I know he can understand me. Excellent!

"Seriously, it's like King Kong and Godzilla had a love child, and you were mauled by a pack of rabid dogs. You're fucking hideous, man! You would actually scare a zombie back to life!"

Oh... here he comes!

He charges forward, his arm held high behind him, ready to swing down for a killer blow. I see it coming a mile away. I sidestep and slam my foot into his weakened leg as he draws level. He drops instantly, sliding to a halt on his knees. I spin around and put my elbow through his temple, as if I'm trying to split his head open. He flies away from me and hits the ground hard, down for the count.

I'm breathing heavily. The adrenaline pumps furiously through my body. I take some deep gulps of air, trying to slow my heart rate down, so I can think clearly. I turn a slow circle.

Oh, yeah... I'm surrounded.

Shit.

Thankfully, they're all staring at me, wide-eyed. I guess that juggernaut was a big deal around here. Their shock buys me a few moments of reprieve, but that doesn't really help me. What am I supposed to do now? I mean—

What's that noise?

I frown and look behind me.

Ol' Juggernaut is getting to his feet!

I momentarily hang my head in disbelief. "You're fucking kidding me..."

I take a deep breath to steel myself.

That's it!

I charge at him, drop my head at the last possible second, and bury my shoulder into his gut. I don't let up, keeping my momentum going and not affording him a chance to realize what's happening. I force him back, using every ounce of strength I have to build up as much speed as I can. I feel him tense as he gathers what senses he has left, but he's too late. I let out a guttural grunt of effort as we collide with the leg of one of the guard towers along the side of the compound. He comes to an abrupt stop, but my shoulder keeps going. I bring both legs up behind me and spear his body through the weak wooden beam supporting the corner of the tower. There's a loud crack as it splinters, and I feel the wind being knocked out of him.

I push off him as he falls, roll away to the side, and spring to my feet again. Time slows down. I glance up as the entire structure starts to collapse. The weight of it proves too much for the remaining beams to support on their own.

"Oh, shit!"

I dive sideways, scrambling away to avoid the falling debris. I hear a scream and look back to see the man positioned at the top of the tower land with a heavy, life-ending thud. His head splits like a melon as it hits the ground. His gun flies from his hands, landing a few feet in front of me.

Ah, thank you very much!

I wait a second longer, just to appreciate the sight of all that wood falling and crushing the giant prick, then lunge for the gun. No time to check the mag. I doubt it's going to be empty. No one here will see that much action. I check the safety, then hold it one-handed as I sprint across the yard toward the housing units, yelling. I turn slightly to fire behind me. It's a fully automatic weapon, so I simply squeeze the trigger and point it in roughly the right direction. I'm not bothered about being accurate as long as I avoid hitting any of the women. I just want to deter them from firing at me for a few seconds while I get some cover.

Everyone's too busy standing slack-jawed and braindead to fight back, anyway. A couple of well-placed sprays as I'm running, and I manage to take out over half the group. In my peripheral vision, I see Mr. Way duck back inside his tent.

Nowhere to run, asshole.

I reach the housing units and slam my shoulder into the side of one to stop myself. Fighting to control my breathing, I drop to one knee and place two hands on the gun. I take aim and start picking off the stragglers before they get the chance to organize themselves. The slightest of touches on the trigger lets off two or three rounds at a time, so I take my shots sparingly, prioritizing the men still up in the watchtowers.

I take out three of them opposite me before the gun clicks empty. I stand and make my way across the front of the units. As I reach the third one along, the door in front of me opens. A man appears, fumbling with his own gun. He looks up, shocked to see me standing there.

I smile. "Hey there."

Before he can reply, I slam the butt of my empty Vector into his face, shattering his nose. He drops like a stone, his face masked in fresh blood. I leave my gun next to him as

I lean down to steal his. Again, I'm assuming it's a full mag, so I click the safety off and turn to start firing once more.

"Jesus..."

There's a sea of men walking toward me with their weapons raised. Not firing... just shouting. There must be forty, maybe fifty, of them.

Save the bullets, Adrian. Pick your fights.

I yank open the door of the next unit along and step inside, then slam it shut behind me. I turn and rest against it, catching my breath.

What the...

There are three men facing me, and they all look... well, terrified, really. They're all in a state of undress—two have pants on but bare torsos. The other is standing in his underwear but with a T-shirt on. Surrounding them, looking equally scared and equally undressed, are well over twenty women. They're trying to cover themselves, despite all being in their underwear. A couple are whimpering, crying with fear, but most are silent and shocked.

Holy shit.

Okay, think fast.

I snap the weapon up and let off three controlled bursts, hitting each of the three men in their chests. They drop lifelessly to the floor, prompting screams from the women and girls who were accidentally sprayed with their blood.

Whoops!

I step forward. "Okay, everyone, listen up. I'm not here to hurt you, but I'm short on time and even shorter on bullets, so I'll be as direct as I can. First of all, I need everyone to be quiet. Can you do that?"

I place a finger on my lips, and a gradual silence descends.

"Excellent. Right, hands up—who can actually understand me?"

Five out of twenty-odd. Hmm. Could be better. Could be worse.

"Okay, the ones with your hands up, pay attention. I'm going to kill Mr. Way and get you all out of here. But I need your help. Can you... y'know... translate for me?"

There's a loud babble of chatter, which prompts even more in response. I give it a minute for it to go quiet...

"Okay, who can drive?"

I'm getting nothing...

Oh, hang on—three hands have tentatively gone up.

That's far from ideal, but it'll have to do.

"Okay, people who can understand me, translate this: I'm going to open this door and start shooting anything that moves. When I do, I want you all to run out of here, single file, and head for the vehicle pool. With me so far?"

I pause while they relay the message. Shock and agreement sound out in equal measure.

"Good. When you get there, I want the three who can drive to get behind the wheel of a 4×4. The rest of you, however many it takes, load a drum of fuel into the back seat. I need two of you to drive over to the corners on either side of the entrance. The third, park it outside Way's tent. Then get out and run as fast you can into the forest, but leave the rear doors open, so I can see the fuel drums. Questions?"

That took a few minutes. While I'm sure a lot of it was lost in translation, I think they got the gist.

I take a quick look around the room. It's sparsely furnished. Rows of beds cover most of the floor space, and a communal bathroom runs almost the width of the back wall.

Where are they?

I look left.

Bingo!

Three Vectors are leaning against the wall beside the door. I *knew* those assholes would have put them somewhere. I walk over, take all the mags, and shove them into every spare pocket I have. I step back, face the door, and then glance over my shoulder.

"Everyone ready?"

They huddle together, crying and murmuring among themselves.

I sigh, setting my jaw with determination.

You really do attract some random shit, don't you, Adrian?

I push the door open and step out. This part is much easier when you don't have to worry about collateral damage. Everyone's a target, so I just snap my aim to the next thing I see move and tap the trigger. Propping the door open with my foot, I take out seven guys before I need to change the mag. I reload as the women and girls file out of the unit.

I hope they understood what I asked them to do. It's a gamble, and it's not the end of the world if they just run off, but it would be nice to make a statement if I can. I want to show Colonel Sanders and his Order that I don't need to audition for anything. I'm the best. Period.

The last of them are out, and they're all heading for the vehicles.

Yes!

I take out a few more men as I dash over to Way's tent and duck inside. I'm not worried about anyone firing at the women. They'll be too concerned about me. Besides, despite this whole place looking like amateur hour, I doubt even *these* guys are stupid enough to shoot the people they sell to make money...

The tent looks empty.

Where the hell is he?

Oh, never mind. Found him. He's cowering underneath one of the tables like a little bitch. I walk over to it and drag it out of the way one-handed.

He's sitting on the floor, hugging his knees, looking up at me with wide eyes. "P-please! Leave me alone! Don't kill me!"

I reach down and hoist him to his feet. I keep my gun trained on him and listen for any movement behind me. "Get up, you sack of shit." I grab his collar and march him over to the seating in the far corner. I shove him into a chair and point my gun at his chest. "You sell women... *young* women... to the highest bidder, and you live off the profits of other people's suffering. You know what? Even if I hadn't been ordered to, I'm pretty sure I'd have wanted to kill you anyway, now that I know what a huge waste of sperm you really are."

He holds his hands up and shakes his head quickly, desperate. "I'll... I'll change! I'll stop all of this, I swear! I'll let them all go and I'll disappear! Please! Just give me a—"

I squeeze the trigger, and a short burst of bullets tears into him. The recoil causes a natural lift that rips his chest and face apart. His body flails in the seat and then slumps to the side. Blood runs from the fresh holes and what's left of his head, quickly staining the sofa.

I stare at him. I didn't hesitate to take him out and feel nothing now that he's dead. What the hell is *wrong* with me? Three days ago, I assassinated the president of the United States in the middle of the Oval Office. I was sentenced to death. Then, by some twist of fate, I was saved. And now here I am, in the middle of a Vietnamese forest, standing over the body of a piece of shit I was *told* to kill, with no justification given. Granted, there was a perfectly valid reason, as it turned out, but even so—that's not me. That's not how I operate. I became the best doing things my own way. And with Josh's help.

But it's too late now, isn't it? I'm officially dead, and I belong to The Order of Sabbah. Maybe they're not so bad. This might be a great opportunity to reinvent myself, start a new life—one that sticks.

But my spider sense is going haywire. I don't know why. I just know never to ignore it.

I smile and shake my head. Ironically, it's taken me being accepted into a secretive, elite group of assassins to realize that maybe, just maybe, this isn't the life I want anymore.

Figures.

I tried getting out of it once before. It worked for a while, but this life caught up with me eventually. I had no choice but to accept that and go along with it. And look where it got me? My entire town got fucking *nuked!* I lost the second of only two women I've ever loved in the blink of an eye, and I haven't even stopped to think about it. It's as if I don't care. Except, I know I do.

What the hell is wrong with me?

I hear shouting outside.

Oh, yeah...

I rush over to the entrance and carefully peek out. The 4×4s appear to be in place, which is good. There's still a large group of armed men taking pot shots at me, but the exposed fuel drum in the vehicle is putting them off, thank God. I reckon that maybe half of them have already run off.

Seriously, what kind of outfit *is this*? All the people who work here are pussies!

I glance over my shoulder at Mr. Way's corpse—a final check that my job is done and the contract fulfilled—then step outside. I crouch behind the 4×4 for cover. There's no sign of the women anywhere, which hopefully means they're hightailing it through the forest as planned.

I look around and count eleven men grouped together along the left side.

They need to be distracted.

I pop up, quickly rest on the hood, and steady my aim. Now that I'm exposed, I only have a couple of seconds before someone risks a shot. I get the fuel drum that's visible on the rear seat of the vehicle next to them in my sights. I take a short breath… hold it… and breathe out as I squeeze the trigger gently.

BANG!

The bullet finds its mark. The vehicle explodes, immediately engulfed in flames. The deafening roar of the blast sends a small shockwave around the camp. Many of the group in front of me are knocked off their feet.

I dash around the hood, firing and picking off the ones still standing as I head for the way out. They go down with zero resistance. I spray a few rounds at the group on the other side, across from me, to give them something to think about. As they dive for cover, I take aim at the other 4×4. As requested, the fuel drum is lying exposed on the rear seat.

Those girls did well!

I stop for a brief moment and fire.

BANG!

Another massive explosion. Bodies fly in all directions. The shockwave takes out three nearby guard towers too, which is a stroke of luck. Smoke billows into the sky, blocking out the sun. The loud crackling flames on either side drown out almost all other noise.

I sprint toward the entrance, running down the center of the compound to avoid as much of the heat as I can. I change mags and lay down my own covering fire, occasionally getting lucky and taking out a straggler as I go.

I reach the guard post. The fence is standing open, and the area is unmanned. That's good. The women must have gotten out with no fuss. I turn and face the compound. The flames on either side are spreading, and many of the guard towers are catching fire. From what I can see, most of the men are dead or have run away. The ones who remain are rushing around in a blind panic.

At the far end, the last of the 4×4s stands ominously in front of Way's tent. I take a knee, control my breathing, and line up my shot at the fuel drum. It's a good distance from here. Considering I have a fully automatic SMG—which isn't the most accurate of weapons—this needs to be a damn good shot.

Luckily for me... I'm me.

I squeeze the trigger.

BANG!

The tent disappears in an instant, quickly consumed in a bright ball of fire. I watch as the flames lash out at their surroundings, slowly burning any trace of Mr. Way's operation to ashes.

Before me is a sea of fire, on which the screams of my victims ride the waves.

I can't remember where I heard that quote. It sounds like something a Viking would say...

It feels appropriate, anyway. I drop my gun, turn, and set off running, back into the forest I landed in not four hours earlier.

5

It didn't take me long to catch up to the women. They're not the fastest of runners, and their crying soon gave away their position. A small group of stragglers at the back all turn as they hear me approach. They all stop and try to hug me at the same time as I draw level with them. I have no idea what they're saying, but they seem happy.

I chuckle nervously, shrugging their hands off me. "Okay, okay... it's no problem. You're all welcome. Just..." I take a couple of paces back, putting some distance between them and me. "There we go. That's right. You're all okay now."

I recognize one of them as someone who vaguely understood me earlier. I look at her. Her face is thin and gaunt, and her eyes are dark and sunken. She looks deflated... beaten. I move toward her. "Have you seen Hong Yun? Was she with you when you left?"

She frowns for a moment, then shakes her head. "Not... with... us."

Shit.

"Okay, thank you."

I look forward and see the main group just up ahead. I break into a light jog and make my way between the trees, avoiding clumps of undergrowth and bushes sticking out as I catch up with them.

I hope she's—

Wait. What's that noise?

I slide to a stop and look up, squinting in the sun. I search the pockets of smoke-filled sky between the treetops. That sounds like...

A helicopter whizzes into view for a split-second, then disappears again. The noise is still loud, though, so it must be landing somewhere nearby.

I let out a long, tired sigh. Now what?

I carry on and draw level with the second group of women.

"Hong Yun?" I say to them, slightly out of breath.

Collectively, they stop and turn, fear etched onto their faces. I can't imagine what they've all been through, but at least it's over now.

Hong Yun pushes her way to the front of the group and stands in front of me. She looks tired and afraid, but she manages to smile at me. "Adrian... you okay!"

I nod. "I always am. I was worried about you. I hoped you'd managed to get out safely."

"Yes... thank you. Mr. Way... is he... dead?"

I nod again.

She looks down. Her shoulders slump forward and she sighs.

I frown. "What's wrong?"

She gestures to the women behind her. "We all hated him... but for many of us... for me... this was all we had. We have... nowhere to go."

I put my hands on her shoulders and smile at her. "Hong Yun, you're free now. Do you understand? You're not in danger. You don't belong to anyone. You are all... *free*. You can go anywhere you want and not be afraid. Don't you have family somewhere? Someone who misses you?"

She glances to the side. "I have... sister. She lives in the city."

"Well, there you go. Go and be with your sister. Start a new life for yourself." I glance over at the rest of the women. "Same goes for all of you. If you have family or friends, go and be with them. Your life is your own now. You can all—"

"Adrian!"

A voice up ahead interrupts me. Without thinking, I push Hong Yun behind me and walk through the group of women, making sure I'm between them and whoever's approaching. The rustling of undergrowth and the sound of heavy footfalls is getting louder. There must be at least five or six of them.

It can't be anyone working for Way. He didn't know my real name. Plus, he wouldn't have been able to reach the phone from under the desk, anyway. Fucking coward.

So, who the hell is—

"Adrian."

A group of men appears before us from behind a tight clump of trees, rounding a slight bend. I was right. There are five of them. They're wearing jungle fatigues and holding handguns. Drawn, ready but loose.

"Let's go," says the man at the front, gesturing to me with his hand. He's quite tall, similar in height to me, with a stern-looking, clean-shaven face and narrow eyes.

I frown. "And you are?"

"Here to bring you back in after a mission well done."

"You guys work for The Order?"

He nods. "The name's Pierce."

"Christ. Okay, *Pierce*, where the fuck were you guys when I had a small army shooting at me a few minutes ago?"

He shrugs. "If you needed our help to get out of there, we wouldn't be here to offer you a ride home."

I roll my eyes. "Oh, yeah. All part of my initiation, right?" I sigh. "Fine."

I walk over to them, and they subtly fan out to surround me without getting too close. I note their positioning. Two behind at wide angles... one on either side, practically level with me... and Pierce, who walked past me and took the lead. If I try to run, regardless of which direction, I'll be tagged before I reach the guy I'm heading toward.

Smart. Effective.

I stop walking. "Hey, wait a minute..."

The men stop and turn. Pierce sighs—a hint of impatience. "What?"

I gesture behind me with my thumb. "What about the women? You're not seriously just gonna leave them here, are you?"

He shrugs again. "They're not my mission. Therefore, they're not my problem."

"They weren't *my* mission, either. But given I'm not a world-class *dickbag*, I don't wanna leave them here to fend for themselves. We're in the middle of nowhere..."

The group of men exchange looks, then Pierce reaches into his pocket and pulls out a cell phone. He presses a button and places it to his ear. After some inaudible muttering and the occasional nod, he hangs up and looks at me. "We'll send another chopper for the women. It'll take a few trips, but we'll get them to safety somewhere in the city. That okay with you?"

I shrug. "Don't tell me..." I glance over my shoulder and then back at him. "Tell *them*."

He sighs and walks past me, stopping just in front of the women. He relays his message, which is met with murmurs of uncertainty. I move and stand next to him. We exchange a glance, and he raises an eyebrow, almost challengingly. I look at Hong Yun. "My friends here are going to return in a helicopter and take you all to safety, okay? I promise you're all gonna be fine. Just stick together until they arrive."

She holds my gaze for a moment and then nods. "Thank you... Adrian."

I smile. "Don't worry about it." I look at Pierce as I turn back. "You need to work on your people skills, man."

I set off walking toward the chopper again, with the group surrounding me keeping pace. Pierce marches past me and resumes his place at the front. A few minutes later, we enter a large clearing. The chopper is standing in the middle, with the pilot and co-pilot visible through the cockpit windows. The four huge blades on the roof slowly start to spin as we approach, and the smaller ones on the tail quickly follow suit.

The speed picks up and the noise gets louder. We duck slightly as we all jog over to the open door on the side. Pierce jumps in first and turns to face us. "Everybody in!"

The two guys on either side of me climb aboard first. One sits facing the cockpit on the far side; the other sits opposite him. Next, Pierce gestures to me. I get in and sit facing the cockpit in the middle seat. I fasten the belt around my waist. The two guys bringing up the rear get in, and the last one shuts the door behind him. One sits on my right, while the other puts his back to the cockpit. Pierce sits across from me.

Less than a minute later, we're airborne, heading to God knows where. We bank right, and I lean forward slightly in my seat, looking past the guy flanking me and out the window. The forest already looks so small and peaceful. It's almost as if I was never there. Then I see a thin plume of smoke in the distance and remember that I always leave my mark on places I visit.

Now... where the hell are they taking me?

6

I'm standing on the balcony of an expensive hotel room, fifteen floors up, leaning on the rail and looking out at the Petronas Twin Towers looming over me. The heat in the center of Kuala Lumpur's business district is already pushing eighty-five, and it's not even lunchtime. I'm only wearing a towel, as I've just stepped out of the shower, but I'm already sweating because of this humidity.

Yesterday, the chopper took us to Tan Son Nhat airport, a few miles north of Ho Chi Minh City. From there, a private jet flew us across the water to Malaysia. Once we touched down, Pierce and his team drove me to this hotel and said someone will be in touch. They told me not to leave my room—and reminded me that I have a tracking device in my neck, so they would know if I did. They said to just sit tight and wait for someone to make contact.

It started out as a long-ass evening. I was pacing up and down the room with all kinds of things running through my

57

head. But eventually, I concluded that worrying and pacing wasn't productive. So, instead, I ordered room service, ate like a king, and crashed out on the bed watching TV.

I slept like the dead.

That makes sense... I mean, that's what I am now, right? Dead.

I took my time this morning, taking advantage of being able to lie in bed and not worry about who might try to kill me today. I ordered breakfast and grabbed a nice, hot shower, then stepped out here for some air. Not that I'm getting much, as it's that hot!

I'm still exhausted after everything that's happened in the last few days. Well, I say *the last few days*, but it's been almost a *month* since fate decided my life would change forever. Almost a month since three assholes walked into my bar and dragged me into *this* shit. And now here I am, nearly four weeks on, standing alone in a Malaysian hotel room with little to show for my efforts besides a heartbeat.

Not that I don't appreciate still having one.

I'm looking out at a world still trying to make sense of everything after witnessing not only the largest terrorist attack in history but also the global war that followed. Far below me, I see people hustling around in every direction, desperately trying to carry on as if nothing's happened. The aftermath of 4/17 hasn't reached this far south of China, so people here in Malaysia, as well as in places such as Thailand and Singapore, are still living relatively normal lives.

But *normal* is now a thing of the past for me. Thanks to Cunningham's master plan, the North Korean invasion was indirectly responsible for my adopted hometown being turned into a three-mile-wide crater. The final stages involved him using the Cerberus satellite to take control of another country's missile and blow up part of his own country with it. He thought the American people would turn to him in their hour of need, pledging undying support in return for him finally stepping in and saving the world. He was beyond deluded, but I still couldn't stop him. He launched a tactical nuke, and that was it—game over. Everything's gone. My bar... my life...

Tori.

I had to watch it happen on a fucking laptop. But I'm still not allowing myself any time to dwell on it. To all intents and purposes, I ceased to exist about five minutes later, so the way I see it, any grief belongs to another life.

That's what I keep telling myself, anyway. Right now, denial seems the sensible option. I'm still trying to wrap my head around this whole Order of Sabbah thing, so I don't want to overload myself with too much shit. I'm on my own now. I have to look after number one. I've never been great at handling all the emotional baggage that comes with the life I lead. I know I'll struggle, so I'm choosing to ignore it completely and focus solely on what lies ahead.

I assume after everything in Vietnam yesterday that I'm in now. I'm officially a member of The Order's ranks. So, I'm also assuming that whoever's going to make contact will be doing so to either give me a proper induction or give me a job.

I wish they would hurry up, though. I'm getting cabin fever in here.

I turn and walk back inside the room, which really is incredible. I remember thinking that place we had back in New Jersey was nice. But this... this is a goddamn *palace*! For a start, there's a water feature in the middle of the room. Seriously! It's a marble plinth about three feet high, with a discreet fountain trickling out of it in a nice pattern. The sound is relaxing, but I can't wrap my head around why any hotel room would ever need one.

The bed is far too big for two people, never mind just me, but it gave me the most comfortable night's sleep I've had in years. It's against the left wall, surrounded by fitted closets and drawers made from dark, presumably expensive wood.

The thick, cream-colored carpet underfoot feels as if I'm walking on clouds. In the middle of the room, facing the opposite wall and the cinema-sized TV mounted on it, is a long, five-seater leather sofa. At either end, angled slightly inward, is a matching armchair. There's a glass table in the middle, with a bowl of potpourri in its center.

And the TV... wow! I watched a bit of news on it last night. It's slightly curved, and the picture quality is so clear, it's like looking through a window. Josh would be in heaven in a place like this.

I sigh, frustrated at myself.

Damn it! I need to stop doing that. Josh is part of my old life. He believes I'm dead. Maybe it would help me to start doing the same. I mean, I'm—

There's a knock on the door.

About time!

I walk across the room. I'm not bothered that I'm only wearing a towel. I'm not exactly having a business meeting, am I?

I grab the handle and lean forward to look through the—

Ooof! Shit!

The door just burst open and hit me in the face!

A woman strides casually past me and into the room. She stops next to the sofa and turns to face me. I push the door closed and rub my forehead where the door hit me. I turn and walk over to her. "Come in, why don't you? Christ... you nearly took my damn—"

I stop talking as I look up at her. She's beautiful. I mean, she's... just... *staggering*. I don't know how else to say it. No words I can think of right now would do her justice.

She's shorter than me but probably slightly above average height for a woman. Maybe five-seven or five-eight. She's slim and toned, and I can tell from the way she's standing that she can take care of herself. There's a relaxed confidence in her body language. Her muscles are constantly tensing and twitching, and her body weight is perpetually shifting, ready to move at a moment's notice.

Her hips are slightly wider than her torso, and her thighs angle inward slightly. She's wearing fitted jeans tucked inside black, knee-high suede boots. A thin white top hangs loose on her slight frame. She has jet-black hair that stops at her shoulders and an Asian complexion, which is accentuated by large, hypnotic brown eyes. She's staring at me, looking a little bemused, with the faintest of smiles on her lips, as if she knows I'm checking her out.

Whoa...

I look down at my towel, then back at her. I smile, a little embarrassed. "Sorry, I wasn't expecting—"

She holds a hand up. The smile fades. "Save it. I don't care what you're wearing. Or *not* wearing, in your case."

Her English is flawless. Her attitude needs a bit of work, though.

I shrug. "Okay, then. So, who are you? Do you work for The Order?"

She nods. "I do, yes."

"And your name is..."

"Unimportant."

"Okay. Well... Miss Unimportant, I'm Adrian, and—"

"I know who you are."

I frown. "You were a cheerleader in high school, weren't you? I can tell. It's your warm, friendly demeanor that gives it away…"

She raises an eyebrow. "Do you think you're funny?"

"Most days, yeah."

"You're not."

"Well, you can't please everyone. Why are you here, Miss Unimportant?"

She sighs. "My name is Lily."

I smile.

She frowns. "What?"

"Nothing. It's just that's a really nice, sweet-sounding, delicate name… and you're… y'know…"

"What?"

"None of those things. Or, if you are, then you need to work on your first impression."

"Please don't assume you know me, smartass."

"I know enough, Lily."

She raises an eyebrow. "Really? Go on, then. What do you know?"

I look her up and down for a moment. "Okay. You're in your late twenties. Definitely single. Left-handed. Well trained—I'm gonna go with Muay Thai. No formal military experience, but you've seen your fair share of fighting. I'm gonna say… only child. Oh, and orphaned."

I'm aware of the cold silence filling the room. The tension is palpable and awkward. I should have added *poker player* to my list, as her face isn't giving anything away whatsoever. I reckon I hit the mark with most things.

She takes a small step forward and lets out a short sigh. "That was… impressive."

"Was I right? I wasn't sure about you being an only child. I was playing the odds there, but—"

She shakes her head. "No. You were wrong about practically everything."

"Oh..."

"Asshole. Have you finished? We have a lot to cover."

"Hey, wait a minute. What did I get wrong?"

She sighs again. "I'm thirty-one. I'm right-handed. I'm incredibly well trained but not in Muay Thai. I've had lots of formal military experience, and I have a sister. Happy now?"

"But you *are* single?"

She rolls her eyes. "Enough. I have no desire to get to know you or allow you to get to know me. Am I clear?"

I hold my hands up defensively. "Crystal."

"Now get dressed. There's much to discuss, and you're buying me lunch."

"I am?"

"Yes, to make up for being such an asshole."

I sigh and shrug. "Fair enough."

I pad quickly over to the bed. The closet was full of clothes when I arrived here, all my size, so I picked out something to wear earlier and laid it all out, ready.

I glance back at her over my shoulder as I reach for the jeans. "Do you mind?"

She shakes her head. "Not at all."

She crosses her arms and stands watching me challengingly.

I sigh again. "Whatever."

11:49 MYT

.   .   .

We're sitting on opposite sides of a small table in the middle of a restaurant downtown. It has an open front that leads directly onto the busy street outside. The noise of the traffic makes any conversation difficult. The Petronas Towers dominate the skyline to our left, and the sun is high and bright overhead.

This place is... cozy. It doesn't matter which table you're sitting at; everyone's sitting next to someone. Plus, I'm twice the size of most folks in here, so I'm feeling a little cramped. I forgot that personal space isn't that big a deal in Eastern culture.

Lily is staring at me curiously, sipping on an ice-cold bottle of beer. The condensation drips over her fingers and onto the thin cloth covering the table. We haven't said much since we sat down. We ordered drinks and a bite to eat, but that's been it.

I take a sip of my beer. "Okay, I'm sorry about before. Can we start over? You know who I am, and I know you work for The Order. So, lay it on me, Lily."

She doesn't do or say anything at first, but after a few moments, she nods and smiles reservedly. "Okay, Adrian. Let's start over. Vietnam was a test, which you passed. Quite impressively, I might add."

I shrug. "Thanks."

"The Order has had its eye on Mr. Way for a while now, monitoring his human trafficking operation. We followed the money—and the girls—to see who his clients were and determine if he was actually the top of the food chain."

"And was he?"

She shrugs. "As far as we could tell, yeah. That's why the contract on his life was activated."

"So, why wait for me to come along to get it done?"

"We didn't wait. It was just good timing. Horizon has had his eye on you for a while too, and after—"

"Okay, hang on. Who the hell's *Horizon*?"

She smiles, more relaxed and genuine than before. "The man who wears the white suit. You've met him a couple times, I believe."

"Yeah, once or twice..." I frown. "What kind of a name is that?"

"The kind people like him are given."

"And who hands out the aliases?"

She shakes her head. "One thing at a time, okay? After what you did in Washington a few days ago, we knew we had to make our move if we wanted to recruit you. Once we saved you from your execution, we had to make sure you have what it takes before revealing the full nature of the organization to you, so we used Mr. Way's contract as a means of testing you."

"And... *Horizon*... thought I was impressive?"

"No, *I* did." She smiles and takes another swig of her beer.

"Uh-huh. So, what happens now? Why bring me here?"

"The Order has a presence in the city, and it's far enough away from your old life that you'll be safe here for now. It gives us time to bring you up to speed on everything."

"Yeah, I do have a few questions..."

"Thought you might."

A waiter approaches the table, carrying our food. He places a bowl in front of each of us and a large dish of rice in the middle. He then puts our individual meals beside us, nods, and walks away.

We both spend a few moments preparing our meals. I dig in heartily, doing my best to eat with chopsticks.

"Okay," Lily says between mouthfuls. "What do you want to know?"

"First of all, what's happened with North Korea? Did GlobaTech kick their asses?"

She nods. "About six hours after President Cunningham's assassination was announced to the world, North Korean forces began to retreat. Footage from all over the world showing GlobaTech soldiers repelling the attacks was on every news channel on every television. Your friend did an exceptional job."

I smile and feel myself zone out, thinking about Josh...

...

...

...and I'm back.

"That's great news. And how is President Schultz doing?"

She shrugs. "Not bad, considering he's only been in the White House a week. He's already tried to rebuild the U.N., but he's outsourced the job of the old Peacekeeping Taskforce to GlobaTech. So, Josh Winters is now on the National Security Council, albeit in an advisory capacity."

My eyes go wide. "Holy shit! Really?"

She nods. "The decision's been met with overwhelming support from almost everyone. GlobaTech single-handedly defended the world against the threat of war. Their security forces can hold their own against any nation's own military —especially now, when so many countries are on their knees. It makes sense."

"Way to go, Josh!"

"Yes, your friend has done well for himself."

"He always was a smartass. So, North Korea has been put in its place... the U.S. is bouncing back after all the conspiracy... things are looking up. How's everyone else doing?"

She shrugs. "As you'd expect. There's no easy fix, but the nations not affected by 4/17 are all playing their part. They're trying to carry on as normal—like these people..." She gestures around the restaurant. "But governments all over the world are jumping at the chance to help President Schultz and GlobaTech Industries rebuild. It'll take some time, but it's good that everyone's banding together."

I smile and shake my head.

She frowns. "What's funny?"

"Nothing. It's just... everything that happened... Cunningham's big plan... ultimately, his goal was to unite everyone. He had an ass-backward way of going about it, granted, but as it turns out, that's exactly what's happened. Only difference is, he's not ruling the world like some wannabe Emperor Palpatine. Kinda ironic, though, when you think about it."

She frowns. "Emperor who?"

"You know... from *Star Wars*? He was the leader of the Empire, ruling the galaxy with fear and..." I stop talking. The look on her face says it all. "You've never seen *Star Wars*, have you?"

She shakes her head.

I sigh. "Another tragedy our world faces... there are still people who haven't watched *Star Wars*."

"You're an odd man, Adrian."

I shrug. "I prefer to think of myself as unique, but whatever."

We both smile and fall silent. We take a few minutes to eat some more.

I wipe my mouth with my napkin and take a sip of my drink. "So, what happens now?"

Lily does the same. "Well, The Order is busy creating a

new life for you. You'll have a new identity, a new house, credit cards... everything."

"Christ... really?"

She nods. "You'll have the freedom to live your life however you want, with only three conditions."

"Hmm, go on..."

"The first one is that you have to be ready on a moment's notice to carry out whatever contract they give you. Always and without question."

I shrug. "Sounds fair."

"The second one is that you can't kill *anyone* without The Order's permission. The punishment for doing so is... not worth thinking about."

"Okay, I can live with that."

"And finally, you cannot—and I can't stress this enough, Adrian—you *cannot* attempt to contact anyone from your previous life. You must remain hidden. You must live like a ghost. Do you understand?"

I clench my jaw muscles repeatedly. That's a big ask. I can imagine the temptation is always there, though it surely gets easier with time. I guess since I woke up to this new life, I've been thinking, somewhere in the back of my mind, there would be a way of letting Josh know I was still alive.

I guess not.

"Adrian?"

"Huh? Yeah... I understand."

"I mean it. That's our only concern about you. Don't make us regret our decision to recruit you, okay?"

I nod. "I won't try to contact Josh. Cross my heart."

"Thank you. Now, apart from those three things, the world is yours. A benefit of being in The Order."

She smiles at me—a gesture I force myself to return. This is my life now. I accept that. The first two rules... they make sense to me. I was half-expecting something along those lines, to be honest. I'm an assassin, after all. Things like that come with the territory. But the third thing...

I sigh.

I know I was told from day one that contact with my old life wasn't an option if I signed up. But I guess I had it in my head that I would be able to find a way around it. Now that I've essentially been threatened over trying to contact Josh, it just makes me want to do it even more. I'm too—

"Are you all right?"

I must have zoned out again. I look at Lily, who's staring at me. "Sorry. Yeah... I'm fine."

She smiles at me, and I detect a hint of sympathy. "Look, I... I know it's hard, leaving people you care for behind. We've all had to do it. But it does get easier. I promise."

That's nice of her to say, despite it being no comfort whatsoever.

"Thanks, Lily. So, what now?"

"Now..." She reaches in her pocket and takes out a cell phone, which she slides across the table. "You need to take this. Horizon wants to meet with you, but before that, I actually have a contract for you. The details are in the message I've just sent to your phone."

I frown. "Is this another test?"

She shakes her head. "No, this is life in The Order. This is your first real contract for us."

I take the phone but don't turn it on. "Does everyone in The Order carry out hits? Do you?"

She nods. "I do, yes."

"But this job is just for me? It's definitely not another test? Because I'm sick of having to prove—"

"Everyone in The Order has a particular set of skills.

Yours, it seems, is finding a way to pull off seemingly impossible contracts, which is why you've been assigned this one."

"Uh-huh. What's your skill set?"

She winks at me coyly. "I have many…"

"I bet."

She certainly seems friendlier than when we first met. To be fair, I probably didn't help the situation earlier. I think starting over was a good idea. My first impression probably wasn't much better than hers was.

I turn on the phone and look at the message waiting for me on the screen. An image loads, showing a man sitting at a table in a crowded restaurant. He has dark hair and is smartly dressed. He's…

Hang on.

I look at Lily, confused. "Is this a joke?"

Still smiling, she shakes her head. "No. He's your target. And you need to carry it out immediately. Rule number one, remember?"

I look back at the screen and sigh.

It's the guy sitting next to me!

7

I stare at the table in front of me until my vision blurs. I've lost my appetite. I have my beer in my right hand, but I'm no longer thirsty. The surprise... the *shock* has me thinking a million different things at once, but I don't yet have the capacity to focus on any of them.

They want me to kill the guy I've been sitting next to for the last half-hour. This has to be another kind of test, surely?

I stare at Lily, who's observing me quietly. "Okay, hang on a minute. I don't—" I glance sideways at the guy and lower my voice. "I don't take someone out just because I'm told to, all right? I need to—"

She laughs. "He doesn't speak English. There's no need to talk quietly."

I roll my eyes. "I'm not bothered about *that*. I was gonna say, I need to know *why* someone deserves to have me coming for them. Why does The Order want this guy dead?"

She shakes her head. "It doesn't work like that, Adrian. That might've been how you did things in the past, and that's fine. But it's not how we do things now. Like I just said, if we give you a target, your only thought should be how quickly and effectively you can take them out. That's it."

"I'm sorry, but I'm not executing anyone just because someone tells me to."

"You did in Vietnam..."

I shake my head. "No, I didn't. I found out what I could about Mr. Way prior to entering his little compound. I knew he was a piece of shit before I tore his world apart. I don't know what *this* guy is supposed to have done, and until I do, I'm not touching him. Are we clear?"

Lily takes a sip of her drink and stares at me. Her jaw is set, and she looks a little pissed off. Her eyes narrow slightly. I can see the internal debate raging behind her brown orbs. After a few moments, she places her drink down and leans forward, resting on her crossed arms.

"He's a customer of Mr. Way's. Or he *was*, anyway. He's a successful businessman and a senior director at a large banking firm here in the city. He's married with two sons, eleven and eight. But he's also a pedophile. He's spent tens of thousands over many years with Mr. Way, having young girls delivered to an apartment he rents behind his family's back. He's a sick bastard, Adrian." She nods at the cell phone in my hand. "Scroll through the images if you don't believe me."

I frown and look at the screen. Using my thumb, I flick through a series of damning pictures that show him walking into an apartment building, then reappearing at the door to greet a couple of men escorting a young girl who's dressed inappropriately. He then disappears back inside with his arm around her.

I clench my jaw so tightly, I think I might actually shatter my teeth. I met a lot of those young women yesterday. They were scared for their lives. They were victims. And people like this piece of shit next to me did that to them.

I look over at her. "Okay, so he deserves it. Give me half a day for surveillance, and he'll be dead by morning."

She shakes her head. "Any recon or additional information will always be done for you and sent along with the details of the target. If you don't receive any, it means there's isn't any. In those circumstances, termination is to be carried out immediately."

Jesus...

I place the phone down on the table. I finish off the beer and place the empty bottle next to it. I look over at Lily. My brow furrows. "You said I have the freedom to live my life however I want now, providing I stick to your three rules, right?"

She nods. "That's right."

"So, what happens if I do something illegal and the police get involved? Would The Order bail me out?"

She pauses for a moment. Her expression tries to hide a slightly bemused smile. "The police... aren't a concern for us."

I raise an eyebrow. "What do you mean?"

"I mean, wherever you are, whatever you do... providing you stick to those three rules, no one is going to bother you. You're free, Adrian."

"Really? Well, that *is* interesting..."

I pick up one of my chopsticks. It's thin but made from something sturdy, like bamboo. I snap it about a quarter of the way down, leaving a sharp, jagged point. I hold it in my fist with the business end facing away from me. I look at Lily and raise an eyebrow.

Screw it. Let's see just how free I really am, shall we?

I lash my arm out to the side in a swift arc. The splintered chopstick connects perfectly with my target, piercing the thin flesh of his throat, just below his Adam's apple. I turn and stare at him. He looks around at me slowly, his eyes wide and his mouth open. I let go, leaving the makeshift weapon sticking out of him. He clutches at it and makes an awful gurgling sound, desperately trying to take a breath but slowly choking on the blood gathering in his esophagus.

No one's reacted yet. The people in the immediate vicinity haven't quite registered what's happening. I stare into the guy's wide, disbelieving eyes, waiting to see the light in them begin to fade.

It doesn't take long.

I reach across and yank the chopstick from his throat. A thin fountain of blood erupts from the wound, soaking both the table in front of him and the person sitting opposite. I quickly place my hand on the back of his head and slam him face-first into his plate. He tries to struggle free, but his efforts are futile. I hold him there for another moment, waiting.

I lean forward to check and...

Yeah... that's it.

He's gone.

I sit back in my chair and look at Lily. Her expression is neutral, devoid of any sentiment or emotion. We stare into each other's eyes until the shock wears off the people around us and the screaming starts. Neither of us makes a move. People leap to their feet and rush around in a panic, fleeing their tables in all directions. We both sit, silently regarding one another like a game of chicken, seeing who will move first.

I shrug. "See, I told you. All I need is a valid reason. Job done."

She finishes her drink. "What if I was lying?"

"You weren't."

"How do you know?"

"Because, believe it or not, I'm better at reading people than you might think. And I trust my spider sense. You weren't lying. You were just reluctant to give me a reason because it's against your rules."

She flicks her eyebrows up and flashes a perplexed smile. "Okay. And what's your spider sense? Is that something out of *Star Wars*?"

She pulls a face, possibly being facetious. I shake my head. "No, it's not out of *Star Wars*... Good God, woman!"

She chuckles and stands. "Come on. The police will be here any minute."

"I thought they weren't a problem?"

"They're not, but that doesn't mean there isn't any paperwork. Let's go."

I follow her outside and we head left. I glance back over my shoulder at the restaurant. There's a crowd of people gathering out front, cell phone cameras going crazy.

Some things never change.

That actually felt quite liberating—getting back to basics and just taking out a target. No fuss, no fallout... just me and the kill, like the old days. It's almost comforting to have something I'm familiar with that makes sense to me. God knows those things have been in short supply lately.

Lily strides confidently and carefree next to me, as if we have all the time in the world. A warm, stifling breeze catches her hair, blowing it gently and causing it to flow like black water behind her as she walks.

She's an absolute vision...

"So, do you always act so impulsively?" she asks.

"I wouldn't say that was impulsive. I tend to operate using calculated risks and instinct more than anything. It's always worked well for me in the past."

"How did you know he wouldn't fight back?"

I look over at her and raise an eyebrow. "Are you being serious?"

She holds my gaze for a moment and then smiles. "No, not in the slightest."

I smile and shake my head. She might be a little frosty at times and really hard to read, but I'm starting to like her. And she seems to be warming to me, which is unexpected but not altogether unpleasant.

"So, where to now, Lily?"

She spins around, so she's facing me and walking backward. "Time to meet the boss."

14:11 MYT

We're sitting at a table outside a small café, silently observing the long lines of people stretching out from the ticket booths at Kuala Lumpur International Airport. Neither of us wanted to sit with our backs to the doors, so after a little debate, we're next to each other.

The airport is crammed and noisy, filled with the monotonous rabble of a hundred simultaneous conversations. Herds of people shuffle in every direction, carrying bags of varying sizes and dragging cases behind them.

Security is insane too. Unsurprising after the last few weeks, I guess. Groups of armed guards are everywhere—

every door, every corridor, even alongside every line of people. Some of them are wearing GlobaTech uniforms, which is making me feel a little self-conscious. I'm trying to ignore them and act normal.

Lily drove us here, which took about forty minutes in traffic. She has a great car. It's a bright yellow convertible—a Porsche, I think. We had the top down all the way here. It was a nice feeling, to be speeding around with little to care about. I've forgotten what a vacation feels like, but I imagine it's something close to how this feels. For the first time in ages, I don't have any burdens or responsibilities. I don't have anyone to look out for or depend on. I just have me.

And do you know what? It's weird, and it'll definitely take some getting used to, but I reckon I've earned this. I'm still not completely convinced The Order of Sabbah is as great as it makes out. In my experience, if something sounds too good to be true, it usually is. Since my test in Vietnam, it's been nice hotels, good food, and a relatively easy kill. I'm not naïve enough to be blinded by it all, but I *am* smart enough to take advantage of a good thing while I have it.

Colonel Sanders is supposed to be meeting us here any time now. I refuse to call him Horizon. It's a ridiculous name. Lily said he wants to talk with me. I just hope he tells me what's going to happen now.

We're both drinking coffee from large paper cups. Mine's black, obviously. No sugar, no cream—just pure caffeine, as nature intended. Lily has this weird, creamy-looking cup of cat sick with chocolate sprinkled on top. To each their own, I guess. She seems to be enjoying it, which is all that matters.

She nudges my arm and nods over at the main entrance. "He's here."

I look over and see the man himself walking toward us,

wearing his trademark white suit and black shirt. There's a guy on either side of him, both dressed in matching black suits, with visible earpieces. No doubt they're armed too.

He stops at our table and nods a curt, professional greeting to Lily. "Hello, my dear. It's good to see you."

She stands, picking up her coffee, and nods back. "Sir." She looks down at me. "I'll see you around."

I go to reply, but she walks off before I have chance.

Colonel Sanders sits down next to me, crosses his legs, and clasps his hands on his lap. He looks out at the sea of chaos flowing around the terminal and takes in a deep, calm breath but remains silent.

I'm not sure what to say, or even if I should say anything at all. I stare at the heaving mass of humanity before us. "Can I... ah... get you a coffee?"

He smiles. "No, thank you. I'll be brief. It's not often I meet with our assets, Adrian."

I look across at him. From the side, he looks quite frail. The loose skin around his throat and on his face makes him appear older than he probably is. He has a tall, strong posture and an easy confidence. I bet he was a real tough sonofabitch when he was younger.

I can't help picturing him with a white beard, though...

"I should count myself lucky, then. This is the third time we've met now."

As I shift in my seat to get comfortable, he finally turns to look me in the eye. "Are you nervous?"

I shake my head. "Not at all. But given the first time we met, I technically died a short while afterward, and the second time resulted in me being thrown out of an airplane, I must admit I'm exercising caution." I pick up my drink and gesture to it with my head. "I just want to finish my coffee before anything else happens to me, all right?"

He nods and smiles, but there's no humor in it. "You have nothing to be cautious about. You're in The Order now, Adrian. This is your life. My name is Horizon."

"Yeah, Lily said. I'm sorry. I just can't bring myself to call you that with a straight face. To me, you're Colonel Sanders." I smile and look at his bodyguards, but they're staring at me blankly. I chuckle to myself awkwardly. "Huh... tough crowd."

"Adrian, when I was given the unenviable task of managing The Order's assets, my life had to change for the second time since being accepted into this organization. I was assigned that name because I was deserving of it. It's more of a title—an acknowledgement of my ability to always plan ahead, to look further forward than other people do. It means I'm always six moves ahead of anyone else and therefore perfect for the job I have. It's who I am, and you will respect that."

I shrug and hold my hands up in silent apology.

"Thank you. Now I understand Lily has already given you a cell phone..."

I nod. "She has."

"Good. Periodically, you'll receive contracts on that device, so keep it with you at all times. There are three rules I want to explain to you, which our people must adhere to. The first—"

I hold a hand up. "Don't worry, Lily has already covered the rules. I—"

"Then you will hear them twice." His tone is sharp and final. "Don't ever interrupt me again."

I nod once and turn away. I pause to take a sip of my coffee, using the time to calm down. Usually, anyone speaks down to me like that, and they're knocked on their ass. But these are exceptional circumstances, and I need to bury that flash of anger.

I place my cup down gently and turn back to him. "You got it, Chief."

He holds my gaze for a moment, almost defiantly. "Thank you. The first rule is that you will always be ready to carry out a contract. You will be provided with everything you need to carry out the task when it's assigned to you, and you should do so without question or hesitation. We expect you to commit to our cause, put your faith in us... *believe* in what we're working for."

"And what is your cause, exactly? Sorry—*our* cause. Blind faith is a lot to ask for without any explanation. For me, trust and faith are like respect. They're earned, not expected."

"I appreciate your point of view, Adrian, but understand that these rules are non-negotiable. The penalty for disobeying any of them is expulsion from The Order and death."

"Bit extreme..."

"We take them seriously. We don't answer to anyone, and consequently don't owe anyone an explanation about anything. But as a show of *faith*, I will say this: The Order has existed for countless years, observing the world around us and working with people in strategic positions to guide it toward the right future. If we believe someone is directly or indirectly working in opposition of this, we see that as a problem, and we assume responsibility for removing that problem. It's a burden we gladly bear."

I take a sip of my coffee. "Fair enough. That all sounds noble, but who put you guys in charge?"

He lets out a short sigh, which I take as a sign of impatience. "The upper echelons of The Order consist of influential people throughout the world. They hide their allegiance but believe completely in the goals we strive to achieve. We put ourselves in charge, and there's no one powerful enough to keep us in check."

Jesus...

I'm not arguing with him. Not here. Not now. I'm going to play along until I find out what the hell I'm meant to be doing.

I wave a dismissive hand. "Okay, fine. Whatever. Rule number two?"

"The second rule is that you're an assassin, not a murderer. There is a difference. You're The Order's weapon, and we will use you when we feel the time is right to do so. But unless we give you permission, by way of a contract, you are forbidden from taking a life."

I have to admit, he's being far more condescending than Lily was when she told me all this. I don't have the tolerance for people like him, but for the sake of argument, I nod along silently.

Horizon—yes, I concede that his reason for the name was impressive—shifts in his seat slightly. "The third rule is perhaps the most important. The life you now have is one that many people cannot imagine. The freedom it affords you is, at times, hard to believe. But we cannot allow you to contact anyone from your former life. You can do whatever you want when you're not working a contract, but you have to actively avoid going anywhere or doing anything that could alert anyone you may have once known to the fact you're still alive. No exceptions. Am I clear?"

I take another sip of coffee, which finishes it. I push the empty cup aside. "You are."

"Good. Now that's out of the way…" He looks at one of his bodyguards and nods. The guy steps forward and reaches inside his jacket. He pulls out a small, thick envelope and drops it on the table in front of me. "Inside that is your new life, Adrian."

I frown and open it up. Inside is a new passport, a couple of credit cards, and some other bits of paperwork. I look over at Horizon. "Is this it?"

He nods. "Your passport is in the new identity we have manufactured for you. The credit cards are limitless, and the bills aren't your concern, so do whatever you want. The other papers in there are a birth certificate and some insurance documents."

Holy shit! Unlimited money, a new ID… are you *kidding* me?

Yeah… I know, I know…

"What's the catch, Chief?"

Horizon shakes his head. "Besides your unquestionable adherence to those three rules? There isn't one. This is your reward, in acknowledgement of the skills that brought you into The Order." He stands and takes a few idle paces away from the table, then turns around to look at me. His bodyguards resume their position on either side of him. With one hand, he gestures to the lines of people, all queuing to buy airline tickets. "It's a big world out there, Adrian. Go and see it. We'll be in touch."

He turns again and walks out the main entrance, leaving me sitting here alone, staring at the envelope. I scratch the back of my head and look around. I'm not really sure what to do now.

Coffee. This definitely calls for more coffee.

I get myself another drink and sit back down. I take a sip

of the steaming hot liquid and let out a deep breath. I look over at the lines of people and all the destinations listed on the boards above the counters they're queuing from, then I look at the envelope again.

I smile. "Anywhere in the world, eh?"

FOUR WEEKS LATER

8

I have the roof down on my car, and I'm resting my arm over the side. I'm cruising at an even eighty on the dusty, twelve-mile stretch of road that cuts through the desert on the outskirts of Abu Dhabi. I've always viewed driving as a necessity, rather than a pleasure. But I've never really done it without a reason. And I'm not a hardcore enthusiast, but seriously—this car is amazing! It's an Aston Martin, fresh off the production line. I think there are only about thirty available. It's jet-black, with large chrome trims and a mixture of brown leather and cloth on the interior. With the temperatures as high as they are out here, if it were all leather, I'd never be able to sit in the damn thing without burning the skin off my ass!

It's electric too, which is big nowadays. Ironic, given this country has always been one of the biggest exporters of crude oil. Having said that, they used to sell a lot more than they are now. Because of everything that's happened

86

recently, it's no surprise that the U.S. is now the gatekeeper for most of the world's oil, so maybe they're playing it smart and covering their asses by investing in alternatives.

As part of their environmentally friendly approach to transportation, all the roads around here have had heavy-duty solar panels laid over them. They look like normal roads, except they're far stronger and more durable, as well as much easier to maintain. All electric cars have paneling underneath the chassis now, so they will charge themselves as you drive around. It was a concept designed a few years ago, but now that the balance of global wealth has shifted dramatically, and with all the uninhabitable land and residual radiation everywhere, the environment has become a priority for everyone. Thanks to GlobaTech—who else?—with their research and funding, it took maybe two months to essentially recover the entire city with these panels. There are many people looking for work nowadays too, so it was a quick and easy job.

I figured I should do my part, which is why, when I spent almost three million dollars on this car, I went for the electric version.

It's the least I can do...

Man, I *love it* here! I've bought a place on Al Reem Island, which is an up-and-coming part of the city near the coast. It's just... beautiful. It took me a couple weeks to acclimatize—to the lifestyle as well as the weather—but I'm actually happy. I'm actively trying to forget my old life. Adrian Hell is dead. His spirit lives on. Don't get me wrong —I've carried out two contracts for The Order since I moved here, both of which were straightforward and relatively easy for me—but the persona is dead.

Thanks to the Order of Sabbah, I'm now legally known as Brad Foley.

I know... weird, right?

I struggled with it at first, but I finally got around to realizing a couple of things. First of all, my life has sucked, badly, for longer than I care to remember. I've fucking *earned* this shit! Even when I had billions of dollars of my own, I didn't really enjoy it—not in the typical sense, anyway. Yes, I bought a bar and started over, but I used what I needed to, so I could have a quiet life. This time, I'm using what I *want to,* so I can actually enjoy myself.

And that's the second thing I've realized. I *shouldn't* feel weird or guilty for doing this. I know Josh would be happy for me and proud of me for finally living my life, instead of simply existing solely to end other people's. Believing that helps me deal with the choices I made that ultimately got me here. A lot has happened in a short time, and I needed to slow things down, take stock, and relax.

I even got a tattoo to mark the beginning of this new life. I wanted a permanent reminder of where I am now but also where I came from and what I've been through. A tribute to my former self, so to speak. I kept it simple. On the inside of my right forearm, in a nice, Latin-inspired font, are four letters: WWJD.

What Would Josh Do?

He might think I'm dead, but he's still keeping me in line.

I hit the Abu Dhabi city limits and drop to a more acceptable speed. The noise of civilization grows all around, and shadows begin to stretch across the streets as immense buildings dominate the skyline.

There's a healthy mixture of everyday life and extravagance here. It's one of the places that didn't become suddenly over-populated by refugees searching for a new life in this post-4/17 world, simply because no one was allowed to. But the government and the Sheikhs have contributed billions to foreign aid initiatives, so they've done more than their fair share to help out. What remains here is a thriving, largely unaffected population, concerned about the rest of the world but living their own lives as normal, with as many luxuries as they can afford.

I fit right in.

I'm actually on my way to an appointment. It may or may not be a bad thing, depending on how you look at it, but there's a lot of downtime when you're in The Order. All the money and freedom in the world certainly helps, but personally, I found I get bored easily. I've enjoyed getting to know the city, but more often than not, I find myself sitting alone in a bar somewhere, drinking 'til dawn.

It's a lot of time to be left alone with only your thoughts for company.

As great as this new life is, and as genuinely happy as I feel, I admit I've... struggled, I guess, with a sense of guilt. I know I *should* ignore it, but I can't. I have no one to talk to— no Josh to keep me sane. It's just my own mind and a lot of beer, which isn't a good combination.

That's why I've sought help.

16:03 AST

I'm sitting in a slightly reclined leather chair, staring out the window at the scorching metropolis sprawling below me. The single room is a converted apartment on the top floor of a four-story building, nestled in the center of a small office complex just a short walk from Mangrove National Park. It's largely devoid of any decoration, which is probably a strategic decision. The carpet is new and still soft underfoot. The walls are plain and painted in a warm, neutral color. The air conditioning is blasting out, keeping the modest space nicely chilled.

Sitting across from me, in a less comfortable looking chair, is a woman. She has dark brown hair tied up in a ponytail and thin, pointed glasses resting low on her nose. Her high cheekbones are pronounced on her thin face. Her smile is friendly and welcoming and accompanies a manner that is never anything but professional.

Her name is Kaitlyn Moss. She's a highly qualified and expensive psychotherapist. I found her purely by chance. She's American but moved out here a few years ago, after qualifying. I've been spending an hour with her four times a week since I moved to Abu Dhabi. I know... weird, right? But I need to talk to someone, and due to lack of options, I figured this was probably the best way to go. I can speak with confidence and without fear of judgment. It may only be a small amount of time, but I've been finding it a big help.

Of course, I have to gloss over some of the specifics when addressing certain topics. While it's confidential, as a therapist, she's still obligated to report me if she believes I could cause harm to myself or others, or if I intend to break the law.

Yeah... there's been a *lot* of glossing over!

Kaitlyn is sitting with her legs crossed and her hands clasped on her lap, with a notepad beneath them. She's just asked me about Lily—how I feel about her and how *that* makes me feel. I'm thinking about my answer. She's watching me, observing.

I take a deep breath and look into her eyes. "I like her. I

admire and respect her. I consider her a friend. Or the closest thing I'll ever have to one."

Kaitlyn nods slowly, not taking her eyes off me. "Okay, allow me to digress for just a moment there, Brad. You say she's the closest thing you'll ever have to a friend. That's an interesting choice of words. What made you phrase it in that way?"

I shrug. "I dunno. I didn't think about it, really. I just... said it."

She looks at me as if she's sympathetic toward the fact that I don't understand something. "Your mind works on two levels—conscious and subconscious. More often than we realize, your subconscious makes choices for us based on instinct and, for want of a better phrase, what comes from the heart. You didn't think about how you phrased it because you didn't need to. In your mind, whether you're fully aware of it or not, you know exactly why you phrased it that way. Just take a moment to think about it."

I raise an eyebrow and laugh. Not in disbelief but at my own phenomenal lack of comprehension of what she just said. "That's some deep and meaningful shit..." I take a deep, slow breath. "I guess... I guess I just don't envisage having much opportunity to make new friends. My job has never really afforded me personal relationships, and..."

"And?"

I sigh. She picks up on every tiny little thing I say and do. "*And*... I lost the only friend I ever had, which was completely my fault. I don't want to replace... I don't want another one."

She smiles as if she's trying to offer me some comfort. "Making new friends doesn't mean you're replacing your old ones. It just means you're moving on with your life. Your past, if nothing else, serves as a reminder of who you are, what you've accomplished, what you've endured to be where you are, and who you are today. There's nothing wrong with embracing that."

I nod. "I know... but I don't feel ready to *embrace* it. I'm not sure I deserve to."

She nods back and makes a quick note on her pad. "Okay, we'll come back to that. I don't want to lose our original thread. You say you like Lily, and you mention a level of admiration and respect. Is that all you feel?"

I raise an eyebrow. "Are you asking me if I'm attracted to her?"

Kaitlyn says nothing. She just makes a small gesture with her hands for me to speak, as if it's up to me how I interpret her question.

I roll my eyes. "I dunno... I mean, it's not like she's unattractive. Any man would find her easy on the eyes, y'know? But I don't think I have any feelings toward her in that way."

"You've mentioned in previous sessions about recently losing a loved one." She pauses to look at her notes. "Tori?"

I nod but say nothing.

That conversation took place in my second... no, third session. Pretty hard to tell the full story, so I succinctly explained that she had been killed in the 4/17 attacks. Easier that way.

"Have you considered the possibility that maybe you're conflicted inside? That part of you actually wants to move on, whether that's with Lily or someone else, but a part of you is trapped in this... cycle of guilt and blame over the loss of Tori?"

I massage my forehead. I feel myself getting defensive. "But I *am* to blame for Tori's death! I should've been there to protect her. I should've—"

Kaitlyn leans forward slightly. "Brad... everyone deals

with things differently. Some people feel their lives will never be the same after suffering a loss, and it can take years for them to feel normal again. Some people never do. Others, for a whole host of different reasons, find being able to close an entire chapter of their lives much easier. It can be an unhealthy thing, like a strong denial, where they consciously or subconsciously choose to avoid the problem, or it can be a positive thing. They can be naturally strong enough to see that their own life doesn't have to stop because someone else's did."

I frown. "Don't you think that's a little callous? Just cutting someone off and forgetting about them like that?"

She shakes her head. "Like I say, some people will do it out of denial, but others can do it without guilt. People of faith, who believe the person they lost is at peace, use the comfort that belief gives them to continue with their own lives."

"Yeah, but what about me? I'm to blame for losing Tori. I should've been there to protect her. I don't deserve to enjoy life knowing she can't because of me."

Kaitlyn sits back in her chair and adjusts herself. "Brad, let me share something with you. Ever since 4/17, people all over the world, from every walk of life you can think of, have struggled in some way. It was the same with 9/11. It's not survivor's guilt. It's more a sense of... helplessness. Of loss. Of fear. The fact that something so terrible could actually happen, the awareness of the impact it had on all our lives forever... the go-to response is to take it personally. The scope of it is too big to comprehend, so we subconsciously personalize it and make it about ourselves. By doing so, we put that tragedy in terms our minds can understand. But the downside to that is that you're essentially making it about *you*. So, you feel as if you're the only one to suffer a loss. You feel afraid. You feel as if you can't do anything to protect the people you care about. And you feel guilty for ever moving on."

I'm staring at the floor. I'm listening to every word she's saying, and it makes a lot of sense. She's clearly good at what she does, and that's why I'm finding it so hard to let her continue. What she's saying probably applies to ninety-nine percent of people who have sought therapy in the last three months. But I was there. I was there when the button was pushed to kickstart 4/17. I was there when it was pushed to blow up my girlfriend. I was *there*, and both times, I should have done more to stop it happening. But I can't say that...

I just nod absently. "That makes sense, I guess. But I know that Tori's dead because of something... because of something I didn't do and should have. It doesn't matter what killed her. She could've been crossing the street and been hit by a car. The fact is, she was vulnerable and alone because of me, and she died as a result. So, I blame myself."

Kaitlyn goes to respond but seems to stop herself. I'm smart enough to know that *she's* smart enough to know there's probably more to this than I'm saying, but I think she realizes I've said all I'm going to about it for now.

She sits back in her seat. "Okay, Brad. Let's look at something else. I think maybe the key to helping you deal with your guilt isn't to address the root cause of it directly."

I raise an eyebrow. "Okay..."

"We've spoken about Tori in some detail. Not only the circumstances surrounding her death, but also the impact she had on your life. You mentioned previously that you retired a few years ago from a job you'd held for... well, most of your life. It was during this retirement that you met Tori, and she became the face of your new life. She symbolized everything your new life was about. A change of scene, a change of pace... your happiness."

I shrug and nod. That sounds about right.

She crosses her legs the opposite way and shifts in her seat. "Tell me, what made you retire from your job?"

I stroke the coarse stubble on my chin. "I'd... I'd done my job well for a long time. I served when I was eighteen, and when I left the Army, I stepped straight into the job and did it, in some capacity, for over twenty years. I felt it was time to stop. To move away from the only thing I knew how to do... from the only thing I was ever any good at... and try to start over."

She nods. "I see. You've never mentioned your time in the military before. Where were you stationed?"

"I was part of Desert Shield, stationed in Saudi Arabia. My unit was ambushed by some local forces a couple of months in. I was shot, and most of them were killed."

Her eyes go wide with genuine disbelief. "My God... and you were eighteen?"

I nod.

"You say most of your unit lost their lives. What happened to the others? How did they survive?"

I shrug. "I don't know. Our squad was split in two. The other half, as far as I know, did survive, but I left the Army soon after I was discharged from hospital and lost touch."

Kaitlyn glances at her watch. "It's almost time to wrap this up for today, but I want to leave you with this thought, Brad. From everything you've told me and how you carry yourself, it's pretty clear, even to someone without three degrees in psychology, that you feel it's your... responsibility to protect people. I think you view yourself as everyone's big brother, and you take it personally if someone you feel is your responsibility is hurt in any way. As honorable as that is, it's an incredible burden for anyone to bear. I think you bear it gladly, but the downside to that is that you end up blaming yourself for things that aren't your fault. It can also be a way of avoiding having to address your own problems.

"In terms of the guilt you say you feel, I think we're at a crossroads now. I think you're intelligent enough to realize what I'm saying makes sense, but I think you're... frankly, stubborn enough to allow yourself to stay trapped in that cycle of guilt we mentioned earlier. You need to understand that any guilt you're feeling is a choice, and you'll continue to feel it for as long as you allow yourself to."

I nod slowly and stare blankly at the floor again, absorbing everything she's saying and trying my best to process what it means. I've never looked at myself that way. No one's ever told me I'm a natural protector. I wonder if she would think that if she knew what I really did for a living? I guess she has a point, but that still doesn't change the fact my actions were responsible for a lot of people I cared about dying, including the woman I loved. What right do I have to move on from that? I *should* suffer the guilt I'm feeling.

I glance out the window, then look at her. "Okay. Thank you, Kaitlyn. As always, I appreciate your time and insight, and it does help me. Really."

She smiles professionally. "You're an intriguing man, Mr. Foley. While I think there's still a way to go, I'm glad you're feeling the benefit from our sessions."

I stand and straighten my T-shirt. "I am, definitely. Are you free tomorrow?"

She flicks through her notepad. "Yes... how does three o'clock sound?"

I nod. "Perfect."

We both stand, shake hands, and I leave her office. I walk down the three flights of stairs, press a button to release the magnetic lock on the main entrance, and get into my car, which is parked in the lot outside. I start the engine, put on a pair of sunglasses, and stare ahead for a moment, lost in idle thought. I always feel drained after my sessions with Kaitlyn. It's difficult having to think about all that shit for a solid hour.

I need a drink.

9

I'm traveling along the E10, heading toward the coast. I exit right and merge onto the road that takes me over the marina to Al Reem Island. The traffic isn't as heavy as in the main city. There are a handful of districts, each with their own micro-communities and points of interest. Lots of money was invested in developing this place over the last couple of years, and so far, it's been thriving quite nicely. Some of the houses over here dwarf mine. That's not to say my place is small, but there are definitely degrees of wealth, shall we say. Plus, I'm trying to stay reasonably discreet.

Because of the climate, natural vegetation and greenery is practically nonexistent, but lots of artificial trees, grass, and shrubbery have been planted all around here. As a result, the place looks a little like Las Vegas, but it's nice.

I drive down the main street for a half-mile or so, then take a left. The road takes me away from the center and out into one of the residential areas. After another quarter-mile,

I turn left again and stop in front of the gates leading into the exclusive community I now call home. There's no security, except for a network of camera feeds that link directly to the local police department. Plus, the wide, wrought-iron gate that blocks the street can only be opened remotely, and only the residents have a remote. I aim mine at the sensor, which is a small black box fixed to the left pillar next to the gate. The fob in my hand beeps, and there's a whirring as the mechanisms kick in and the gate begins to slide open.

I drive through, and it closes automatically behind me. The street is a long cul-de-sac, separated down the middle by a strip of grass roughly three feet wide, which has tall, thin trees planted at even intervals all the way along. There aren't that many properties within the community, but each one is enormous, set back from the road behind a big driveway and front lawn.

My place is the third one along on the left. It's a single-story house made from brilliant white brick, with a decorative pillar standing on either side of the front door. Inside is a large reception area that leads straight through to the kitchen. The hallway stretches away in both directions. Left leads to the first of two living rooms at the front of the house, as well as another room at the back that families would probably use as a dining room. I haven't bothered furnishing it. Some free weights are stored along the left wall, with a heavy punch bag hanging from the ceiling in the middle. To the right is a second living room—which, again, I haven't bothered too much with—and my bedroom, which has an en suite bathroom and shower.

I ease my Aston Martin into the drive, kill the engine, and climb out over the side—mostly because I can, and it's fun. I walk toward the front door, reaching for my keys, but stop when I near it.

It's open.

What the hell?

I look over my shoulder, glancing up and down the street. There's no sign of anyone. No movement. No unfamiliar cars.

Instinctively, I move my hand to my lower back and grab the Beretta I have holstered there. I've moved away from carrying two around with me all the time. I've even refrained from personalizing this one. It's just a boring, stock 92FS.

I quietly work the slide, chambering a round, and flick the safety off. I cautiously step forward and lean gently against the wall on the left. I place my hand on the door and hold my gun low by my side. I take a deep, quiet breath and slowly push it open, just wide enough for me to sidestep inside.

I pause in the doorway and flash a glance along the hallway—first left, then right.

Nothing.

I continue slowly, just a few steps into the foyer. Only now do I bring my gun up, ready to fire if necessary. You should always lead with your head, not your hands. You only need a second to see if anyone's there. Whereas, if you hold your gun out in front as you walk in, anyone who *is* there will see your weapon before they see you, which means they know you're armed and can prepare for you before you even know they're there.

I don't close the door behind me; I want to keep any noise to a minimum. I tread carefully, silently, across the foyer and head left. There are two doors leading into the living room, which slide apart. They're standing slightly separated. I ease the left-hand door back, just enough to give me a view of the room.

Empty.

I continue down the hall, reaching the dining room-slash-makeshift gym. The door is wide open. I press my back against it, both hands on my gun. I quickly peer around it. The split-second glance is all I need to see this room is empty too.

I turn back around and walk down the hallway, past the front door and on toward the second living room. The doors are the same as before. I slide them gently back and look inside, but there's no one there.

Whoever this is better not be on my goddamn bed!

I turn around and—

"Jesus Christ!"

Lily is standing right in front of me, smiling and eating an apple.

I shake my head. "What the hell? Are you fucking crazy? I could've shot you!"

She smiles. "Nah... you're too good to make a silly mistake like that, aren't you?"

I breathe out heavily and relax. I flick the safety catch on and tuck my gun back into its holster behind me. I shake my head again. "Come on."

I turn and head toward the kitchen, diverting only to shut the front door on my way past. I walk inside and open the refrigerator, which is one of those huge, two-door things with an ice dispenser built into the front. I take out two beers, pop the tops, and hand one to Lily, who's standing next to me. She takes it with a nod, places her half-eaten apple on the side, and takes a grateful gulp.

She's wearing a thin, yellow crop top, which is stretching over her obvious, impressive chest. It's actually difficult not to stare. Her exposed midriff is toned with a visible six-pack, and her navel is pierced with a small vertical bar topped by a bejeweled butterfly. She's also wearing tight white jeans and black heeled boots.

Heels?

I nod at her feet. "How the hell did you sneak up on me wearing *them*?"

She shrugs. "Good question. You should really think about that, shouldn't you? I could've been anyone."

She flicks her eyebrows, smiles playfully, takes another sip of her beer, and walks across to the counter in the middle of the room. She sits on one of the stools and continues drinking. She doesn't say anything. She just stares at the microwave in front of her.

I move over to join her, relishing the sensation of the cold bottle in my hand. "So... what are you doing here, Lily? Not that it isn't nice to see you, but... it's a little out of the blue."

She doesn't look up. "I was bored. Thought I'd say hey."

I smile. "You could've just called. Why break into my house?"

She looks at me and shrugs. "Like I said, I was bored."

There's clearly more to it than that, but I'll play along and let her tell me in her own time.

I sigh. "Okay. So, how've you been?"

She stands, takes a breath, and has a deep swig of her drink, emptying the bottle. She places it heavily on the counter and turns to face me. In her heels, she's not that much shorter than me. Her eyes are level with my chin. "What do you do for fun around here? Besides sweat..."

I laugh. "Yeah, it can get a little warm. Fun? What do you want to do? We have pretty much everything here."

"I want to drink. And dance."

I raise an eyebrow. "Okay... a club it is. Let me grab a

quick shower and change." I gesture to the refrigerator behind me with my thumb. "Help yourself to another beer."

I head out and left, toward my bedroom. I hear her behind me.

I look over my shoulder. "You all right?"

She's smiling. "Yeah..."

I nod slowly. "Okay, then. I'm... gonna go shower now..."

She's still following me. This is weird!

I walk inside my bedroom, and she stops just outside, still smiling. I frown at her and close the door behind me. I pause for a moment and then re-open it. She's still there. Still smiling. I shake my head, feeling confused, and shut it again. I lock it this time.

I walk into my bathroom and turn the shower on, peel my T-shirt off, throw it on the floor, and stare at my reflection in the mirror over the sink.

"What the hell is going on?"

21:23 AST

The music—if you can call it that—is loud. The bass is thumping to the point where my chest is vibrating. It's still early, but this place is already busy. It's one of the more popular nightclubs in the city. I've been here a few times on my own. Not because I like partying, and *definitely* not because of the music... but because it's easy to have a drink and turn invisible in a place like this.

The black floor tiles have spotlights in them, and alternating colors flash in sync with the song the DJ is playing. The house lights are turned way down, but the tables and the bar are illuminated by pulsing neon, providing more than enough visibility.

Lily and I are sitting next to each other at a small, round table in a booth against the back wall, looking out at the large dance floor, crammed with bodies. The surface is glowing pink. I have a half-empty beer in front of me. Lily opted for a cocktail that looks like a fruit salad with a firework sticking out of it.

We haven't said much to each other since we arrived. I don't know whether that's because it's hard to hear each other speak, or simply because she doesn't feel like talking. I'm happy either way. I'm comfortable sitting in silence.

I can't figure her out, though. She's just sitting here, moving her head slightly to the music and looking around absently at the people dancing, drinking, and having fun. When we first met, she was pretty frosty with me. Then she seemed to warm to me a little. Then she was all business. Then she walked away, and I haven't heard from her in almost a month. Then she broke into my house because she's bored and felt like saying hello...

I don't know if it's just her or women in general that I don't understand.

I nudge her arm with mine to get her attention. She looks at me and I smile. "Is everything all right?"

She nods. "Great."

She says it with a smile, but even I can tell there's something on her mind.

"Be straight with me, Lily. What's going on? Why are you really here?"

She shrugs. "Can't I just call in on a friend when I feel like it?"

"Yeah, that would be perfectly fine. But I didn't think we knew each other well enough to be friends. And you didn't call in. You *broke* in, which you still haven't properly explained or apologized for..."

She finishes her drink and sighs heavily. She goes to speak but stops herself. After a moment, she rolls her eyes. "All right, fine. I was working a contract The Order gave me, and it didn't quite go as planned. I needed to lie low for a while..."

I frown. "What happened?"

"I missed my target. I've been trying to stay under the radar while I track him down again. I can't fail. Horizon will have my head."

"And you haven't been able to find him?"

She shakes her head. "Oh, no, I've found him..."

"So... what's the problem?"

She looks at the table for a moment, then at me. The regret and apology in her eyes is obvious. She doesn't need to say anything else.

I sigh. "Your target's here, isn't he? You didn't call in to see me at all. You need my help."

She holds up a hand defensively. "Hey, I don't *need* your help, okay? I just... thought you might want to tag along."

I shake my head and smile. "Uh-huh..."

"Oh, whatever. I'm getting another drink. You want one?"

"Yeah, I'll have a beer. Thanks."

She shuffles out of the seat and walks across the dance floor, toward the bar. I can't help but watch her go. Her hips are like poetry in motion, swaying with a natural flick to the side with each step. She really is—

"Excuse me?"

Distracted, I look to my right and see two women standing there, smiling at me. Both are gorgeous. They're not in Lily's league, but they're undeniably attractive all the same. They could be twins. Both have long blonde hair, and both are wearing tight black dresses that leave little to the imagination. They're holding small handbags and standing close together.

I raise an eyebrow. "Can I... help you?"

They look at each other and giggle. The one on the left steps forward and leans against the table. "We've... ah... we've seen you around here before. What's your name?"

I take a sip of my beer and try to remain casual. I'm doing my best to stay optimistic, but sadly, I'm too old and too experienced to avoid being cynical. I've been coming to this club, on average, maybe twice a week for the last three weeks. I come here for the atmosphere and for the beer. I don't come here to dance, socialize, or pick up women. And while I don't consider myself to be bad-looking, I wouldn't ever assume I can attract any woman I want. So, when two stunning, seemingly eager women approach me and start flirting—which I think is what this is—I'm immediately skeptical.

I look at each woman in turn and smile courteously. "The name's Brad. Brad Foley."

The one leaning on the table moves to my side. Her friend sits down and slides across the seat, so she's next to me. Both of them link my arms, laughing.

"Nice to meet you, Brad," says the one on my left. "I'm Nicki. That's Hannah."

Her friend squeezes my arm. "Hi, Brad!"

I smile politely. "Hi... Hannah. So, what are you two doing in Abu Dhabi?"

Nicki shrugs. "We're on vacation. We wanted to see the world, y'know? After everything that's been happening, we decided life's too short, so we should seize the moment. Hannah, what's that saying?"

Her friend frowns. "Crap a dime, or something?"

I smile, trying not to laugh. "You mean *carpe diem*?"

"That's it!" squeals Nicki.

Crap a dime? Seriously...

"You're so smart!" gushes Hannah. "And handsome. Oh my God, that watch is gorge! Can I try it on? It looks heavy..."

And my skepticism prevails!

I admit I may have been a little indulgent with my newfound wealth. I bought some nice sunglasses—Oakley, gold-rimmed, tinted lenses—and this watch, which is a gold Rolex, complemented with diamond and platinum highlights on the hands and face. It's a bit extravagant, I know, but I thought I should allow myself a few luxuries to go along with my new life.

I gently remove her hand from my arm. "I don't think my watch is really your style. Sorry."

She looks a little deflated but quickly bounces back. "So, Nicki and I are going to hit another couple of bars before going back to our hotel. Do you wanna join us? You would have a wicked time. Promise!"

Nicki leans in close. "You *so* would, Brad!"

I annoy myself sometimes. Put me in a room full of guys armed to the teeth, all trying to kill me, and I'm fine. I'll either talk my way out or shoot my way out, every time. But give me two young, scantily clad, willing women with dollar signs in their eyes, and I turn into an over-polite, apprehensive teenager who doesn't have a clue.

"Friends of yours?"

I look up and see Lily standing here, holding our drinks. Oh, thank God!

"Hey. So, Nicki, Hannah—this is my... ah... this is Lily."

The girls turn to look at her. I see their faces change in

an instant. The territorial instincts of the wild woman in her natural habitat instantly take over. These two can't be older than twenty-five. They must know they're attractive, but they'll know that neither of them can hold a candle to Lily. She's stunning on a whole other level, and it's effortless. She doesn't need short dresses and make-up... she's just *that* hot. And she's probably aware of it too, but she doesn't let it influence her behavior in any way.

Lily's staring at each of them challengingly. I don't know if it's just because I know she's an assassin, but she looks really fucking scary right now! Hot... but scary.

Hannah slides out of the booth and moves to stand beside Nicki. Both of them are a little taller than Lily, but that's likely to do with their heels. Not that it matters—Lily's not exactly going to back down from them.

They're standing with their backs to me. I take a sip of my beer and watch. Even I know it's best to stay quiet when women are doing... whatever *this* is.

Without a word, Lily pushes between them and stands next to me. She holds my gaze for a brief moment, and then leans forward, places one hand behind my head and—

...

...

...

—kisses me.

Sorry—I was always taught it's rude to talk with your mouth full.

Holy crap, that was incredible! Her lips were soft, her tongue was warm, and I could feel the passion in her touch.

She pulls away and smiles at me, then turns to face Nicki and Hannah. "Beat it, you pair of whores. And if you come near my man again, I'll shoot you."

Their eyes nearly pop out of their heads, and they both

turn and run across the dance floor and out through the main doors. Well, I say run... it's more of an awkward totter in those shoes. Without saying anything, Lily slides my beer across the table to me and shuffles in beside me. She gets comfortable and has a sip of her drink.

I'm not entirely sure what just happened there. Or why. Not that I'm complaining. I just feel... guilty, like I've been unfaithful. I think back to my session with Kaitlyn earlier and the things she said about misplaced guilt and how people react differently to loss. In a split-second, I summarize a month's worth of therapy and decide that, right now, I need a drink.

I take a large gulp of my beer and turn to look at her. "So... *that* was new."

She shrugs, stares at her drink, and waves a hand dismissively. "They were only here for your money. I was just doing you a favor."

"I know they were. I had it handled..."

She looks up at me. "*Sure,* you did. *I don't think my watch is really your style...* Please!"

I frown. "How do you—"

"I can lip read. I was watching from the bar. You're hopeless. D'you know that?"

I nod and stare at the table. "I do."

Out the corner of my eye, I see her smiling at me. "Okay, Adrian. I... I do need your help. I'm sorry for randomly interrupting your new life like this, but—"

"Hey, if this is your idea of interrupting me, don't feel bad. I can learn to live with it!"

We both laugh, and she goes a little flushed. "Listen, can we get out of here? Go somewhere quieter? I can fill you in on the details of my contract."

"Sounds good. Come on."

We both stand and head across the dance floor, navigating our way through a growing sea of people, all jumping up and down to the music. We step out into the humid evening and take a right, walking side by side in the direction of the coast. Lily slides her arm around mine and leans in slightly.

"Tonight's been nice. Thank you. It was just what I needed to unwind."

I smile. "I'm glad it helped. So, are you gonna tell me what happened?"

She stands straight, as if she's steeling herself for the unenviable task of telling me. "Well, it all—"

"There they are!"

We both frown, confused, and look behind us. Nicki and Hannah are walking purposefully toward us, striding confidently in their heels. Behind them, six men are huddled together, looking angry. They're all big guys, and they look capable and organized. They all have tanned skin and thick, black beards, painstakingly groomed in a variety of different styles.

Nicki steps forward. "Hey, asshole... no one turns us down. Do you hear me?"

Lily and I exchange another glance. She smiles. "This should be fun!"

I rub my eyes with tired frustration. "I think you and I interpret fun *very* differently..."

10

I turn to face the approaching mob. My mind is already running at full speed, playing out my first few moves. I glance at Lily. "Just follow my lead, okay?"

She pats my arm. "All yours, hotshot."

We don't make a move. We just stand and let the group come to us. The girls stop a few feet away from us, standing defiantly with their arms crossed and a hip cocked to the side—the universal position that pissed-off women assume right before a confrontation.

The men fan out to surround us, taking up the full width of the sidewalk. The few passers-by hurry to give us a wide berth. Nicki and Hannah push their way into the middle, smiling arrogantly as if they've gotten one over on us both.

A man from the right steps forward and moves next to the women. His hand disappears inside his pocket and comes out a moment later wearing a set of brass knuckles.

I take a deep, calming breath, trying to keep my heart

rate steady. I can sense Lily doing the same beside me. We both stand loose, ready for anything.

Hannah shakes her head. "You should've just come with us, Brad. Yeah, we were gonna rob you, but chances are, you wouldn't have been hurt that much."

Nicki nods in agreement. "Plus, you *are* pretty cute. We might have taken pity on you..."

I ignore them both and look at the man standing with them. He's a powerfully built guy, a bit shorter than me but wider, with more obvious muscle mass. His bulky fingers look swollen, forced into the grip of the brass knuckles. He's staring at me, trying to look intimidating.

Dick.

In my head, I've already planned how I'm going to take out all six of these pricks. Shouldn't be too difficult, especially seeing as I have Lily with me. But I want to understand something first...

I point to the guy in front of me. "Are you in charge?"

He doesn't say anything, but I notice the two women glance at him expectantly, so I guess he is.

"I'll take your silence as a yes. So, what is this, exactly? Are you really just a gang who go from club to club, using these two bicycles..." I nod at Hannah and Nicki. "...to lure rich, gullible idiots outside, so you and your boys can rob them?"

Hannah tuts loudly. "Hey! Who are you calling a bicycle? What does that even mean, anyway, asshole?"

I smile. "I'm insinuating that, like a bicycle, I suspect most people have ridden you at some point..."

Next to me, Lily snorts as she laughs aloud.

Hannah's eyes go wide, and she scoffs with shock. Nicki looks angry and lunges at me, winding up a big slap. I barely need to move to catch her hand, but I do, firmly, as it comes around aimed at my face. I grip her wrist tightly enough to stop her moving but no more than necessary. She's just a dumb kid at the end of the day, and I don't want to hurt her.

"Don't be silly..." I push her arm away. "Now be quiet, darlin'. The grown-ups are talking."

The circle of men all visibly tense, dropping their arms and getting ready to fight.

I ignore them, focusing again on the main guy standing with us. "Let me save you some time here, Chief. There aren't enough of you to take anything from me. I appreciate the gesture. I'm sure it's a sweet little set-up you have here. But I'm the wrong guy, all right? So, let's save everyone some time and some pain. Just cut your losses and walk away. No harm, no foul."

He shakes his head and smiles. "You don't know who you're fucking with..."

I raise an eyebrow. I actually feel pretty bad for the guy...

I look at Lily. "Are you still bored?"

She cracks her neck and winks at me. "Believe it or not, I'm starting to feel a little entertained."

"Glad to hear it." I look back at the guy. "Okay, you little fucktrumpet, this is your only warning—your only shot at walking away from this unscathed and unaided. I suggest you take it before it's too late."

He steps toward me, raising both arms and clenching his fists.

Here we go...

I don't move forward to meet him. Instead, I stay still and simply push my foot forward and down, connecting with his kneecap. *Then* I take a step forward, keeping the momentum going, so I follow through as if I'm stomping a cockroach and want to put my foot through the ground. All his weight is currently on that leg, and it snaps like a twig.

He screams and buckles, falling quickly to his side. He lands hard, clutching his injured leg, which is flopping lifelessly around in his hands.

"Oh, *nice!*" shouts Lily, hitting my arm in a congratulatory fashion.

The two women are stunned. They gasp and hug each other, shuffling outside the circle to safety. The remaining men exchange uncertain glances, but no one moves.

In my experience—which is, sadly, quite vast in this area—if you have a group of adversaries like this, the best strategy is to hit the first one who moves or talks. Put them down, hard and fast, with little or no warning. Usually, the one who acts first is in charge, and if you drop *them*, the rest of the group will be shocked and confused, which gives you a great advantage.

I look at each one in turn. "Anyone else still think *this* is a good idea?"

There's a guy on our left, maybe a step or two behind us, who's the only one close enough to grab us if he wanted to. He needs to go next, just to hammer the point home. I subtly nudge Lily's arm. She quickly steps toward the guy, turns counterclockwise, and slams her forearm and elbow into his temple. He didn't even see her move, let alone process the strike or attempt to block it. He was just standing there, minding his own business, preoccupied with trying to look imposing. She caught him right on the money, and he dropped like a stone.

I look back at the group, who have now all taken a step back. "Seriously... anyone else feel compelled to finish what you started?"

Silence.

"...is the smart answer. Well done. Now fuck off, all of you."

Without hesitation, they scoop up their unconscious friends and walk away from the club, tails between their legs, leaving Lily and me with the two women. Hannah and Nicki look terrified. As they should. I take a step back, and Lily moves toward them. They visibly shrink on the spot.

Lily lets out a tired breath. "You two should choose your friends better. Do you actually realize how close you both came to dying tonight?"

They exchange a glance and look confused.

"Wha-what do you mean?" asks Nicki.

Lily steps backward, drawing level with me. In a lightning-fast movement, she reaches behind me and takes out my Beretta. She levels the gun at the pair of them, her arm steady.

"I mean... I'm trying hard not to shoot you both, you stupid bitch."

They both scream. Loudly.

I hear the faint sound of a siren in the distance. They're playing our song...

I think it's time we were somewhere else.

I move beside Lily and push her arm down gently with my hand. I ease my gun from her grip and slide it back into its holster. "Come on, Lily. We're done here."

I put my arm around her shoulder and usher her away from the screaming women and the retreating men, walking hurriedly in our original direction. After a few minutes, we turn off down a side street and drop to a more discreet, casual pace.

I turn to look at her. "So, are you gonna tell me what happened that really brought you here?"

She turns to meet my gaze. Her brown eyes sparkle in the glow of the streetlights. "I will but not now, okay? After all that, my adrenaline's pumping, and I just want to drink and dance. We can talk tomorrow."

I nod. "Fair enough. Drinking sounds good."

"And dancing..."

I shake my head and smile. "You can dance. I'll drink and watch."

She rolls her eyes at me, and we share a laugh.

I have a feeling our night is just beginning...

11

Holy shit... what was I drinking last night?

I open one eye. I'm lying in bed, face-down, buried in my pillow. It's daylight outside. Far too bright for my liking. I glance at the alarm clock on the bedside table and close my eye again.

Ugh! The inside of my mouth feels like the desert, and my head is banging louder than the music was in the club last night. I'm not cut out for this shit anymore. I'm too old.

I frown.

Wait a minute...

I snap both eyes open and quickly roll over on my back. I look to my right and see Lily lying next to me, seemingly still asleep. She's sprawled on top of the covers. She still has her crop top on, but she's dispensed with her white jeans. Her underwear doesn't look like it offers much in the way of warmth.

Oh... my... God...

I stare at the ceiling, massaging my temples. What the hell happened last night?

I roll out of bed carefully, so I don't disturb her, and make my way to the kitchen. I grab some juice from the refrigerator and look out the window at my pool. It's already hot, and there isn't a cloud in the sky, so the glare from the sun is unrestrained. Neither are prime conditions when dealing with a hangover.

I hear something behind me. I look over my shoulder and see Lily padding barefoot into the kitchen, looking tired but decidedly more awake than I feel. She waves silently and heads straight to the fridge. She takes out a beer, pops the top, and takes a big gulp, then walks back out. I force myself to look away, so I don't stare at her ass as she goes.

She really is something else...

I finish my juice and follow her out. I push open my bedroom door to see her sitting on the bed, leaning back against the pillows.

She smiles weakly. "Morning, sunshine."

I nod a quick greeting. "It sure is. You okay?"

"Yeah, I'm all right. Those cocktails were stronger than I thought, though..."

"Yeah... what happened last night? I remember going in the first place we found after the fight, but then things get a little blurry..."

She chuckles. "Yeah, I think that was where we discovered that really expensive tequila."

I raise an eyebrow and try desperately to recall anything about what happened last—

Wait...

Tequila?

I remember shot glasses.

I hold my head with both hands and breathe a heavy

sigh. It's as if remembering it is actually *increasing* my hangover.

"Oh, yeah... tequila."

I sit down on the end of the bed, lean forward, and rest my elbows on my knees and my head in my hands.

Lily moves next to me and pats me on the back. "Don't worry, big boy. It's just your age."

I don't bother looking up. "Gee, thanks. How are you so perky, anyway? You're way too skinny to absorb that much alcohol, surely?"

She giggles. "Practice. I'm gonna jump in the shower... that okay?"

I wave a dismissive hand. "Go for it."

She disappears inside my bathroom. I quickly throw some clothes on, pick up my cell phone from the bedside table, and walk back out to the kitchen. I make a pot of coffee—I need the caffeine to wake me up—and check my phone.

No messages.

I let out an impatient sigh.

Considering all the hoops I jumped through to get in The Order and the fuss they made about recruiting me, things have been annoyingly quiet. I guess I envisioned being busier than this...

I sit down and sip my coffee. Ten minutes pass easily enough before Lily appears next to me, wearing the same clothes as yesterday, looking more refreshed and smelling amazing. She pours herself a cupful of the good stuff and sits down opposite me.

I gesture a silent *cheers* with my mug. "Feel better?"

She nods. "Yeah. Thanks."

"Okay, down to business. I don't know what, if anything, you told me last night, but I'm damned if I can remember any of it, so we need to run through it again. Or for the first time—whichever. Who's your target, and what went wrong?"

She sighs and stares at the counter, seemingly reluctant to tell me. I can understand that. It's a pride thing. We're meant to be the elite in our profession. It's not easy to admit you failed.

"Horizon activated a contract on a man called Sayed bin Mawal. He's a Saudi prince visiting the city for a few days. Naturally, he's well protected. My plan was to use what God gave me—" She gestures to her chest with her hand. "—to get close to him, then take him out once we were alone."

I shrug, trying not to stare. "Makes sense. So, what happened?"

"I couldn't get close enough. His security was too thorough, and they didn't trust me. When I pushed the issue, they threatened me, and I was forced to defend myself, blowing my cover. I barely got out of there alive. I won't get within a mile of him now."

"Don't beat yourself up over it, Lily. That happens sometimes. Just regroup and try again."

She shakes her head. "No, you don't understand... I told Horizon it was done. I said I'd killed him."

I frown. "Why would you do that?"

"I don't know! I panicked, I guess..."

"But won't Horizon and The Order find out he's still alive?"

She nods.

"And I'm guessing they frown upon the whole *failing and lying about it* thing, right?"

She nods again.

"Shit. How long d'you think you have?"

She shrugs. "Twenty-four hours, max."

I nod, processing the information. Instinctively, I start thinking about the hit, looking at every option, every eventuality. I play out the contract in every possible way, considering every possible scenario, until the target's dead. Then I rewind everything in my mind, right back to the beginning, and focus on the single most important question.

"Why does The Order want this guy dead?"

Lily sighs. "Not this again, Adrian. I don't know, okay? I didn't ask and Horizon didn't tell me. Besides, who cares?"

"You should. You're putting your life on the line here. Don't you wanna know why?"

She shakes her head. "No, I don't. We've been through this. That's not how things work. It's not for us to ask why. I trust that Horizon has his reasons. I'm just his weapon."

I roll my eyes. "Jesus, Lily. When are you going to wake up and smell what you're shoveling? You sound like you're brainwashed, reading out of the welcome brochure! We're highly trained killers, but we're not animals. We're professionals, and you can't honestly tell me, if you were working for yourself, you wouldn't ask that question..."

She pushes her mug of coffee away from her slightly and sits up straight in her chair. "No, Adrian, I wouldn't! I don't work for myself, but even if I did, I wouldn't care. I'm an assassin. People pay me to kill other people. I'm not interested in why. All I've ever cared about is how much I'm getting paid for it. And I respect the fact that, like many other jobs around the world, there are people who know things others don't—now even more so. I'm not here to know what he knows. I'm here to shoot who he tells me to. End of story. Why is that so hard for you to come to terms with?"

"Because I'm the absolute best at what we do, Lily. Without exception. Not finding out why you're killing someone is amateurish. It leaves you vulnerable to potential repercussions. You have to—"

She stands and slams her hand on the counter. "Fuck you! Who are you calling *amateurish*, you fucking asshole?" She paces away, toward the back door. "I can't believe I came here..."

Jesus.

I'm a little taken aback by her outburst. I hold both hands up. "All right, take it easy. I'm not questioning your abilities, Lily. Knock it down a notch, okay? All I'm saying is that it's a mistake not to ask that question, and mistakes get people like us killed."

She doesn't say anything, holding my gaze for a moment. There's a confused rage in her eyes that I can see her wrestling with. She slowly sits back down, grabs her mug, and takes a sip. I can see her jaw muscles tensing as she thinks about what I've said. I can see the doubt slowly creeping in, replacing the anger.

I smile to myself.

I've been there, sweetheart.

"Lily, I'm sorry, all right? I didn't mean to give you a hard time. Old habits, I guess. We'll do this one together. That's not against the rules, is it?"

She fixes me with an unblinking stare. I can see her trying hard to stay angry at me, but after a moment, she relents. Her expression softens and she smiles. "No, there's no rule against a helping hand... providing it's from someone in The Order, obviously. Thank you."

"Forget about it. I've been looking for something to do anyway. This playboy lifestyle gets a little boring after a while."

She laughs. "A bottomless bank account, total anonymity, *and* immunity from everyone... it's every man's dream, surely? You've barely been at it a month. How are you bored already?"

I shrug. "You were bored when you got here. What's your excuse?"

She rolls her eyes. "Yes, but I was *lying*, remember?"

I sigh. "Whatever."

She smiles. "So, what now?"

I finish my coffee and take a breath. Resting on the counter, I glance down at my right arm.

WWJD.

What would Josh do?

I smile, mostly to myself. "Research."

10:07 AST

I grabbed a quick shower, threw on some fresh clothes, and set my laptop up on the kitchen counter in front of Lily and me. She's sitting on one of the stools, transfixed by the screen. I'm just pouring us both another glass of juice. It's hotter than hell, and despite the AC blasting cool air throughout the entire house, it's still unbearably warm.

I sit next to her and pass her a glass, which she takes silently. I watch her studying an article on the page for a moment, looking uncomfortable. I bet she feels as if she's betraying The Order by showing some initiative. She's probably never done research before. I know The Order says they will provide you with all the information you need to carry out the contract, but I would bet my bottomless credit card they only give you half the story. I can guarantee they leave out the important bits, such as why you're killing them.

JAMES P. SUMNER

I don't think it's just me being stuck in my ways and stubborn, either. It's a perfectly legitimate question that I think we have the right to have answered. Lily, me, probably countless others... we're the ones on the front line, risking everything to kill these people. The least The Order could do is tell us why. They're not a religion. They don't operate on unquestioning belief and donations.

Besides, I know from experience never to ignore my spider sense. Every time I do, it nearly gets me killed. And it's not as if I'm asking for an in-depth report. I just want a simple explanation. *The guy's a terrorist...* or *they profit from other people's misfortune...* Hell, even *they're a bit of a prick.* All of those statements are more than adequate reasons to shoot someone. But saying nothing immediately makes me question things.

Anyway... to business.

As much as I'm an advocate of research and preparation, I have to say it's actually pretty fucking boring and definitely not my thing. I've just spent about twenty minutes doing it, and I have a whole new level of respect for Josh. Here I am, feeling bad about making him think I'm dead, when I've been making him do this shit for over a decade! I'm surprised the guy hasn't tried to kill me himself.

Okay, so Sayed bin Mawal wasn't exactly a hard man to track down online. It turns out he's one of the richest men on the planet. He was loaded before 4/17, but in this unstable new world, he's one of the few who has actually maintained his wealth.

Despite only being the tender age of thirty-one, he's the majority shareholder in numerous companies across the world. The most prominent of those companies is Fuelex— a public, multi-national corporation and one of the largest exporters of crude oil in the world.

124

So Forbes says, anyway.

Now I have to admit... I glossed over the details here because they weren't really about him, but the basic gist of why he's so rich is that Fuelex stock rose significantly in the aftermath of 4/17.

The attacks affected Eastern Europe and Asia, mostly. The West was largely left alone—with the obvious exception of Texas—as was Africa and parts of the Middle East. Consequently, there's been a power shift in certain areas. International trade agreements have mostly been ignored in favor of the greater good. No one can afford anything anymore. Millions of people are homeless. Half the world is drowning in poverty and economic recession, despite the other half, to its credit, doing everything it can to help out.

Some of the key players in the crude oil industry who were based in countries hit by the attacks are no longer in business. Consequently, their substantial share of the pie has now been split between the only remaining players on the field—the U.S. and the Middle East. Both regions have always been prominent in the industry, but now they completely monopolize it.

The U.S. still charges above-average prices to its customers *not* affected by the recession. This serves to keep the commodity afloat on the stock market, which, in turn, helps strengthen the market as a whole.

But the people who *are* affected by the recession still need oil. They can't afford to pay what the U.S. is asking, so to counter this, Fuelex—arguably the largest single entity in the business—have begun exporting it at a loss, purely to satisfy the massive demand from millions of people who couldn't afford it otherwise. It helps everyone out, which is great, and it's ultimately only the good prince himself who's losing money—and he doesn't care because he has lots of it.

The problem is that him doing that devalues the commodity on the stock market, which is causing all the rich people in the States, who are desperately trying to carry on as normal, to lose money. Lots of money. Like, billions of dollars.

So, I think—if I understand all that shit—I've found the reason The Order wants him dead. They, or the people who have reached out to them, want the prince gone because it's simply too costly to let him live.

I understand it, but I don't like it. They basically asked Lily to murder Robin Hood.

I massage the bridge of my nose and pause for a drink. It's too hot to think...

Maybe I *should* try learning to go with the flow. Stop asking so many damn questions and accept the fact that life's different for me now. It shouldn't matter to me why I'm being sent to kill someone, should it? This is my job. Hell, this is my *life*. Back in the old days, when it was just Josh and me on the open road, I know that was more about running from my past than anything else. I needed that moral justification, so I felt better about myself and what I was doing.

But now?

I don't know. As I said to Lily earlier, old habits die hard.

"Check this out," says Lily, distracting me.

"What is it?"

She scrolls down a page on a local news website. "It says here that bin Mawal is staying in a penthouse suite at the Jumeirah Hotel for the next few days."

I raise an eyebrow. "Oh..."

"Is that a bad thing?"

I nod. "If that's true, it puts him either on or above the sixty-fifth floor of the Etihad Towers. In Tower One, I believe."

"Oh..."

"Yeah... *Oh*. If he's as well protected as you say, it'll be near-impossible to hit him while he's in the hotel."

She raises an eyebrow and half-smiles at me. "*Near* impossible?"

I smile back. "Yeah... there's no such thing as a truly impossible shot. You can get to anyone, providing you make the right approach." I stand, finish my drink, and grab my keys from near the edge of the counter. "Come on."

Lily stands. "Where?"

"We should start with some recon. We'll take my car. Chances are you'll be spotted, and we want to avoid that if at all possible."

"So, we're going to the hotel?"

I shrug. "Yeah, why not? That's where he is."

I turn and head for the door.

"But Adrian, what if someone sees us? This is reckless. This is insane! Why on Earth would you go and stand outside the guy's hotel? It'll be swarming with his security. I can't believe you're—"

I stop listening to her as I open the door and step outside. The heat hits me like a freight train as the effects of the AC are left behind. I jump over the door of my Aston Martin and start the engine. Lily appears in the doorway and stares at me defiantly.

"This is stupid!" she shouts.

I smile back.

She's not the first person to say that to me when I've had an idea, and I doubt she'll be the last.

12

I pull over to the side of the road and kill the engine, parking in the shadows of the Etihad Towers. The temperature is unholy, and the shade is doing little to compensate. I lean back in my seat and stare up at the dizzying height of Tower One.

Christ, it's big.

I think Tower Two, which is just to the left of it, is a little bigger, though. I'm looking up at the top floor, trying to figure out a way of getting up there without being seen.

Nothing's springing to mind...

I look across at Lily. She seems distracted, staring blankly at the dash.

"Hey, you okay?"

She nods vacantly. "Yeah. I'm just thinking what I'm gonna say to Horizon when he finds out Sayed bin Mawal is still alive."

I smile. "It won't come to that, I promise. The guy's

gonna be dead by the end of the day. Don't waste your time and energy worrying about The Order, okay?"

She looks at me. "You can't *possibly* be that confident?"

I shrug. "Like I said, no hit is impossible. But... some of them can be difficult, so a little bit of thought is required. That's all."

She scoffs. "Only a little bit?"

"Yeah... too much and you jeopardize the mission. Our business is about instinct. Get too weighed down with a plan, you lose sight of your objective. You become more bothered about doing it a certain way than you do about simply getting it done. That's when shit starts to go wrong."

She shifts in her seat, turning her body toward me. "Okay... you're the expert here. You're the *best there is*..." She air-quoted that. Bitch. "How do we kill this bastard?"

I raise an eyebrow at the not-so-subtle edge in her tone. I'll chalk it up to concern for now.

"Let me see what we're dealing with first."

She frowns. "What are you going to do?"

I nod toward the entrance of the hotel. "I'm gonna go ask what room he's staying in."

She shakes her head with disbelief.

I laugh. "It'll be fine. But maybe don't wait around for me just in case you're spotted. Drive around for twenty minutes. Meet me back here after that, okay?"

"Yeah... whatever."

"Oh, and my Beretta's in the glove compartment, should you need it."

She furrows her brow with confusion. "Won't you need it?"

I shake my head. "No. If I get close enough to him, they'll search me, and having a gun will be hard to explain away. I don't want them to think I'm a threat."

She flicks her eyebrows up. "Your funeral..."

I climb out of the car, and she shuffles sideways behind the wheel. She starts the engine, revs it harder than I'm happy with, and then speeds away.

I watch her go and then walk over to the entrance. It's a large revolving door made of tinted glass, with polished brass handles affixed to the outer edge of each pane. I push the right-hand side and step through as it spins counter-clockwise. A blast of refreshing, cool air hits me as I walk out the other side and into the main lobby.

I glance idly around, then head over to the front desk, which is in front of the wall facing me, running almost the full width. There's a decorative logo of the hotel chain mounted above it. Straight away, I spot three guys sitting on the circular sofa away to my left. They're wearing dark suits, with their white shirts half-fastened underneath. No ties, but my trained eye spots the bulge of their weapons holstered beneath their jackets easily enough. Same on my right, except there are only two. They have to be bin Mawal's men.

I need to be discreet here... subtle.

I know, I know—I'm screwed!

My shoes squeak on the polished, marble floor as I approach the desk. There are four people behind it, sitting side by side—three women and a man. The counter is waist-height, so I can only see their upper bodies. They're all smartly dressed. One of the women, on the far left, is talking on the phone. The man, sitting on the far right, is dealing with a young couple who look as if they're checking in. They have suitcases with them, and they look happy, so it's unlikely they're on their way home.

I stop in front of the young woman sitting to the left of the guy. She's attractive but has a little too much make-up on for my liking. She has straight black hair that rests comfortably on her shoulders and an easy smile that just reaches her dark eyes.

She looks up at me. "Hello, sir. How may I help you today?"

I smile a quick greeting. "Hey, yeah, I'm just wondering if you can tell me which room one of your guests is staying in, please? They're an old acquaintance, and they mentioned they're staying here a few days. I was passing, so figured I'd call in and surprise them."

"I'm sorry, sir. We can't give out that information. However, if you give me their name, I can call their room and let them know they have a visitor? At least it will still be a surprise."

She smiles, which I reciprocate. Not ideal but not her fault.

"That would be great. Thanks. His name's Sayed bin Mawal."

To her credit, she didn't skip a beat. In fact, I doubt anyone would've noticed the split-second flash of concern that registered in her eyes. But I'm not just anyone. And I did notice it.

"My apologies once again, sir, but His Royal Highness, *Prince* Sayed bin Mawal is not available for visitors. I would be happy to take a message to him on your behalf?"

Any friendliness has left her tone. She's now completely professional, all business, despite sounding a little defensive. I think I might have asked the wrong receptionist...

I frown. "How do you know he's not available? You didn't even check."

She smiles again, but this time, it doesn't reach her eyes. It's simply a sign of impatience. "With respect, sir, it's highly unlikely you're an old acquaintance of His Royal Highness, and because of an earlier security concern, he doesn't wish to receive any more guests. I'm afraid I will have to ask you to leave."

Before I can say anything, the five men in suits appear and surround me—one on either side of me, with the other three forming a loose semicircle behind. With the desk in front of me, I'm pinned in. Nowhere to go.

I ignore them and look at the young woman. "Okay, I don't want any trouble. I'll leave. But do you think you could pass a message on for me anyway?"

She goes to speak but doesn't get the chance. The man on my right steps forward and grabs my arm with a firm grip. He stands tall, authoritative. He has short, styled, dark hair. His beard's similar. He has a Middle Eastern complexion and emotionless eyes. "She said leave. So, leave."

I look at his hand, then up at him. I hold his gaze and don't blink. "Son, you got three seconds to let go of me."

He glances around and smirks at me. "Or what, asshole?"

"Or... I'll pull your arm out of its socket and beat you to death with the wet end."

His arrogant smile fades. There's a bustle of noise as everyone's suit jacket is brushed aside, making their firearms easier to reach, should they need them.

I don't take my eyes off him. I still don't blink. I'm openly challenging him to disobey me. To push me and see where it gets him. I know I shouldn't, but I can't help it. It's in my DNA. Hearing the phrase *or what* triggers a genetic, almost primordial rebellion inside me.

That being said, I'm not allowed to draw attention to myself or kill anyone anymore, am I? Order's orders...

Spoilsports.

Plus, while I would normally be relishing the opportunity to take these pricks out, if just one of them draws their gun, it'll change everything. There are too many innocent people standing around. The receptionist might have been rude to me, but I doubt she's on the prince's payroll. Or her colleagues, for that matter.

No, I can't get involved here. But I'll be damned if I'm letting him think he can get away with still holding onto my arm.

I raise an eyebrow. "I'm waiting..."

His eyes narrow, and he takes a deep, reluctant breath. Then he moves his hand.

I should fucking think so, too...

I look back at the woman behind the desk. Time for plan B.

"Listen, the prince is gonna be *really* interested in my message. You should hear me out."

She looks at the man on my left momentarily. "Okay. What is the message?"

"Someone's hired an assassin to kill him. He should increase his security and get out of the city right away."

She frowns and shakes her head slightly, clearly not believing me. "Really? And how, may I ask, do *you* know this?"

I smile. "Because I'm the guy they hired."

All five guns are drawn and aimed at me in a flash. I hold my arms out to the side, palms facing up, showing I'm no threat. Or at least, making them think I'm not.

The guy who grabbed my wrist steps forward again. He presses the barrel of his gun to my temple. "Who are you?"

"I'm Adri—" I stop myself. Shit. No, I'm not. "My name's Brad Foley. I work in the... private security business. I sometimes freelance if the money's right. Anyway, someone's offering me an awful lot of money to kill the prince."

One of the men behind me places his gun on the back of my head. "So, why are you telling us? And what's to stop us from killing you right now?"

I turn my head slightly, so it's clear I'm addressing him despite not looking around. "There's nothing stopping you. But a man of the prince's standing... I'm guessing he'll want to know who his enemies are. Am I right? I might do this sort of thing on the side, but I'm not an amateur. I know who he is. I don't care what reasons someone else might have for wanting him gone. I don't want to be the one to do it. When I told them, they were pissed—as you might expect —and now they want *me* dead too. So, to get back at them, I thought I could warn the prince and give him the opportunity to prepare himself."

Silence falls on the scene, and I find myself holding my breath. I'm not sure this was the best plan B I've ever had. I have the barrels of two guns resting against my head, and I'm unarmed. My only chance is—

"Come with us," says the guy to my right. "Prince Sayed will want to meet you before we kill you."

I close my eyes for a second, breathing a quiet sigh a relief. Then I re-open them, turn to look at the guy, and smile. "Excellent. Lead the way."

11:14 AST

It took three elevators to reach the penthouse levels, with each one taking us up twenty-odd floors at a time. I think

134

they do it that way so you don't have one long cable running top to bottom. Probably safer.

The doors open with a ding on the sixty-fifth floor. I'm surrounded by the five assholes from downstairs. They usher me out into a small lobby, with corridors stretching off to the left and right.

"This way," says one of them.

We all head to the right and make our way down the long hallway. The plush chocolate carpet muffles the marching of our collective footfalls. Artwork hangs at sporadic intervals on the cream walls. Stationed between the doorways, statues and busts atop marble plinths stand like sculptured sentries. Overhead, chandeliers that must cost a small fortune hang down, providing ample lighting.

I look around, trying to appear casual. I even let out a low, impressed whistle along the way to give these asshats the impression that I'm stunned at the opulence around us. I guess I am, to an extent, but the truth is that I'm scoping the place, and I'm a little worried. There are few doors, which suggests each room is sizeable. There are security cameras everywhere. I also have to assume everyone else in the prince's entourage is as armed and as well organized as these pricks.

Seriously, the White House was easier to get inside than this!

We stop outside a set of double doors. Four of the men take a step back, training their guns on me. I glance at each of them in turn. Their fingers are tight on the triggers, their arms unwavering. Just waiting for a reason...

I'd best try not to give them one.

The fifth guy knocks on the door. After a moment, the left-hand side opens slightly. A thin crack offers no view of the interior, blocked by the body behind it. There's a brief, muted exchange in a foreign language, and the door closes again. A moment later, it re-opens fully.

I feel a cold, metallic pressure in the middle of my back. Someone's using his gun to urge me forward.

"Inside," says a voice behind me.

I begrudgingly comply, stepping over the threshold and into the room. I hear the rest of the group file in behind me. I immediately begin looking around to—

Whoa...

The room's fucking huge! It must take up the entire side of this floor, easily. It looks like... Christ, I don't know what it looks like. It's like a ballroom. Maybe a palace. It's bright, on account of the far wall being nothing but floor-to-ceiling windows overlooking Abu Dhabi. The midday sun is shining in, and it feels as if I'm level with it as I gaze out, squinting at its glare.

The room stretches away to my left, probably all the way back to the elevators. I was thinking there were a few different rooms that were just pretty big, but it turns out the entire floor is one massive suite!

There's a wide ledge running around the perimeter, with steps leading down to the middle every few hundred yards. There's a piano in the far corner, multiple tables and sofas, at least ten doors in total...

I genuinely forget myself for a moment. "Holy shit..."

"Impressive, isn't it?"

Huh?

I look to my right and see a man approaching. He's wearing a light-gray suit that's probably so expensive, my bottomless credit card couldn't afford it. He has dark, smooth skin and jet-black hair, which, like his beard, is groomed and styled to perfection. He's wearing gold-rimmed sunglasses, and I can see a watch on his left wrist that's likely worth more than a small nation's GDP. Two men with submachine guns over their shoulders, hanging loose by the strap, flank him. Both are smartly dressed and look like professionals.

I raise an eyebrow at him as he smiles a polished, politician's smile.

"The room... it's beautiful, no?"

I shrug. "Yeah, it's not bad."

I'm surprised—his English is impeccable. He sounds normal. Nothing like I would have imagined. I know there are all sorts of customs and traditions usually observed by Saudi princes and their staff, but this guy is acting... dare I say it? *American.*

He gestures to the rest of the room with his hand. "All the money in the world, yet places like this never fail to take my breath away. You see, I never take anything for granted, my friend. I appreciate every luxury I have. My wealth may have been inherited, but I've worked hard to grow it to what it is today. And I like to think I've put it to good use."

"Yeah... congratulations on being so loaded."

"I consider myself an honest man, my friend." He gestures to me. "A trait I believe we share."

I shrug again but say nothing. I'm aware of the close proximity of his armed guards—and I doubt these guys are all he has. I have no move. I just hope this works.

"My staff tells me you freely admitted to being sent to kill me. Is that right?"

I nod. "Yeah. Sorry."

He holds his hands up and smiles. "No need to apologize. You are simply doing a job. I assume there is no personal animosity here. But what I don't understand is why you would tell me? Why endanger yourself like this? And make no mistake, my friend—you *are* in significant personal danger right now."

I flick my gaze around. "Yeah, I see that. Truth is, the people I work for aren't crazy about giving out explanations. Me? I have no issue killing someone, but I have to believe they deserve it. They didn't tell me why they want you dead, which didn't sit right with me. And when I did a bit of research on you, it seemed to me that you're a pretty decent guy."

He shrugs modestly. "Thank you."

Every good lie is ninety-five percent truth. I *can* understand why someone would want to kill him. But given I'm not one of the rich people losing money because of him, I can also acknowledge the good he's doing. If I weren't in The Order, and someone approached me to do this job, I would decline based on what I know right now.

But... that's not an option. Bottom line, I *am* in The Order, and he needs to go whether I agree with it or not because Lily's already said he's been taken care of. If Horizon finds out he's still alive, it's her ass in the crosshairs.

I nod at him. "No problem. Anyway, I told them to shove the job up their ass, which they didn't take too well. So, now they've put a contract out on me as well. I just wanted to give you a heads up."

He's stopped a few feet away from me, and his bodyguards have fanned to the sides, covering me from a wider angle. He appears to be thinking about what I'm saying, nodding thoughtfully to himself and staring into space.

"Well, I appreciate you telling me, of course. But you must have known the risk in doing so, which makes me think maybe there's something you want from me? Something you want to get from this? Money?"

I shake my head. "I don't want anything from you. I just

want to screw over the people trying to kill me. That's all. You surviving long enough to get out of the city would definitely do that, which is fine by me. I don't need your money."

He smiles, but it's not through humor. It's more apologetic. "My friend, I think you have underestimated my position. It's not an issue of me *surviving*, as you put it. Take a look around. I'm surrounded by some of the best personal protection in the world. We're sixty-five floors up. No one can get to me here."

I shrug. "I did."

"True, but you're not here to kill me, I assume?"

I shake my head. "No, I'm not."

"So, I'll be fine. I'm thankful for your concern, but it was unnecessary. Now all that remains is to decide what to do with you."

"Oh, that's easy. I'll just walk out the front door, and you'll never see me again."

He laughs. "My friend, I admire your confidence, but I'm afraid it's not that simple. Tell me why I should just... let you go. You were hired to murder me, after all."

Wait a minute.

I've just noticed that bin Mawal has a diverse security detail. Lots of different ethnicities. They're also well organized. Clearly, the prince has spared no expense on his protection.

Why is that standing out to me?

I think back to my therapy sessions with Kaitlyn, how she goes on about conscious and subconscious. I subconsciously picked up on this, like an instinct. And I trust my instincts, which means it's an important fact.

Oh, no...

I turn to the guy standing on my left, who accompanied

bin Mawal a few moments ago. "Hey, buddy, who do you work for?"

He frowns, glances at the prince, and then shrugs. "Him."

"Yeah, I know that. But you're a contractor, right? You work for a company *he's* hired. Who?"

He stands tall and pushes his shoulders back. His chest swells with pride. "GlobaTech Industries."

I smile. Then I laugh. And I can't stop laughing. That is just... *brilliant!*

13

Okay, so, here's my dilemma. I'm not allowed to let Josh find out I'm still alive. If I do, The Order kills me. Probably Josh too. And here I am, standing in a room full of GlobaTech employees.

Do you see how that screws me on so many levels?

There I was, thinking I was being really clever, coming up with a plan B. Never thought about needing a plan C!

Ah, I'm new to the whole planning ahead thing. I'll forgive myself.

Still need to figure a way out of this, though.

...

...

...

Shit.

I'm an idiot.

I just assumed bin Mawal would use his own people for his security, not someone else's. I genuinely had no intention of killing him when I came in here. I was just scoping the place out, planning how I would take him out later. But now, if I leave just one of the men in this room alive, I risk word of *Brad Foley* having been here getting back to Globa-Tech HQ... and, therefore, back to Josh. With all the goddamn security cameras around here, it would take him all of ten seconds to hack the footage, see me, and then all hell would break loose.

That's something else. I'll need to destroy the security footage.

Christ.

Okay, one King Kong-sized clusterfuck at a time.

I look over at the prince. My cheeks are aching slightly from the genuine laughter. He's frowning at me, probably confused.

"Have I... missed something?" he asks.

I shake my head, still smiling. "No, sorry. I've just realized what an astronomically bad day I'm having. You know those moments where things are so outstandingly fucked up, all you can do is laugh?"

He nods and smiles. "I do, my friend, yes. But forgive my ignorance... I don't understand why you're just realizing this *now*."

I sigh.

Shit, shit, shit!

I need to start thinking of a plan C, don't I?

I stare at him, momentarily studying my reflection in the lenses of his glasses. "Okay, honestly? Prior to my little moment of clarity just then, I didn't really consider myself to be in a bad position."

He chuckles. "Well, your confidence is certainly honorable, if a little unjustified. Why, may I ask?"

I shrug. "There's no reason you would want to hurt me.

I've explained I came here in peace. I'm doing you a favor. Despite the faith you have in your security detail, you need to understand that the people who hired me... the people now coming after *both of us*... are dangerous and far bigger than you or I. Why would you want to hurt me or kill me?"

I gesture to the men surrounding me.

"Would these guys even obey an order from you to take me out if I weren't a threat? They're GlobaTech employees. They're the golden boys at the moment, aren't they, with everything that's been happening? It wouldn't look good on the company if their staff murder people because their clients tell them to."

Prince Sayed smiles humorlessly. His seemingly warm and friendly persona is leaving him. Maybe he doesn't like being proved wrong? It's like a physical change, as if he's removing an item of clothing. He's just... different.

He points to each one of them individually. "*They* will do whatever *I* tell them to. That's what I pay for—their protection and their obedience. The wealth I have affords me a freedom not available to most. If I deem you a threat, they *will* execute you."

I breathe out a slow, calming breath. In much the same way I just saw him change, I suspect he's now seeing the same thing in me. The act has stopped. The lie is no longer valid. The change in him was all I needed to satisfy my own moral code. For all the good he might do, the fact he's capable of such arrogance and anger tells me there's probably more to him than meets the eye. More than what the public figure shows the world. In that moment, I was left with little doubt that The Order's contract is fully justified, whatever the reason.

Besides... he just threatened me. *Nobody* threatens me.

This used to be the type of situation where my Inner

Satan would take over. Where I would *hulk out*, as Josh so eloquently put it. But that doesn't happen anymore, which is actually even worse news for these assholes. No... my demon's no longer some out-of-control beast that escapes from time to time. Now, in much the same way I would pull a gun and load a magazine, he is a trained weapon—something I use in addition to my normal skillset.

I can feel him next to me, patting me on my shoulder, offering his support. He limbers up, ready to go to war *with* me, not *instead* of me.

I take another deep breath and plan in my mind how this is going to go down.

There are four guys behind me, two on my left, one on my right, and bin Mawal in front of me. Eight targets... seven of them armed, five of them already aiming their guns at me... maybe two within reach on a moment's notice.

Well, Prince Sayed can wait. He's not a threat and he's not going anywhere. His two personal bodyguards aren't a priority either. They're armed, but they're not holding their guns. It'll take them two or three seconds to prepare themselves and aim, by which time I'll have shot them. So, my focus needs to be on the guy to my immediate left—who, luckily, is within reach—and the four douchebags behind me.

I raise an eyebrow and smile at the prince.

Showtime.

I step quickly to my left, grab the guy's extended arm by the wrist, and turn into him, putting my back against his chest. Grabbing his hand with mine, I squeeze, forcing him to fire four shots. Directing his arm by holding the wrist, I put a bullet in each of the four guys behind me. The lethal and accurate gunshots are deafening in the silence of the large suite. The sickening squelch of bullets penetrating skulls follows a moment later.

Before the lifeless bodies thud to the floor, I push back, using my weight to turn us both counterclockwise. As we do, I squeeze off a round at the guy standing farthest from me, next to the prince. It punches him in the chest, sending him flying backward, but I'm not stopping to celebrate. I continue the turn, shoving the guy away from me and easing his weapon from his hand. He goes flying into the remaining bodyguard, who is slowly starting to register what's happening and reaching for his own weapon.

As one guy collides with the other, I spin in a quick circle, stopping to face Prince Sayed. Using the gun I've just acquired, I aim under my left arm and fire three rounds. The first hits the guy I had a hold of squarely in his back, between the shoulder blades. He falls away to the side, sprawling to the floor. The other two bullets hit the remaining bodyguard in his chest. He flails backward and lands heavily, sending his own weapon skidding away to my left.

Silence falls once again. I'm breathing heavily, partly from the exertion and partly from the adrenaline rush. I grip the gun tightly in my hand and stare at the prince, who stands slack-jawed before me. He looks around quickly, the panic evident, despite not being able to see his eyes.

He lunges to his left, presumably heading for the main door. It's a really stupid move because he's nowhere near it, and unless this guy's actually Clark Kent, he's not going to run faster than—

BANG!

—a speeding bullet.

I just shot him in the leg. Right above the knee. He buckled mid-stride and collapsed in a heap on the floor.

He's screaming with understandable agony, clutching at the wound as it gushes blood across the tiled floor.

Hmmm, thinking about it...

I walk over, crouch beside him, and deliver a stiff jab to the side of his face, just below the cheekbone, on the bend of his mandible. His eyes flash wide for an instant, then he stops screaming.

There we go. He could have woken the dead with all that noise. But more likely, he will have alerted the rest of his significant security detail. I need to get the hell out of Dodge.

I stand and walk a quick circuit of the room to make sure every door is locked. It won't keep people out for long, I know, but it'll buy me an extra minute or two, which is better than nothing.

I make my way back over to the prince. I reach down and drag him by his collar into the middle of the room, pulling him unceremoniously down the small flight of steps and over to one of the exquisite leather sofas. I sit him down and position him so that his recently ventilated leg is resting up on a small, tinted glass table in front of him.

I lean over and slap him. "Hey... wakey, wakey, your Highness."

He snorts back to consciousness and snaps his eyes open, disoriented. He looks around for a moment and then focuses on his injured leg. His eyes go wide and his mouth opens, preparing to scream once more as the pain begins to register. Before he can, I shove the barrel of the gun between his lips.

"Ah, ah, ah. Don't be making all that noise like last time, or I'm gonna have to hit you again."

He tries to speak, but his words are muffled by the gun. I take it out slowly and gesture to him to repeat himself. He spits blood on the soft, cream cushion beside him. "I said... just kill me and get it over with, you bastard!"

I nod. "Oh, I will. Don't you worry about that. But there are a couple of things I need to know first."

He scoffs. "What makes you think I'll tell you anything?"

I shrug. "Because if you do, I'll end it quickly and painlessly."

He smiles challengingly. "And if I don't?"

I shrug again. "Then you'll die in a manner that's neither of those things, and that would suck for you."

He sighs, spits out some more blood, and stares at his leg, snarling through a fresh wave of pain.

I rest my foot next to his on the table and lean forward. "First question—who do you think would want you dead?"

He genuinely thinks about it for a minute. "I don't know... I'm not an idiot. I know I have made many enemies recently. It could be anyone."

"Huh... fair point, I guess. But why you, specifically? I'm guessing Fuelex has an entire board of rich investors and shareholders. I admit, I admire what you're doing, but you wouldn't have made the decision to do it alone. Why go after you and no one else?"

He shrugs but says nothing. He looks away to grimace at the excruciating pain in his leg.

"Is there something you're not telling me? Something personal? Something unrelated to Fuelex? There must be *something*. What have *you* done to warrant having me sent after you? Are you a thief? A liar? A murderer? A pedophile? What?"

He frowns, apparently offended. "I'm none of those things, you... you disrespectful *prick*! I don't know why anyone would want me dead. Anyway, why do you care? You're just a hired gun, here to pull the trigger, right?"

"Honestly? No, I'm not." I use the gun to scratch my fore-head, rubbing the tip of the barrel up and down my temple. "Truth be told, I'm doing someone a favor. A colleague of mine was sent to kill you. She's gorgeous. Unbelievably so. That previous security risk everyone is so bothered about—that was her."

He frowns again. "Who? That stupid Chinese bitch?"

"Well... I don't think she's Chinese. Or stupid. And if you feel brave enough to call her a bitch, you go right ahead. Anyway, she obviously failed, but she told our employer that you were dead anyway. She then got into a bit of a state because our employer happens to be quite powerful and resourceful, and she figured they would find out you were still alive and then go after her for lying to them. So, she came to me for help."

"And here you are... such a good friend!"

His disdain isn't hard to miss.

"Actually, I was against killing you at first. My employer isn't big on telling me *why* they want people dead, as I've mentioned. Personally, I like to know such things before I put a bullet in someone, so I figured I'd come here, bullshit you a little, and see if I could find out for myself why someone would want you gone."

"And?"

"And... I still have no fucking clue, beyond the obvious. I was hoping to get an idea of the kind of people my employer is involved with but no such luck. Anyway, along the way, I decided for myself that you're worth killing because you threatened me."

He shakes his head. "Wait... so in the last fifteen minutes, you just *decided* to kill me? What the fuck? Do you have any idea who I am? I mean, really, who I am. How much money I have? How powerful I am?" He shifts in his seat as best he can with his injury. He hunches over a little too, almost as if he's shrinking and losing his confidence. "Listen... I can give you anything you want if you let me live. Please! I don't want to die... I've done nothing to deserve this. I'm begging you, I—"

BANG!

I put a bullet between his eyes, shattering his expensive sunglasses in the process. His head snaps back violently, then sags forward. Blood trickles from the hole in his head, down the front of his suit, and onto the cushion he's sitting on.

He was starting to get on my goddamn nerves. *Do you know who I am?* Really? Who says that?

Wait... I've said that before, haven't I?

Yeah, I have. But that was different. I obviously would have meant it ironically, to entertain myself in what I'm sure would have been an otherwise humor-free situation.

Ah, fuck it.

Now... how do I get out of here?

14

Shit. I should really start thinking about this kind of thing in advance. I'm sixty-five floors up, trapped in a room with seven dead GlobaTech operatives and a dead Saudi prince. I'm likely to be all over the hotel's security feeds, and if there's less than thirty armed men coming for me right now, I'm a lucky man.

I take out my cell and call Lily.

"Where the hell are you?" she asks when she answers.

I glance around. "Yeah... funny story. Now don't shout at me, but things got a little out of hand."

She sighs. "What have you done?"

"Well, Sayed bin Mawal is dead."

"What? How?"

"I shot him. And his seven bodyguards."

"Oh my God, are you fucking insane?"

"You'd be surprised how many people ask me that..."

"Would I? Really?"

"Okay, no. Probably not. Look, I'm in his suite on the sixty-fifth floor, and I have no way out. I need your help, Lily."

She's silent for a moment. "And I thought *I* was in deep shit. Okay, you can't go down, right? So, you go up. I'll arrange an extraction team to come get you. There's a helipad on the roof."

I stare out the window. I hate heights. I close my eyes for a moment. "Up... got it."

"You need to buy yourself ten minutes."

"Okay. Ah... Lily, there's one more thing."

She sighs again. "What?"

"I may have been captured on their security feeds. A lot."

She gasps with disbelief. "Fucking *seriously*? Remind me never to ask for your help again!"

"Yeah, well..." I pause for a moment to think of a suitable retort. "Okay, I've got nothing. Just sort it, will you? You know how The Order deals with this shit."

"Fine, whatever."

The line clicks off. I look around at the bodies of the GlobaTech security team. I feel really, really bad about that, for many reasons. First, they're the good guys. They were just doing their job and happened to be in the wrong place at the wrong time. Second, they're ultimately Josh's boys, and this is a slap in the face for him. But third, and arguably the most important, The Order doesn't like it when you kill people they haven't asked you to kill. It's in their rules. And they only made three of the damn things, so they must take them seriously. I reckon I might get sent to my room after this...

Screw it. I'll deal with that later. For now, I need to focus on getting out of here.

I walk over to the main door and place my ear carefully against it, listening for any hint of movement outside.

...

...

...

I can't hear anything. I didn't give any of these guys a chance to call for back-up before I took them out, so I might be lucky enough to make it up one final floor without being spotted.

I grip the gun tightly in one hand and ease the door open with the other, creating a gap maybe an inch wide. I peek out. There's no one in the hall that I can see.

I open it fully, trying to stay as quiet as I can. Cautiously, I peek out again, this time looking both ways. Still clear. Good. Now all I have to do is reach the elevator at the far end and ride it up a floor, and—

Shit!

I duck back inside as a guy appears at the end of the corridor. I wait a second or two, holding my breath...

I don't think he saw me. I roll my eyes with relief. He must be patrolling the floor. Annoying but not too much of an issue.

I chance another look out.

Double shit!

He's not alone. There are three of them. They're just pacing idly around in front of the elevators. I need to get past them, preferably without...

Wait a minute...

I look over my shoulder at the interior of the suite. Specifically, the layout and positioning of the rooms and other doors.

Light bulb!

I gently close the door and walk quickly across the room, all the way to the opposite end. There's another door here. If I'm right, it opens up almost directly in front of the men and, more importantly, the elevator. I forgot how big this suite actually is...

I crouch in front of it and peer through the keyhole.

Yeah, I was right. I can see the three guys standing in a loose triangle.

I tense my jaw as I play out in my head every possible way this could go down. I could do this several ways, but I don't particularly want to kill them, which immediately reduces the number of options. Plus, non-lethal takedowns aren't exactly my specialty...

I keep watching until the guy closest to me is where I need him to be—next to this door, with his back to me. I stand and glance down at the gun in my hand, mostly for reassurance.

Don't hesitate. Don't think... just do.

My rules.

I yank the door open and push the man in front of me forward, hard. He flies into his colleague, who's standing side-on a few feet away, talking with the third guy. As the first two collide and fall to the floor, I rush out and bury my shoulder in the third guy's sternum, forcing him backward into the small strip of wall next to the elevator. I feel the wind leave him, and he sinks to the floor. I spin around to face the other two, who are just starting to gather themselves and realize something's not right. The guy I pushed initially had dropped his weapon, so I kick it away from them and aim mine at the second guy before he has chance to think.

I gesture to the side with my head. "Throw your gun away, sweetheart."

He glares at me angrily but does as I ask. I kick it over to the other one.

"Now both of you, on your feet, nice and easy."

They stand and hold their hands out to the sides. I'm facing them with the elevator on my right. The one on my left smiles. "You have any idea what you're doing, asshole?"

I shake my head. "Not usually. I figure it's harder for people like you to anticipate my next move if I don't know what it is myself."

He doesn't respond.

"Okay, whether you see tomorrow depends on the answer to my next question. How many of you are there on the floor above us?"

The men exchange a glance, then the one on my right looks at me. "The suite upstairs belongs to the prince. There's maybe fifteen of us."

And of course... triple shit!

I nod. "This is good. We're being honest with one another. Is there a way to the roof from here without having to go up a floor first?"

The first guy shakes his head. "No, you have to be upstairs. There's a maintenance stairwell against the west wall and a private elevator that runs up to the helipad. Why?"

I shrug. "I'm meeting some friends of mine up there, and I'm trying to avoid any more violence."

The second guy smiles. "You're shit out of luck there, man."

"Story of my life. Right, here's what's gonna happen. You —call the elevator." He does. I look at the first guy. "You—if you move before I want you to, you're dead. Understand?"

He nods reluctantly. I look over at the elevator and watch the lights count up as it approaches.

"So, there are fifteen guys above us?"

The first guy nods again but stays silent.

I raise an eyebrow. "Wonderful."

Hey. Adrian. It's me. Listen, I know we're, y'know, partners nowadays, but seriously, this is some dumb shit you're planning on doing. You know that, right? I mean, you'll be in a metal box, with nowhere to run, most likely facing a large group of armed guys who want to shoot you. You're making it too easy for them, man. It'll be like shooting fish in a fucking barrel! Listen to your Inner Satan, man... Find another way.

Believe it or not, I actually told Kaitlyn about my Inner Satan in one of our early sessions. I didn't call him that, but I told her I had this voice in my head sometimes. It wasn't as if I had an angel on one shoulder and a devil on the other. It was more like my devil had grabbed a hold of my angel, snapped its neck, and was now just whispering sweet nothings in my ear while drinking whiskey.

She had laughed at the analogy, then launched into a detailed explanation as to why people like me—and by that, she meant people suffering with survivor's guilt—seek independent reassurance or support for our actions. And if we can't find it, we create it to help us get through the ordeal we're reliving.

I didn't have the heart to tell her that she was way off. I am, in fact, listening to one of my more prominent and useful demons.

But I'm—*he's* right. Simply going up in the elevator is pretty stupid. That's why I'm gambling on them not expecting me to do it.

The elevator arrives with a ding, and the doors slide smoothly open. I gesture toward it with my gun. "Inside, both of you."

They step into the carriage, and I follow quickly behind

them. I maneuver myself behind them and press the button for floor sixty-six. I raise my gun, holding it with both hands, keeping them covered. "Now turn around."

They both comply as the doors close, and we begin the short ascent.

I'm taking slow, deep breaths, keeping myself calm. It's so easy in situations like this to allow your adrenaline to flow freely and let your instincts take over. I know because I used to do it. Whenever I was neck-deep in shit like this, I'd just step aside and let my Inner Satan take over. He was the side of my personality that cared little about my own well-being. He simply got the job done when I couldn't find the strength to do what I needed to.

But nowadays, that doesn't happen. I take my time. I access that hidden reservoir of violence when I choose to and use it the same way I use my gun. It's nothing more than a weapon I'm trained to wield.

DING.

The doors slide open. I take one more deep breath, and time slows to a crawl. My eyes flick in all directions, absorbing every detail of what lies before me, allowing me to plan my attack.

Ahead of me is a wall of windows that offer a breath-taking view of the city outside. There are three steps leading down from them into the middle of the suite. Six men armed with SMGs are standing casually in a line, holding their weapons loosely by their sides. Just in front of them, standing on either side of a low, glass table in the center of the room, are two more guys—equally armed, and equally casual.

I take one step forward, extending my peripheral view of the room. Away to the right, three sofas form a U-shape. They're white leather, pristine, and look comfortable.

There's one guy sitting with his back to me and another standing by his side.

Across from them, on my left, three large decorative pillars are positioned in front of more windows, following the slight natural curve of the room. Three men stand like sentries, more alert than the others. Just beyond them, I see a set of doors leading out to the roof and, presumably, the helipad.

Jesus...

For the first time... ever, I think... I don't know where to start. It's not so much the numbers that I have an issue with. It's their layout. There's too much space between the different groups. If I aim at one side, I won't have time to spin around before I'm shot by the others.

I'm not second-guessing my abilities. I'm not being negative or thinking too much. I'm not scared. I just know a lost cause when I see one. It might look as if I rush blindly into every situation, but I only do that when I know enough about that situation to know I can handle it. This... this isn't happening. I need to find another—

Holy mother of God!

Just as time resumes its normal pace and people start to look over at us, a helicopter appears in front of me, rising from below and hovering level with the windows. It's an attack chopper, painted jet-black. I know the kind, but I've never seen a model like this one before. It's a fucking beast! It looks like a flying tank. The level of armor alone is terrifying. It's symmetrical in design, with two sets of vertical blades on the tail—one either side—and four large horizontal blades on the roof. Attached to both sides of the undercarriage is a frighteningly big rotary cannon. Basically, it's six miniguns joined together in a long cylinder, which spins quickly, essentially causing an endless stream of bullets. A few years ago, you could be looking at upward of six thousand rounds a minute. God only knows what this thing would do...

Everyone in the room is reacting as I am. They're all standing, frozen and stunned, staring out the window. I can't see inside the cockpit because the windows are tinted, but I can tell from the position and the angle of the chopper that I'm going to need to find some cover when that thing—

"Holy shit!"

I push both guys standing in front of me out of the elevator and press myself against the side as the chopper opens fire. It takes a split-second for every pane of glass to shatter, letting in the deafening noise of its blades as it hovers menacingly outside. The roar of the bullets is insane! There's an almost continuous cracking as the tile floor splinters under the onslaught from the twin cannons.

Screams sound out for a brief moment and then end abruptly as every man in there is annihilated. I'm holding my breath, forcing my body against the side of the elevator, almost pushing my way through it, desperate for some cover.

The whirring of the cannons sounds loud but quickly fades as the firing stops. I wait a few moments, then stick my head out to look around.

I raise an eyebrow. "Sweet Jesus..."

The place looks like a warzone. Remember the lobby scene in *The Matrix*? When Keanu Reeves brings all the guns through the metal detector, and half the world tries to shoot him? And when it's over, all the walls are destroyed, and chunks of plaster and marble are scattered everywhere?

Well, this entire suite kind of looks like that, only a million times worse!

I walk out and hold my gun with both hands, keeping it

low but ready. I scan the whole room, opting to ignore the chopper for a moment. I'm assuming whoever's in there is on my side.

I hear a shuffling behind me. I spin around and see a guy crawling slowly toward me across the floor. Half his right leg is missing, and the trail of blood behind him is... significant. His face is a mess. He's looking up at me, trying to speak, but there's no sound. His mouth is just—

BANG!

One side of his skull disappears in an explosion of deep crimson. I spin around, raising my gun. The chopper has turned side-on, and the door is now open. Pierce is standing there, holding on with one hand and still aiming his pistol in the other. He smiles at me and signals with his weapon for me to head up to the roof.

I nod, tuck the gun in my waistband behind me, and walk quickly toward the doors in the far corner. I pull them open, brushing two piles of rubble aside as I do. I walk through and head up the small metal stairwell to the fire door at the top. I push it open and step outside. Despite the temperature, at this height, there's still a cold wind, made even more prominent by the blades of the chopper that's slowly landing in front of me.

As the wheels touch down, Pierce steps out. He makes his way over to me, ducking slightly as he passes under the blades. I haven't seen the guy since back in Vietnam.

"Heard you could use some help," he says, smiling.

I tuck my gun behind me. "Yeah. Thanks."

"C'mon. Get in."

I follow him over to the chopper. Seeing it hovering outside before didn't give me a clear sense of how big this thing really is. The design is flawless. It's a flying fortress, heavily fortified, and could probably win a war single-handedly. I don't know where they got this kind of machine from, but I'm glad it's on my side.

I climb aboard, and we're airborne before I even sit down. The interior is deceptively spacious, with enough room for ten people, easily. I know that, because in addition to me and Pierce, there are eight people sitting down. One of them is Lily. She's sitting on the far left, nearest the opposite door. I sit with my back to the cockpit, and Pierce moves next to me. He pulls a gun and jams it into my ribs, then reaches behind me and takes mine. He casually tosses it to another guy sitting across from him. Everyone except Lily and me are armed.

Pierce leans close. "Sorry, Adrian—orders from up high. See, unlike you, I actually obey the rules I'm given."

I turn and stare into his eyes. "You gonna kill me so soon after saving my ass?"

He shakes his head. "No. Horizon wants to see you both. I'm just here to make sure you don't do anything stupid on the way there."

"Now what makes you think I'd do something stupid?"

He smiles humorlessly but doesn't say anything.

"Oh, and Pierce? Just so we're clear, when all this is over and the dust has settled, you and I are gonna have words about you pulling a gun on me. Understand?"

He remains impassive, smiling and staying silent.

I turn and look at Lily. Her large brown eyes are full of regret and apology. I nod at her. "You okay?"

She nods back. "For now, yes."

I sit back in my seat and stare at the riveted chrome floor.

I think this is one of those times when shit's going to get a lot worse before it gets better.

15

We've been flying for about an hour. No one's said much since we left Abu Dhabi. Lily has barely looked at me. I don't want to say she seems afraid because I don't think she even understands the concept of fear, but there's definitely some concern there. And judging by our current predicament, I'd say any concern was completely justified.

I look around the cabin. I recognize the rest of Pierce's team from Vietnam, and they've brought along three more guys for good measure. This is a big unit to send after two people. Even if we are elite assassins, you could argue this is overkill, considering how well trained these guys are. It says a lot about how much they respect our abilities. I guess I should be flattered, but I'm not. I'm trying to figure out what's coming next, and I have no idea.

We bank left, and I feel the chopper begin its descent. I lean forward slightly and gaze out the window. I see the outline of the Burj Al Arab Hotel below us, getting closer with every second that ticks by.

You have to hand it to them. The Order sure knows how to treat its employees.

I feel Pierce's hand on my shoulder as he forces me back in my seat. "You've done so well. Don't go getting any ideas about misbehaving now, asshole."

I glance at him, then stare at the floor again. I try to make it look as if I'm completely dismissing him as a threat. I'm not—far from it—but there's no harm in having him think I'm underestimating the trouble I'm in. But right now, I'm more concerned about what's waiting for us both down there.

The Burj Al Arab is easily the most opulent and luxurious hotel in the world. It sits about six miles east of the manmade Palm Island in Dubai. As we fly low and circle around to approach the helipad, I'm given a good view of the place.

The hotel is shaped like a huge, three-dimensional sail. Clear blue seas surround it, and the glare of the scorching sun is blinding as it reflects off the copious windows. I can make out a small group of people standing on the helipad, all dressed in black.

Another welcoming committee. Great.

I stretch my leg out and tap Lily's foot with mine. She looks over at me, and I smile, trying to look calm and reassuring. "You all right?"

She nods vacantly but doesn't say anything.

"It'll be okay, Lily. Don't worry."

One of the guys sitting across from me chuckles. "You keep telling yourself that, hero."

I look at him for a moment. He's not one of the guys Pierce had with him in Vietnam. He looks young, but the network of scars on his face say otherwise. He's smirking at me, comfortable in his own arrogance.

Prick.

I lean forward and rest my elbows on my knees. "Hey, buddy, just so you know, the only reason I haven't killed you and all your friends here already is simply because I've chosen not to. That's it. You need to appreciate that doing something like that is well within my skillset. You also need to understand that I'm not somebody you want to piss off. Next time you think about opening your mouth, compare the importance of what you're about to say with the sensation of falling head-first out of a chopper and decide if it's worth it."

Pierce nudges me in the ribs with his gun. "Sit back and shut up. There's no need to turn this into a pissing contest. We were asked to bring you in, so we are. Maybe the only reason you're so uptight is your own guilty conscience?"

I glance over my shoulder at him, then sit up straight against the back of the seat. "I'm not uptight, and I'm certainly not guilty. What I *am* is slightly aggravated and running low on patience. I don't appreciate being summoned back and forth like this. Feel free to tell your boss that."

Pierce shrugs. "Tell him yourself. I couldn't care less. I know who you are, *Adrian*. I've read your file. Shit, I was one of the people who insisted we made our move to recruit you when we did. But don't for one second think you intimidate me. You've been a big fish in a small pond for a long time. You're good, but you're out of your depth here. The Order will make you disappear in a heartbeat if they want to. And I'm the guy they'll send to do it. So, I'll say again—shut your goddamn mouth and relax."

I hold his gaze for a few seconds, then look away.

I don't like him, but I'll let him have his moment.

The chopper touches down on the helipad. One of the men to my right slides the door back and steps out, ushering everyone else out after him in a loose formation. Pierce gestures to Lily, who reluctantly stands, walks past me without looking, and climbs down onto the clean blacktop of the helipad. I follow her out, stretching and looking up to the sky. I close my eyes and feel the cold wind brush across my face, countered by the intense heat.

There are six guys waiting for us, all wearing identical black suits. They move efficiently and surround us in a wide circle. Pierce and two of his men step inside it and form a triangle around Lily and me, completely trapping us. He takes point, with his two men behind us. Everyone starts walking, leaving us little choice but to do the same. We're moving toward a large brick square near the far edge of the helipad, with a set of double doors in the middle.

I feel Lily slide her hand into mine and squeeze gently. I look across at her. She's walking tall, like she's regained some of her confidence.

"I'm sorry I dragged you into this," she says, without looking at me.

I smile. "You didn't drag me into shit. I walked beside you willingly, just as I am now. We'll be fine."

She doesn't respond, which makes me think she doesn't agree.

Two men break away from the circle. They stride quickly over to the doors, push them open, and hold them for the rest of us. We walk through and down a short flight of stairs to a small lobby. In keeping with the rest of the hotel, the area is decorated with eye-popping extravagance. The burnt orange carpet underfoot is thick and clean. The walls have mahogany paneling on them, with thin-framed gold light fixtures spaced evenly along both sides. At either end is a set of double doors, but I can't tell where they lead. Seems a bit much for them just to be stairwells.

Ahead of us is an elevator. Pierce steps through the outer circle of men and presses the button to call it.

I glance around at the lavish decoration. "Hey, Pierce, tell me something. The Order's meant to be this big, secretive organization that's been around forever, right? Yet they're not particularly big on discretion, are they? I mean, look at this place..."

Pierce half-smiles. "There are degrees of wealth and power, Adrian. Someone like you, you probably chose to hide in plain sight, spending a fraction of your fortune so as not to draw attention to yourself, right?"

I shrug but say nothing.

He continues. "Then you have the people who frivolously spend their millions, living a life many people only dream of and relishing the attention that kind of lifestyle brings them. Finally, you have the people who are so rich... so powerful... they go beyond the materialistic pleasures of money and live in a way that isn't dissimilar from people like you. The Order operates in a world beyond normal men and women, where their level of wealth and power affords them unparalleled freedom and anonymity. We can go anywhere and do anything." He squares up to me, moving so that he's only a few feet away. He looks me in the eye. "I hope bringing you into this world wasn't a mistake, Adrian."

I take a deep breath. I'm doing my best not to rise to him or feel threatened here. I've done nothing wrong. I simply did what I had to in order to survive. Anything they criticize me for is nothing more than a learning experience. For the sake of every man here, I'm trying hard not to feel as if I'm in danger.

I shake my head. "I'm not here to rock the boat, Pierce. I'm here to live out the rest of my life doing something I'm good at. That's all."

Behind him, the elevator arrives with a ding, and the doors slide open. He nods at me and smiles. "Good." He gestures behind him with his thumb. "Now get in."

The carriage is surprisingly spacious, and we all fit inside comfortably. I can't see what button is pushed, but the doors close, and mechanisms rumble into life as we begin our descent. I glance sideways at Lily. She's tapping her foot and cracking her knuckles.

She's worried.

The elevator slows and stops with another ding. The doors slide open, and everyone files out, sticking to the same relaxed formation. We're in another lobby. It's a modest square, smaller than the last one but still decorated with the same luxury. A single hallway stretches away before us, lit subtly by strip lights overhead.

The group starts walking. We pass a couple of doors on either side. It reminds me of the Jumeirah hotel back in Abu Dhabi. Less doors means bigger rooms. I can only imagine what lies behind some of these...

We're maybe halfway along. Pierce steps to the side and turns to face us. His two men take a few more paces past him and stop. The men behind hang back. They're giving us space but making it perfectly clear that there's nowhere to go except where they want us to.

Pierce knocks twice on the door. "Go on. He's expecting you."

I glance back at Lily, who nods. I reach for the handle, but Pierce puts his hand up. "Just remember, hero... this is the only way in or out, and we'll be waiting here for you. Don't do anything stupid."

I roll my eyes and open the door, pushing it as I step inside. I hear Lily follow behind—

Holy crap...

The suite is incredible! And I mean, *really* incredible! The first thing I notice, away to my left, is a large statue of Ganesha, the Hindu Elephant God. It's maybe nine feet high and made of marble. It's colorful and adorned with jewels that must cost a small fortune. Lights in the floor illuminate the base from below.

I let out a low whistle as I gaze around in genuine awe. The wall opposite is all windows and offers a stunning view of the ocean. The living room is split into sections by groups of seating and low tables. In the far corner is a spiral staircase. Straight ahead is a large double door, standing slightly open and leading into what looks like a bedroom. To the right is—

"Oh, c'mon... I don't need to see *that*!"

There's a huge oval hot tub against the right wall, with thin pillars leading up to the ceiling. Sitting in the middle of it, with his arms stretching out to the sides, resting on the edge, is Horizon. He has a woman on either side of him, pouring water over his exposed chest from a decorative bowl and then rubbing him down with a cloth. Each woman looks—

Yup... they've just stood up.

They're completely naked.

I look away. Not because I feel awkward. Not because I'm trying to be polite. And certainly not because they're not amazing to look at. But I don't want to associate two wet, naked women with a wet, naked Horizon. That kind of mental image stays with you forever.

I hold my hand up as if shielding myself from the sun.

"Jesus Christ, Chief. Can you at least get dressed for your meetings?"

Lily strides past me, into the room, and I hear the door close behind me. I watch her look around. She doesn't seem as impressed as I am. She glances briefly over at Horizon but simply rolls her eyes, turns her back on him, and casually paces toward the statue of Ganesha.

I get no response from Horizon. I look back over at him to see—

"Oh, seriously! For fuck's sake!"

He's standing up in the hot tub. The two women are patting him down with a towel. I've just seen things that are the stuff of nightmares. I might never be the same again...

I turn my back and walk over to Lily.

I lean toward her slightly. "I didn't realize the guy was a nudist."

She leans into me and smiles. "He's not. He just doesn't give a shit."

I nod. "Ah, I see. Neither do I, but you don't see me—"

I stop because Lily's looking at me with an eyebrow raised.

I frown. "What?"

"What were you wearing when we first met?"

Oh, yeah.

I shrug. "That was different. I wasn't parading myself around. I'd just stepped out of the shower."

She smiles. "Uh-huh..."

"What? It was totally different! Besides... I'm better looking."

She makes a point of looking me up and down. She shrugs. "Huh... I guess."

She turns around and walks slowly back over to Horizon, who's now wearing a white robe and standing in the middle of the room with his arms around the two women. They're still naked and dripping water on the carpet. They're both cozying into him with a hand on his chest and one leg slightly bent, resting against him—possibly in an effort to hide some of their modesty.

It isn't working.

"Thank you for coming, both of you," he says.

I walk over to join Lily. "Not like you gave us much choice." I gesture to the room with my hand. "Nice place, though."

He nods. "This is the closest thing I have to an office. And you two are the first assets ever to come here." He looks at each woman in turn, then moves his hands down and grabs their asses. "Go wait for me in the bedroom, okay?"

They both nod, giggle, and trot away toward the double doors, holding hands.

I look at him and raise my eyebrow. "When I get as old as you and need a care home, remind me to ask for the sponge bath service you just had."

He smiles. "Just a little perk I occasionally allow myself. Now, Adrian, if you would take a seat, I'd like to discuss a few things with my dear Lily."

I look over at her. "You gonna be okay?"

She nods. "It's fine."

I walk over to one of the sofas in the middle of the room. It's a large U-shape and could easily seat thirty people. It's a deep purple, with red and gold cushions arranged across it. I sit down heavily and watch.

Horizon moves over to Lily and places the back of his hand gently on her cheek, stroking it. "What happened in Abu Dhabi, my dear?"

She flinches slightly at his touch, but I can see she's trying not to. She takes a breath. "I had a plan for the hit, and it went wrong. When I realized Adrian was living in the city, I asked for his help." She moves her head away from him and turns to look him in the eye. "That's not against The Order's rules, is it?"

He shakes his head. "No..." In the blink of an eye, Horizon strikes her across the face with the back of his hand. The slap sounds like a whip crack in the otherwise quiet room. "But lying to *me* is!"

I spring to my feet. "Hey!"

He snaps his head around to look at me and points his finger. "Sit... the fuck... down. I'll deal with you in a moment."

I'm a little shocked he would speak to me like that. I'm not just saying this, but I actually *have* killed people for less. Stunned by his response, I just sit down and watch.

He turns back to Lily. "If something goes wrong, you tell *me*. You come to *me*. That is your only priority if you fail a contract. To lie to me is unacceptable."

She takes a small step to the side, away from his hand. She doesn't look at him. "I was embarrassed and ashamed that I'd failed. I knew, with help, I could get the job done, and I didn't want you to worry or think less of me."

He grabs her by her elbow. "The Order consists solely of the world's greatest assassins. It has for countless years. Pride has no place among our ranks. Do you understand?"

She nods.

"You have disappointed me, Lily. You have always been one of our most reliable and effective weapons, but this was an amateurish mistake."

I clear my throat. "Can I... say something here?"

Horizon looks over at me again, still holding onto Lily's arm. "Something tells me you're going to anyway..."

I shrug. "I just wanted to point out that, regardless of

who or how, the job got done, and there was minimal fallout and exposure. I'm not saying what Lily did was right in the first place, but she found a solution, and the job got done. Can't you just let it go?"

He holds my gaze for a moment, then turns back to Lily. "We're done here. You will be contacted when we have another contract for you. Now leave us."

She stares at him for a few tense seconds. I can see the anger on her face, but I'm not sure how much of that is directed at Horizon and how much is directed at herself.

She yanks her arm free from his grip and marches toward the door. She glances at me as she passes. Her expression is difficult to read. I watch as she leaves the suite, shutting the door gently. I turn back to Horizon, who's staring at me.

I walk over to him. "C'mon, lay it on me…"

He shakes his head. "You shouldn't have helped her."

"All right, look. She came to me and asked—"

He holds a hand up. "Don't talk to me like I'm your colleague. I'm telling you, you shouldn't have helped her. It's not always about just getting the job done, Adrian. Some jobs have to be done a certain way to have the maximum impact."

Don't lose your temper…

I nod. "I know that. I just—"

"Oh, and you mentioned minimal exposure. Please, tell me… what part of your face appearing on the security footage of twenty-seven separate camera feeds in one of the world's most famous hotels would you class as *minimal*?"

Okay, I can't get angry about that one.

I chuckle. "Yeah… funny story about that. My plan was to—"

"Your plan was bullshit. It was reckless, unnecessary

bullshit, and it resulted in seven dead bodies no one asked for. I specifically remember telling you not to do that. Ever. I'm starting to think recruiting you maybe wasn't in everyone's best interests."

I take a short breath. "Finished?"

He stares at me blankly but says nothing.

"Good. First of all, if you ever cut me off like that again, I'm gonna knock you back in time, all right? Secondly, my plan to get to bin Mawal was sound, but even the best-laid plans sometimes turn to shit. If I hadn't handled things the way I did, I'd be dead for real, and as grateful as I am to your little group for saving me, I'm not willing to *actually* die for you. Now answer me this: did you manage to find a way to delete all traces of me from the security footage?"

He nods but remains silent, his lips pursed together stubbornly.

"Right, so that's that problem solved. The prince is dead, so there's your other problem solved. I completely get why you're pissed at Lily and at me, but the job got done. A difficult job, I might add. So, how about you cut me some slack? First offense, et cetera."

He looks at me for another moment, then smiles— mostly to himself, I think. He walks over to one of the sofas and picks up a cell phone resting on the arm. He starts typing something.

"Do you have your phone with you?" he asks, still staring at the device.

I take it out of my pocket and hold it up. "Yeah, it's here. Why?"

He looks up at me. "I'm going to be honest with you, Adrian. Regardless of circumstances, you killed seven people you weren't asked to, which is a direct violation of our rules. Expulsion from The Order is the bare minimum punishment for such recklessness, but in this case, I would normally have no other choice than to authorize your execution."

I stand up straight and take a deep breath, involuntarily steeling myself for what might come next.

Behind me, I hear the door open. I look around and see Pierce stride in. He leaves the door open, and I can see his men in the hall outside.

I look back around at Horizon and raise an eyebrow. "Normally?"

He shrugs. "I'd be lying if I said I didn't think you're an outstanding talent. Your skills are largely unmatched, and while your attitude leaves a lot to be desired, you're an asset we simply can't afford to lose."

"So... what now? A slap on the wrist?"

My phone vibrates and beeps in my hand as a message comes through.

Horizon nods at me. "I've just sent you details of a new contract. You will do this one alone, and you will carry it out immediately. Think of it as a way to redeem yourself."

I frown and open the message. I use my thumb to scroll through the details.

My eyes go wide. I look over at him. "You're fucking kidding me?"

On the screen is a full-color image of Lily.

16

Horizon stares at me. "I don't make jokes, Adrian. I don't make idle threats, and I don't bluff. You have your job. It doesn't warrant justification, before you ask me for any. Failure to carry out this task is not an option."

I watch him walk away, toward the bedroom. He pauses outside the door and glances over his shoulder. "Something you want to say?"

I go to speak, but I can't think of any words that would be relevant. I'm angry that he's managed to get one over on me so easily and that he's done it brazenly. He smiles at me, steps inside the bedroom, and slams the door shut behind him. I look back at my phone and stare at the image of Lily on the screen.

Shit.

"Let's go, asshole."

I turn around to look at Pierce. He's standing with his

arms folded across his chest, smiling at me. I fix him with my coldest stare. "I'm not doing it."

His smile fades, but the arrogance doesn't. "When are you going to understand? You don't have a choice. You belong to The Order now. You owe us your life. You do what we ask without question. End of story."

I step toward him, so our faces are mere inches apart. "I don't *belong* to anyone. Not you, not Colonel Sanders back there, not anyone else. This is who I am and what I do, and I'm here purely due to lack of a better option, all right? I'm grateful for them saving my ass, but I'm not gonna change who I am and start blindly pulling the trigger just because they tell me to."

Pierce raises an eyebrow. "Finished?"

I shrug. "Yeah, I guess."

He takes something out of his pocket and holds his hand out to the side. I glance at it. He's got something that looks like—

"Argh!"

My eyes go wide and I drop to my knees. I cradle my head in my hands. The pain is sudden and blinding. It's—

"Argh! What... the... fuck?"

I fall to the side and roll on my back. My jaw's aching from grinding my teeth together so hard, trying to manage the agony. There's a pulsating sensation of intense burning behind my eyes. I screw them shut and let out an involuntary growl.

What the—

It's stopped.

I open my eyes and look around. My vision's blurry, and I have to squint against the brightness of the lighting in the room.

I'm breathing fast. "Holy... shit! What just... happened?"

I slowly get to my feet. I massage my temples, trying to reduce the pounding inside my head.

Pierce grabs me by my collar and shoves me into a nearby chair. "*That* was a warning."

I frown and shake my head, still feeling groggy. "I don't... understand..."

He crouches beside me. "Let me break it down for you, hero. You know that tracking device in your neck? Well, it's not *just* a tracking device. There's an explosive charge embedded in it that can be activated and detonated remotely. Normally, once a device like this is active, it's not uncommon for the low frequency of the electrical pulse in the device to cause some... discomfort. But with it being so close to your brain, the effects are amplified exponentially—which is what you just experienced.

"The charge itself is obviously small enough to be contained within such a tiny device, but make no mistake—if it's detonated, it'll take your head clean off your shoulders. Well... maybe not clean. It's actually quite messy. So, I will say this to you one more time, Adrian. You *will* do *exactly* what The Order asks of you, and you will do it with no further hesitation or doubt. And if you don't, I will personally blow your fucking head off. Do we have an understanding?"

Well...

That sucks.

I move a hand to the back of my neck, suddenly aware of the small bomb stuck in there. I can't believe I was so careless... so stupid as to think The Order wanted anything more than to make me their fucking slave. I wasn't thinking clearly, back when I escaped that room. I wasn't prepared for them sticking me with anything, and I should have been.

I glance down at the tattoo on my forearm.

WWJD.

What would Josh do right now? First of all, he would definitely insult me using a British phrase I'm unlikely to have heard of. Something involving *muppets*, probably. But once he'd gotten that out of his system, he'd start working on a way to get it out of my body, or at least disable it. Then he'd—

What's that noise?

I realize my mind's been wandering. As my vision re-focuses on my surroundings, I see Pierce clicking his fingers near my head to get my attention.

"There we go. Did you hear what I just said?"

I frown at him and nod at his hand. "That's really annoying. And no, I stopped listening to you shortly after you told me about the bomb in my head."

He smiles. "I figured. I said... and before you get any ideas, you can't remove the device. It has a sensor on it that acts as a failsafe, causing it to detonate the second it comes into contact with the air."

Shit!

Okay, poker face...

I shrug. "The thought hadn't crossed my mind."

"Uh-huh..."

I get to my feet. "Listen, if you're done with the science lesson, it turns out I've got a job to do. Any chance I can catch a lift back to Abu Dhabi?"

He steps back, giving me room to move. He puts the detonator back in his pocket and shakes his head. "No, you're on your own. But... we did have someone drive your car over here. It's parked outside. Make your own way home."

"Huh... that's actually pretty nice of you. Thanks."

He shrugs. "We're not trying to be your enemy. If you

would simply commit to what we're trying to achieve and stop all these mindless acts of rebellion, there wouldn't be a problem."

I stroke the stubble on my chin. "And *that* is exactly what isn't sitting right with me. What we're trying to achieve... Is The Order simply a collection of the best killers for hire, or does it have its own agenda? You seem pretty well informed about what The Order's working toward, Pierce. Maybe you could share some details? Y'know, purely out of curiosity..."

He rolls his eyes. "You just don't learn, do you?"

His hand disappears into his pocket again. I hold a hand up. "Now, now... there's no need for that. I'm not questioning the jobs I'm given. I get that, okay? That's not what this is. The job's done. I'm just asking, like I say, out of curiosity... one colleague to another. Just some friendly, water cooler conversation. We're all on the same side, right? I just want to understand what I'm a part of."

Pierce holds my gaze for a moment. I can see the cogs working behind the scenes, as if he's trying to figure out if I'm being serious.

He stays silent.

I sigh. "C'mon, man... I'm pretty sure I know *why* Sayed bin Mawal was taken out, but whose benefit did The Order do it for?"

He arches his brow. "Okay, I'll play along. Why do you think he was eliminated?"

I shrug. "Money. He was happily giving something away that other people were trying to sell at a decent margin. I'm not an economics professor, but I know what he was doing would have had an impact on the stock exchange, which would've cost people millions of dollars. Without him, that doesn't happen."

He regards me silently for a moment, then shrugs. "Nice theory. It makes a lot of sense."

"So, am I right?"

He shrugs again. "I have no idea. I'm not told the reason, and I don't fucking ask."

I'm going around in circles here!

"Look, I get it. You're a company man, happy to accept and feed others the company line. But what I'm asking is, if I'm right about bin Mawal, why does it matter to The Order if some rich prick in the States stays rich or not?"

"It probably doesn't. But there will be a valid reason why we wanted bin Mawal to stop doing what he was doing. Same reason we asked you to take out Mr. Way when you first joined. Doing something bad isn't justification enough to be killed. Lots of people do bad things every day. But we don't go around killing every drug dealer, murderer, and rapist. We take out the people whose actions are likely to have a profound effect on the larger picture."

I shake my head and let out a short sigh. "Okay, fine. Whatever. I can see I'm wasting my time. The organ grinder won't tell me anything, so why would the monkey, right?" He smiles at me, which I ignore. "Now if you'll excuse me, I apparently have a job to do."

He steps to the side. I walk past him without another look and head out into the hall. I make eye contact with everyone standing here as I push past them and make my way back toward the elevator.

This is turning out to be a really shitty day.

15:13 AST

. . .

I'm sitting in my car in the driveway outside my house. I can't quite bring myself to go inside. Maybe it's on principle. I don't know. I mean, the place is bought and paid for by The Order, and in the last couple of hours, I've come to realize they're nothing but a bunch of maniacal, sadistic, delusional bastards. I'm not sure I want anything from them anymore.

I wonder how many of the assets they have on their books are aware that they have a bomb in their neck...

I wonder how many know they're working for a cult of arrogant pricks with a God complex...

Probably not that many. I bet the others aren't stupid enough to keep asking questions.

Actually, no. It's not stupidity that makes me do it. It's fucking talent! You hear about it all the time. Well, at least, I used to, when I had Josh as my link to the underworld community professional killers. Assassins who were supposedly at the top of their game, making big money, living the fast life... suddenly disappear because they were set up, or because they were ambushed, or because their target got lucky.

That won't ever happen to me. You know why? Because I ask questions. I find out information for myself. I don't take things at face value from the people who hire me because I'm a paranoid sonofabitch. I make sure the job is done cleanly and that the target deserves to be on the business end of my Beretta. If I'm not satisfied by what I find out, I turn the job down and walk away.

D'you know what? If The Order of Sabbah doesn't like the way I do things, they can kiss my ass! They hired me for my skills, not my personality. They would've done their research on me, they would've asked around... they would've known my reputation before they approached me.

As far as I'm concerned, I'm well within my rights to ask for some information when I'm putting my ass on the line.

Pierce was surprisingly helpful earlier, offering me some much-needed insight into how The Order works. But I'm not happy with what he said. A handful of people making decisions on behalf of everyone else never works out well for everyone else. I can guarantee that any decision made is in some way beneficial to the person or people making it—or, at a push, to the highest-paying clients.

He mentioned Mr. Way. For me, that was a cut-and-dry job. The guy sold women and girls to wealthy men, essentially for the purposes of sexual slavery. No one will ever convince me that killing him wasn't the right thing to do. But I'm not convinced there wasn't a bigger picture being considered when the contract was taken out on him. I think they do go around killing all sorts of bad people, for no other reason besides they were bad—which I consider almost honorable. But what I don't like is when they start serving their own agenda and disguising it as the greater good. Shit like that sounds a little too familiar, and history proves it's never a good thing when people do it.

I slam the palm of my hand down hard on the wheel.

"Goddammit!"

I can't believe I've been so blinded that I didn't see any of this coming. I knew something was off from the moment I woke up in that bed. But I carried on anyway. And where has it gotten me? I only have one friend in this new life, and now I have to kill her or risk having my head blown off my shoulders.

I grip the wheel tightly with both hands until the color drains from my knuckles. I can feel myself getting angry and frustrated. I haven't been myself since waking up in that weird room. I rolled with it for a while, but when the honeymoon was over, even I managed to recognize that there was something fundamentally wrong with me. Hence the therapy. Don't get me wrong. Therapy has been helping much more than I thought it would. But there's still something not quite right. It's as if a part of me is missing. It's not the killer instinct. It's more...

I let out a long sigh.

It's the desire. The passion. My heart's just not in it anymore. It feels as if I was doing this for so long simply because I had to. But when I moved to Devil's Spring, it was over for me. I didn't have to do anything. And that made me happy. But this life caught up with me and ruined everything. I was forced back into this world, and I resent it for making me pick up my guns again. And now, after everything I've been through, I'm stuck in this vicious cycle, unable to ever walk away from this life again.

All this therapy has changed the way I look at things I would otherwise have taken for granted. Maybe that's why I've been questioning everything and why I've been so reluctant to put my faith in The Order. I've been looking for a reason to back out, to stop myself from committing to my new life. I don't want it. I either want my old life, to be me, or nothing at all.

I should have just...

I reach behind me and take out the Beretta tucked into the back of my waistband. I hold it low, resting it on my lap. I look down at it, admiring its beauty, finding comfort in the feel and the weight.

I look around casually. The neighborhood is quiet. The temperature's at its hottest right now. The light blue sky is free from the blemish of any cloud, and the sun is bright and intense. I could be the only person in the world.

I lift the gun up, bringing it closer to my face. Everyone

I've ever cared about is either dead or thinks *I'm* dead. I'm essentially a prisoner in my own life, condemned to an existence of violent slavery, working for an organization that exists only in myth. I have no freedom. I can never rest. My life, such as it is, belongs to someone else, and I'm not sure I can live with that.

I flick the safety off, work the slide, and place the barrel against the fleshy underside of my chin, in the middle of my jaw. I take a deep breath and close my eyes.

Fuck it. There's no one to miss me. I'll finally be free. Free from the guilt. Free from the sadness. Free from...

I open my eyes and breathe out slowly.

Fuck!

Who am I kidding? We all know I'm too proud to take the coward's way out. It's too easy, and I don't deserve that. If I'm going to find peace, I should be made to suffer first. To fight for it.

I put the safety back on, place the gun down on the seat beside me, and start the engine. I check my watch.

Shit. I'm already running late.

17

I sit down heavily in my usual seat and glance out the window. The glare from the sun is still reflecting brightly off the windows in the nearby buildings. I let out a long, tired sigh and look over at Kaitlyn Moss. She looks slightly disheveled, which I suspect is due to a full day in a warm office. She takes off her glasses and cleans the lenses with a piece of cloth.

"Sorry I'm late, Doc."

Kaitlyn puts her glasses back on and nods. "It's no trouble, Brad, though I do usually prefer a bit of notice if you can't make the original appointment time. Luckily, I had a cancellation this afternoon. Otherwise, we'd have had to reschedule."

"I know. I'm sorry. I've just... it hasn't been a great day, and you're pretty much the only person I trust enough to talk to about things right now."

She shifts in her seat, re-crosses her legs, and clasps her hands on her lap. "So, tell me what happened."

I feel a little overwhelmed. I have to tread carefully here. I can't say anything that would give her the impression I've broken the law, but it's difficult to think of a metaphor that tells the story accurately enough that her feedback can be useful but remains vague enough that I don't get in trouble.

I take a deep breath. "Well, I... acted without thinking earlier today. I put myself in danger to help someone close to me, and I've ended up putting her at risk through my actions."

"This person who you're close to... is it Lily?"

I nod. "That obvious, huh?"

She shakes her head and smiles. "Not obvious but an educated guess."

"Yeah, she came to me for help, but I didn't consider the consequences of my actions, and now I think she might be in danger."

Kaitlyn nods along thoughtfully. "Could you perhaps be seeing danger where there isn't any? Yet again, you've assumed this natural role of protector. Are you possibly looking for danger to justify your actions?"

I can't help but feel as if I'm wasting her time. While I've no doubt what she's saying is phenomenally accurate based on the information I'm giving her, I'm not giving her a true account of what's happening in my life. That means her advice is irrelevant and, ultimately, worthless.

I shake my head. "I... don't think so, no. I happen to know she's in real danger right now, and that's a direct result of what I did. I wanted to do the right thing. I wanted to help her. But I didn't think far enough ahead to consider the consequences, and now she's—"

Kaitlyn puts her hand up. "It sounds as if you're

assuming the blame for something you had no direct control over. No one can plan for something that may occur unexpectedly. All you can do is what you feel is right at the time. It's as if you've expanded the guilt cycle we spoke about, and you're allowing it to encompass every aspect of your life. That's no way to live, Brad."

I nod. "I know. I... ah... I considered killing myself before I came here today."

She's visibly shocked but only for a moment. She recovers quickly and frowns. "How long have you had those thoughts?"

I think about it. I remember back before everything went to shit, when it was just Josh and me, blasting out classic rock songs as we ran from the loss of my family. In the early days after losing them, I thought about eating a bullet every second of every day. It was Josh who kept me going until I began choosing to keep going myself. That feels like a life-time ago.

I shrug. "Not long. I was just sitting in my car before, lost in my thoughts, and my mind just kinda... drifted toward the idea. It made sense at first. I even put a gun right here..." I point to the flesh underneath my chin. "But when I actu-ally—I dunno—*entered* that moment, I just felt detached. It was almost as if I knew exactly what was happening and simply talked myself out of it. I see that as the coward's way out, and that's not who I am. I think maybe I needed to test myself—to put myself in that position to see how it would make me feel."

"And how *did* you feel?"

"Honestly? Like I should live, if only to suffer through life for the choices I've made that have hurt other people. The memories of the people I couldn't save deserve more. They should be able to rest knowing that I'm being torn up inside, over and over again, for the pain they felt because of me."

"Okay... ignoring for a moment the fact that you've just admitted to possessing a firearm, the fact you put yourself in that position and chose to live is a good thing, whatever your reasoning. That's a big step forward. I don't believe you're a risk to yourself or others. I think you needed to test yourself, like you say, to see how far you could allow yourself to go, and I think you satisfied that curiosity. I think the next step for you is learning *how* to live."

She's looking at me expectantly, but I'm not sure what I should say. I mean, she's right. *Obviously,* she's right. But what can I say? I can't exactly tell her the situation I'm in...

Or can I?

No, I can't. Don't be stupid, Adrian.

That's not the kind of shit you can just—

A red dot has just appeared on Kaitlyn's chest. I feel my eyes grow wide as I process the million different thoughts currently bombarding my mind. I know exactly what it is. Someone's aiming a sniper rifle at her, but I don't know why.

The large window on my left looks out at the neighboring office buildings. Whoever's holding the rifle has to be in one of them. The dot is steady, which means either the rifle is mounted, or the shooter has a strong arm. I glance sideways out the window. There are three buildings with line of sight, but only two of them are as tall as the one we're in.

Fuck!

I don't know who it is, why they're doing it, or even how they know where I am, but right now, all the questions can wait. I need to keep Kaitlyn safe. I need to—

"Brad, is everything okay? You look a little... alarmed."

I nod slowly. "Yeah... listen, this might sound a little

weird, but do you mind if we sit somewhere else?" I point to the large space next to me, away from the window. "If I move my chair there, will you sit where I am now?"

Kaitlyn frowns. "May I ask why?"

The dot hasn't moved a fraction since it appeared.

Shit, shit, shit!

I need to remain calm, but I need to hurry up.

I shrug. "I'd just feel more comfortable facing the window. That's all."

She seems to think about it, then she stands. "Of course, if that's what you would prefer."

I get to my feet and dash over to pick up her chair, making sure I'm standing between her and the window. "Allow me."

I'm not worried about getting shot. If whoever has the rifle wanted me dead, they would aim at me. The fact they're aiming at Kaitlyn tells me they know who I am, and they want to send me a message by attacking someone I'm close to, so to speak.

She smiles politely. "Thank you."

I reposition the furniture and sit facing the window. I scan the buildings opposite for any sign of movement but can't see anything. The dot has disappeared.

Doesn't mean the threat has, though.

Who could possibly know I'm here?

Kaitlyn clears her throat. "Brad, are you sure you're all right? You seem distracted all of a sudden..."

"Sorry, I just—"

I snap my head left and stare at the door.

What was that?

I frown. There was a loud noise somewhere below us. It sounded as if it came from outside, on the street. I look across at her. She clearly heard it too, but the look on her face is one of confusion more than concern, thankfully. It wasn't on our floor—it was too distant—but we're three floors up, so whatever it was had to be big for us to hear it at all.

An explosion?

Perhaps, but I think we would've felt some kind of physical repercussion from the blast. Whatever that was, it wasn't powerful enough to shake the building itself. So, it wasn't a bomb...

A breaching charge?

Hmmm... that's a little more likely. That would be bad. Most normal people wouldn't use something so specialized to attack a building, which means whoever's coming in is trained and has access to that kind of equipment.

Kaitlyn stands. "Do you mind waiting here a moment? I'm just going to see what that—"

I get to my feet and grab her wrist as firmly and as gently as I can. "Ah... actually, I think you're maybe better off staying here. Let *me* check it out, okay?"

She pulls her arm free of my grip and furrows her brow. "Brad, I appreciate the sentiment, but while you're here, you're in my care. For insurance purposes, unless there's a fire, I can't let you leave the office if there's something wrong."

She moves for the door, but I step in front of her. "Okay, Kaitlyn, you have to stay here. This isn't my protective older brother thing kicking in, all right? You have to trust me. My spider sense is off the scale right now, and I think we're about to be in some serious trouble. You need to let me handle this."

"Brad, what's going on? What aren't you telling me?"

I go to speak but hesitate. What can I say? I can't exactly—

"And I read people for a living, so don't even think about lying to me. I know sometimes, for whatever reason, you tend to be a little... vague about certain subjects. If you've learned anything at all from our sessions, I hope you know you can trust me enough to be honest with me. Tell me what's *really* going on. You swapped the seats around moments before what sounded like a small bomb went off outside the building. Trust that you can open up to me, Brad."

I sigh. "Adrian."

"What?"

"My name isn't Brad. It's Adrian."

"Okay... so, you felt the need to conceal your true identity during our sessions. I can maybe see why—"

I shake my head. "No, Doc. Don't try to analyze it. Right now, I don't have the time to explain why you've been missing the mark with so many assumptions you've made about me. I just need *you* to trust *me*. I'm pretty sure we're about to find ourselves knee-deep in shit, and if we're gonna get out of this in one piece, you need to listen to what I'm about to say."

She holds my gaze. I can see in her eyes that she's both afraid and professionally curious at the same time. And maybe a little pissed off, which I can understand.

She nods. "Okay, *Adrian*. Tell me what's going on."

I glance over my shoulder at the door, assuring myself it's still closed. "Have you caught the news today?"

She shakes her head. "I haven't had the chance. I've been with clients most of the day."

"Okay. Well, there was an incident at the Etihad Towers a few hours ago. Most of the top floor in one of the towers was decimated by a helicopter gunship, and close to thirty people lost their lives."

Her eyes widen with shock. "Oh my God! Was it North Korea again? Do you think there's still a threat in the city? Is that what this is?"

I shake my head. "There's no threat in the city. I haven't seen the *official* story on the news myself. I'm just assuming the incident was at least mentioned on it. But I was there. The chopper came to rescue me because I was trapped up there with a significant number of armed security guards who had designs on killing me."

"I... I don't understand. Is this some kind of metaphor you're trying to use?"

I smile weakly. "I'm afraid not. This might be hard to believe, Kaitlyn, but sometimes my job requires me to do some... questionable things. And one of those things involved being in that tower today to kill someone."

Her expression is neutral, as if she's not committing to believing what I'm saying, but she's not dismissing it either. It's probably the professional in her—stay detached, look at the facts, and try to help the person in front of her without letting her own emotions cloud her judgment.

She nods. "And did you?"

"Did I what? Kill him?" I shrug. "Oh, yeah, obviously. But I also killed his seven bodyguards, which I wasn't supposed to do. I did it because it was either them or me. They left me no choice. But—"

I look back at the door again. I can hear footsteps outside. They're only faint, but I think they're getting closer. We're in an old apartment building, which has been converted for commercial use. It's not a typical office block, so there's one central stairwell and a handful of rooms on each floor. I think the footsteps are coming from two floors below us.

I look back at Kaitlyn. Her bottom lip is trembling. She's breathing fast. She looks afraid.

I let out a heavy breath, not of impatience but of regret. "Look, Kaitlyn, we really don't have time for this. I'm sorry, but here are the facts—I'm an assassin, and the people I work for have ordered me to kill Lily. She's also an assassin, and the guy I killed in the Etihad Tower was a favor for her because she was meant to kill him and failed. As punishment, our mutual employer has ordered her dead and given me the job. I don't wanna do it, obviously, but it turns out I have a small bomb implanted in my neck, which means if I don't kill her..." I make the explosion gesture with my hands. "Ka-boom—off comes my head. Hence me coming to you, so you can help me make sense of my shitty life. I think whatever's going on below us has to do with that, and I don't think it's gonna be good. I need you to do as I say, so I can get you to safety."

"I... I... You're—"

The footsteps are getting louder outside. Whoever it is, they're on our floor.

I pull Kaitlyn close to me, put my hand over her mouth, and step to the side, resting against the wall next to the door. Her body is pressed close to mine, and her eyes are wide with genuine fear. I feel really bad about this, but there's nothing I can do about that right now. I look into her eyes and place a finger to my lips.

Oh, man... what the fuck is going on?

I try to slow my breathing. My heart's hammering against my chest as the adrenaline begins its familiar surge around my body. The low, rumbling march of multiple boots outside the room is growing louder. I close my eyes, trying to pinpoint how many people there are.

Four... maybe five. I can't tell.

Shit.

Think, Adrian...

It has to be The Order, right? But why would they send a team after me when they've given me the job of killing Lily? And that red dot... Who even knows I'm here? And why would whoever it is target Kaitlyn and not me? Why send a message by hurting someone I'm linked to?

Goddammit, I hate not knowing what's going on!

The movement outside has stopped.

Whoever it is, they're standing right outside our door.

18

Kaitlyn lets out a muffled moan. I press my hand harder over her mouth and shake my head, willing her to understand that she needs to stay quiet.

BANG... BANG... BANG...

A heavy, methodical knock on the door sounds out.

I slowly shake my head once more at Kaitlyn, signaling to her not to move or make a sound.

BANG... BANG...

"Brad, I know you're in there. Stop being a pussy and open the goddamn door, will you?"

I frown. That's Pierce...

What the hell?

I let go of Kaitlyn and chuckle nervously. "Sorry about that. Wait here."

I quickly step over to the other side of the door and put my back to the wall. I reach over and grab the handle, then glance over at Kaitlyn and place a finger to my lips again. She nods hurriedly.

"Pierce, is that you?"

"Yeah. Open the door."

"Why should I?"

"Because I'm telling you to."

I laugh humorlessly. "Try again..."

"We need to talk."

"Now's... not a good time."

Silence.

"I don't care. Open the door, or I'll blow it off its fucking hinges."

"Oh, excuse me, *Big Bad Wolf!* Look, this is a private appointment, all right? Little piggies only. If you wait outside, I'll be with you in about... a half-hour?"

"Brad, don't kid yourself by thinking you *have* privacy anymore. You've got a job to do, and that should be your only priority."

"What's it to you how I go about doing my job?"

"Horizon asked me to keep an eye on you and make sure you don't do anything stupid."

"Who? Me?"

"Just open the fucking door."

I sigh. He's not going anywhere, is he? He's probably not alone, and he's almost certainly armed. I'm pretty much trapped here. I have to assume that, whoever the sniper is, they're still watching the window. Plus, this isn't exactly a large office. It's a modest, open-plan space with a small bathroom built into the far corner. That's it. Nowhere to hide. No way out.

Shit.

"Okay, Pierce, here's the thing. I'm not alone, and the person in here with me has nothing to do with any of this.

You hear me? She's innocent and unaware of the life we live. I need you to promise you won't hurt her. I'm not trying to make a big thing out of it, but if I let you in, and you're all confrontational and shit, I'm gonna have to whoop your ass a little bit and maybe even kill you. We clear on that?"

More silence.

"I'm not here looking for a fight. I'm here to help you."

Huh. Well, I wasn't expecting that. Help me? How?

Probably best to let this play out for now. I can't think of any reason why he would actually want to hurt me or Kaitlyn, so I think I'll be okay.

I look over at her and smile, trying to reassure her, and then look back at the door. "Well, why didn't you say that in the first place?"

I turn the handle and pull, letting the door swing open. Pierce is standing casually in the hall. He has an assault rifle hanging loose over his shoulder, and he's with the same four guys who picked me up in Vietnam. They're all standing to his left, looking more alert than he does.

I move in front of him. "How did you find me here?"

He rolls his eyes, as if I've just asked a stupid question. "That thing in your neck I can detonate? It is still an *actual* tracking device. I know exactly where you are at all times."

"Great. So, what's up?"

He gestures to the room behind me. "You're not gonna invite me in?"

"No."

He smiles. "I'm sure Miss Moss won't mind."

What?

I raise an eyebrow but say nothing.

"No privacy, remember? You gotta learn to keep up. This is getting embarrassing."

"Hey, fuck you, all right? What do you want?"

"We think you're being hunted."

"Yeah, I think so too. What's it to you?"

"Horizon gave you a job to do. My job is to make sure you do yours. Sometimes, that means I gotta give people... an incentive. Other times, it means I gotta watch their backs."

"And which is this?"

"The latter. For now."

I step to the side, and he strides into the middle of the room. He turns to face me and catches sight of Kaitlyn. He nods a polite greeting. "And you must be the therapist. Nice to meet you."

She looks at me. I can see concern and confusion in her eyes. "Adrian, what's going on?"

Pierce turns to me and raises an eyebrow. "*Adrian*, eh? You've told her your real name? Tut tut..."

I wave my hand dismissively. "She's bound by confidentiality, so she won't say anything to anyone. She's not a threat. Anyway, I hadn't told her anything. I was forced to when you stormed in here like a stampede of wild assholes. I had to say *something*."

"Whatever. I'm here because you've got bigger problems."

"So, what else is new? What is it this time?"

"Lily."

I frown and actively avoid making eye contact with Kaitlyn. "She's not a problem. I've been told to kill her, and I will. Admittedly, only because I have no choice, but even so —I will."

"Oh, I know. *That's* not the problem. The problem is that we're pretty sure she's showing some initiative and actually hunting *you*."

I take a breath. "Ah..."

"She's found a way to hack into our network, which means she has access to the information received from the tracking devices. She has eyes on every asset The Order has."

"Oh..."

"We've been monitoring her movements, and we know she's in a nearby building right now. I think it's obvious she's making a preemptive effort to get rid of you."

I pace back and forth, processing what Pierce has just said.

Kaitlyn steps close to me and puts a hand on my arm. "Adrian, what does all this mean?"

She didn't hide the tremble of fear in her voice.

I stop and look at her. "You need to... just... gimme a minute, all right? I'm trying to wrap my head around this myself."

I carry on pacing for a moment, then turn to Pierce. "I don't understand why she would suddenly want to kill me. We were—"

He raises an eyebrow. "Friends? Adrian, she's been in The Order a lot longer than you have. She knows how we work. She'll know Horizon gave you the contract to take her out, and she knows you can't turn it down, which means she knows it's only a matter of time before you try to kill her. Fuck friendship, man. It's basic survival tactics."

"Yeah, but she has the same device in her neck, right? Surely, she knows that if she were to somehow take me out, Horizon—or you—could just push a button and blow her head clean off her shoulders?"

He shrugs. "I didn't say it makes sense. I just said it's happening."

I let out a heavy sigh. "Shit."

Kaitlyn moves over to me. "Adrian, you *have* to tell me what's happening! I don't understand!"

I face her and put my hands on her shoulders. "Kaitlyn, I appreciate this is a big ask, but I need you to trust me. Once I get you to safety, I promise I'll explain everything. But right now, you need to focus on the fact that there's a dangerous assassin trying to kill me, and anyone who's with me is just as deep in the shit as I am. I'm the only one who can protect you right now, so you have to stick with me." I gesture to Pierce with my thumb. "Hopefully, this guy's gonna get us out of here and then I can get you out of the city."

"But Adrian, after everything you've told me about Lily, do you really think she would just try and *kill* you without at least talking to you first?"

I nod. "Everything I've told you about Lily is only half the story. I'm sorry. And yeah, under the circumstances, I think she would. Neither one of us has much choice in the matter. We either kill the other one, or we die." I turn to Pierce. "So, what's the plan?"

He gestures to his men standing in the hall. "My team and I are gonna make sure you get out of here in one piece. You're in no position right now to take her out. She has the advantage, so it's my job to protect you long enough for you to get your head out of your ass and do your job."

I go to say something but stop myself.

I've always had this ability to make my surroundings... I don't know... slow down. I've learned how to stay calm to the point where things seem to start moving slower than normal, which ultimately helps me see things other people don't. It helps me plan my next move, react quickly, and find resolutions to problems others probably won't even identify.

It also seems to be linked to my spider sense, as if my subconscious automatically activates the ability when it knows I need it. It only ever happens when shit's hitting the fan... or when it's about to.

I stopped myself from saying anything because the world is slowing down right now. The room is unchanged. The people in it aren't doing anything different. But... there's definitely a noise that doesn't belong. It's like a roaring, whooshing sound, and it's coming from outside.

I turn to look out the window.

"Shit! Everyone move!"

I lunge to grab Kaitlyn by the arm and sling her through the open door. She stumbles and falls to the floor. I ignore Pierce and move to follow her, but I'm not fast enough. Time resumes its usual speed as the RPG hits the building just below the window. The impact shakes the foundations, like an earthquake. The thunderous explosion completely shatters the glass, hurling thousands of tiny shards into the room.

I grit my teeth. "Fuck!"

I didn't make it out of the room. I was blown into the far corner by the blast, and I'm lying face-down in agony. My back feels wet and sticky, torn to shreds by the glass. With the exception of the loud, constant ringing in my ears, I'm completely deaf, and my equilibrium's all kinds of screwed.

What the hell just happened?

I push myself up with one arm and look to my left. Pierce is lying a few feet away from me, looking almost as bad as I feel.

I frown. Christ, it's hot...

I look behind me at the window.

It's gone. There's a sizeable hole in the side of the building, and flames are climbing into the room. I shake my head, trying to clear some of the fog. Background noise is slowly starting to register. The crackling of the flames is prominent.

I can also hear what sounds like... crumbling, maybe? And screams. Definitely screams...

Shit, Kaitlyn!

I turn the other way and look over at the door. I can see a pair of legs lying motionless but nothing else. Man, I hope they're still attached to someone...

I take some deep breaths, but because of the smoke filling the room, I start coughing. "Kait... Kait... Kaitlyn!"

I close my eyes and frown, summoning all the focus I can to drown out the extraneous noise.

I still can't hear anything.

"Kaitlyn!"

I listen carefully.

"...ian!"

Was that...

"Kaitlyn?"

"Adrian!"

That's her!

"Kaitlyn!" I grimace as I try to move, which sends a pain shooting across my back like a lightning strike. "Where are you?"

"I'm—"

Whoa!

Shit!

I'm sliding backward uncontrollably because the floor's just crumbled away! My arms are stretched up, my hands desperately searching for something to—

"Ugh! Fuck me..."

—get a hold of.

Ah!

Some of the thin, metal framework used to reinforce the concrete is sticking out in places. I went to grab one piece in particular, which is jagged and sharp but mistimed it. It sliced my palm open and is now sticking *in* my hand! I ignore how much it *fucking hurts* and grasp it as tight as I can because my legs aren't resting on anything.

I close my eyes for a moment. This is one of those times where I know I really don't want to know the answer, but I need to ask the question anyway.

I open my eyes and look down.

"Oh, shit!"

I look back up quickly and close my eyes again.

Yeah... there's nothing below me except a three-story drop. That crumbling noise is getting louder. The building looks pretty old, and the blast must've damaged the structural integrity. The impact of the RPG has compromised the entire east wall of the office block, so the floors below are starting to disintegrate too, like a domino effect.

I take a deep breath, trying to calm myself, but this is one of those rare moments where I'm finding that hard to do. I hate heights. Like, seriously fucking detest them. Planes are okay. I can even handle jumping out of them because I usually have a parachute on my back, at least. But this... there's no 'chute. There's no safety net. Just a big fucking drop.

Three stories is probably about... what? Thirty feet? Maybe forty? That's enough of a drop that I wouldn't just fall. I'd plummet. And while that might not kill me, it'd do some serious damage. But this isn't a normal drop. Scattered thirty-to-forty feet below is a huge pile of burning rubble. Falling... *plummeting* onto that shit would *definitely* kill me.

My arm is getting tired. The only thing keeping me hanging on is the fact that the metal piping is stapled to my hand! There's nothing for my left hand to grab, and everything around me is crumbling and falling slowly away to the ground below.

I take another long breath, trying to block out the pain from my hand and my back... I ignore the fact I'm hanging out the side of a building, three stories up, surrounded by flames... I also ignore the fact that, right now, Lily is most likely looking on from whichever building she's in, watching me through the sights of her sniper rifle. She could shoot me at any moment and put me out of my misery. Or, assuming she's a good enough shot, she could shoot my hand and make me fall to my death instead. *That* would suck.

I sigh.

I am so screwed right now.

I look down again and immediately wish I hadn't. This is fucking surreal. This morning, I woke up beside Lily, nursing a hangover. And now, six hours later, I'm dangling above certain death because she's trying to kill me.

I really can go from *normal* to *fucked* in the blink of an eye, can't I?

"Adrian?"

I frown.

Huh?

I look up and see Pierce staring back at me. He leans over and lowers his arm.

"Adrian, gimme your hand!"

You don't need to tell me twice!

I reach up...

Ah! Just short.

I shake my head. "I can't reach you."

He sighs. "Okay, hang on." He disappears again.

I roll my eyes. "*Hang on*... really?"

He reappears, leaning over farther than before. "Try now."

My right hand feels as if it's being ripped in two! I swing my body slightly from side to side, once... twice... and...

I throw my arm up and grab hold of his hand.

He grimaces from the effort. "Gotcha!"

He pulls me up as best he can, just far enough that it takes pressure off my other hand and allows me to find some footing. I manage to heave myself up the rest of the way and climb up onto what's left of the floor in Kaitlyn's office. I roll over onto my back and stare at the ceiling.

"Holy... shit..." I take a few deep breaths. "Thanks..."

I lift my head and look over at him. He's lying on his front with his feet hooked around the legs of a small table. He's wedged the table in one of the gaps that's appeared in the floor. Risky move, but I'm grateful, nonetheless.

We both struggle to our feet and quickly move out into the hall. The structure out here seems more stable, but I don't want to hang around any longer than necessary. Kaitlyn is standing over by the stairwell with three of Pierce's team.

Three?

I frown and look behind me.

Oh, crap.

Those legs I saw before *are* still attached, but the poor bastard has a pretty big hole in his chest. Looks as if something impaled him during the initial blast.

I turn to Pierce, who's staring at the body. "I'm sorry, man."

He shakes his head. "No time for that now. We need to get you out of here. Follow me."

He pushes past us all and takes point, heading down the flight of stairs for the exit. Two of his team go next, with Kaitlyn just behind them and me just behind her. The final member of his team is bringing up the rear.

We make it to the first floor and dash out onto the sidewalk. We don't stop until we're across the street and around the corner. There's a large crowd of people standing nearby, looking on with morbid fascination. Sirens are blaring in the distance and getting louder by the second, so the emergency services will be here any moment.

We keep moving until we're far enough away from the building that we can safely stop to catch our breath. We all stand in a tight circle. Pierce looks hurt, but it's not obvious where. He's taking some deep breaths and seems to be managing. The rest of team looks mostly unscathed. Kaitlyn's sitting on the edge of the curb, staring blankly at the ground. I know the onset of shock when I see it. I'll give her a minute. She's smart, and it's her job to understand how the mind works. She'll know what's happening to her, so I'll give her some time to process things before I say anything.

I look down at my right hand. Goddamn, it's a mess! There's a deep gash running horizontally across my palm. I try to clench my fist, but I can't. It's as if there's something physically stopping my fingers from moving that close together.

"You need to get that looked at."

I look over and see Pierce staring at my hand.

I nod. "Yeah, it's pretty bad, but there's no time for that now. What's our next move?"

He gestures down the street with his thumb. "Our SUV is parked down there. We have plenty of ammo and some spare guns in the trunk. You can take it and get the fuck outta the city. You need to regroup before you try taking Lily out."

I shake my head. "I'm not running. Not my style. I know roughly where she is right now, so I'm gonna finish this before she causes any more damage. Unless... y'know, *you* wanna go and do it?"

Pierce smiles and shakes his head. "That's not my job. It's yours. My job is to keep you alive long enough to do *your* job."

"Fine." I turn to nod at the building, which looks like it's getting ready to completely collapse. "But right now, she's desperate. She's not thinking straight, which makes her all the more dangerous. I can handle myself, and shit like this... innocent people could die. I can't allow that."

He smiles faintly. "Ever the white knight, eh, hero? But this isn't a discussion. Collateral damage isn't your concern. You work for The Order. Don't forget that. I saved your ass because I was told to. Now don't be a dick. Don't stop using your brain after what we just went through. Get... the fuck... out of here. Regroup and come back stronger. As things stand, you're in no position to take her out, so don't try. If you turn cowboy, everything I just did for you will have been for nothing, and that'll really piss me off."

I take some deep breaths and stare at the ground. My vision blurs slightly as I consider my options. There aren't many.

I refocus and look at my arm. WWJD. Yeah... Josh would tell me that, as much as I hate it, Pierce has a point. I need to get Kaitlyn out of harm's way and get back to full strength before I try to do anything else. I'm sure The Order can clear up this mess. It's not my problem.

I move over to Kaitlyn and sit beside her. I nudge her gently with my elbow. "Hey. You all right?"

She turns to me.

Oh, man, she looks pissed!

"No, I'm not okay, Brad... Adrian... whatever your name is!" She points to the smoke billowing in the air from her office building. "That was my *life*! I moved here to start over. To start up a private business, which I did—quite successfully, I might add. And you've just reduced it to dust! I have nothing now!"

She lashes out and hits me twice in the chest. Compared to all the shit that hurts right now, her strikes don't even register. But I let her hit me, and I'll keep letting her for as long as she needs to. She has every right to be pissed at me. I brought this on her. Like an idiot, I thought I could offload the emotional crap from my life onto her without consequence.

This is me. There are *always* consequences.

She hits me maybe five times before she runs out of steam and simply starts crying. I put my arm around her, and she falls into me.

"I'm gonna keep you safe, okay? You have my word. But we gotta get out of here, all right?"

I stand, and a moment later, so does she. I look at Pierce and hold out my good hand. "Gimme the keys to your SUV. You're right. This is gonna take some time."

He nods and throws them to me. I catch them easily. "Thanks for this. I know what my job is, and I'll do it."

He stands tall. "I know you will. All this..." He shakes his head. "It doesn't change shit, Adrian. The Order understands that sometimes a job isn't straightforward. Sometimes things go wrong, and sometimes we have to react, as opposed to being the preemptive machines we're all trained to be. For those times, people like you have people like me. Now get the fuck out of here."

I nod once, take Kaitlyn's hand, and set off walking along the street as quickly as we can without drawing attention to ourselves. The SUV is parked one street over, maybe a block away. It's a black Suburban. I throw the keys to Kaitlyn. "You need to drive." I hold up my right hand. "I doubt I'll be able to steer with this."

She nods and climbs in behind the wheel. I get in beside her and slam the door closed with my left hand.

"Where to?" she asks.

I shrug. "Not sure. Just get us away from here. Head out into the desert. It's away from the city, away from people, and the open terrain will make it easy to spot anyone following us. I'll make a call once we're out of Abu Dhabi, and we'll go from there."

She takes a deep breath and seems to compose herself. She doesn't question me. She just guns the engine, quickly spins the car around, and hits the gas. We drive away, leaving the carnage in the rearview.

19

Kaitlyn and I are sitting side by side, leaning forward and resting on the bar in a small restaurant. It's a discreet little place just off the main strip running through the center of Doha. The décor is shiny black, with a blood-red trim all around. It's filled with the low noise of multiple conversations from the modest crowd as they finish their meals. Families, couples, large parties... all sitting together, laughing without a care in the world.

We got here about ten minutes ago. As soon as we hit the city limits, we found an underground parking lot and ditched the Suburban. They're not exactly the subtlest of vehicles, and from this point on, we need to keep a low profile. We both loaded up with as much weaponry and ammunition as we could carry between us without it looking obvious and set off on foot through the center of the city. This is the first place we came across that looked quiet.

We told the waiter who greeted us that we weren't hungry but needed a drink. I ordered a beer and Kaitlyn a large glass of red wine.

I glance sideways at her. She's vacantly staring at the counter. She hasn't said anything since we sat down. We didn't speak much on the journey here, either. We chased the sunset all the way along E11 until we reached Qatar. Credit where it's due, she's been a real trooper. She drove all the way here without any questions or hesitation, and we only stopped once for a bathroom break. We were pretty lucky with traffic, and it took a little over five hours.

I take a sip of my beer. "How are you doing?"

She doesn't reply.

I let out a long, heavy breath, which hurts more than it should. "Look, I know you're angry. I know you're afraid. But we need to be on the same page if we're going to survive this. I can protect you. I can take Lily out. But I need your help. I need you—"

She snaps her head around to look at me. "You need *my* help? How can *I* help *you*, exactly? By carrying around your..." She pauses and leans in closer to whisper. "...your guns? Or maybe you need my help making someone disappear, or whatever you people call it? Or how about..."

She trails off. She's breathing fast and not blinking. I can see the resentment in her eyes, which I completely understand.

I nod. "It's okay, Kaitlyn. You have every right to be mad at me. I blame myself for everything that's happened to you."

"Good. I blame *your*self too."

I look away for a moment. This is turning into one of those times where, despite agreeing with the person who's pissed at me, I'm starting to lose my patience with the whole *blame Adrian* thing. I'm trying to remember that she's not like me. She's... normal. She won't understand my frustrations. She won't think I'm entitled to them.

I look back at her. "Okay, look. I understand you need to be angry at me. But you need to start moving past that. Now. We have bigger problems to deal with than whose fault this is. Do you get that? We have somebody..." I lower my voice. "We have somebody trying to kill us. Normally, that wouldn't bother me all that much, but this person knows exactly where we are at all times, which means we don't get to rest. We don't get to recharge and regroup. It means we have to keep running until we're in a position to fight back." I hold up my right hand, which I crudely bandaged using the first aid kit from the SUV on the way here. "Which might be a while. And it's not just anyone who's after us, either. Lily's an assassin good enough to be recruited by the organization responsible for recruiting the deadliest killers the world has ever known. The same organization that recruited me."

Kaitlyn's eyes grow wide as my words slowly start to sink in. "I don't understand. What do you mean? What does *any* of this mean?"

I sigh. "I know this is a lot to process. But I need you to understand the real danger we're both in right now. I'm essentially one-handed, and I have to focus on protecting you, as well as figuring out how to take someone down who has the distinct advantage of knowing where I am at all times. We're pretty much swimming into a shit tsunami, and I don't need you being mad at me while I'm trying to save your ass, okay?"

She doesn't say anything. She stares at me for a moment,

then looks away. She's quiet for a few, long minutes, then she picks up her drink, downs it in one, and slams the glass back down on the bar.

She takes a few deep breaths and then looks back at me. "I want answers. I need to understand what's happened that could lead me here, to this moment, sat with you."

If she were anyone else, I have no doubt she would've crumbled under the pressure of this long before now. I guess it's her training as a therapist that's given her the ability to remain mentally strong and focused, almost detached... despite the dire circumstances she's in.

I nod. "I know you do, and I promise, I'll tell you everything. But now isn't the time. What I will say is that I've never lied to you. I admit I... substituted certain elements of what we discussed with metaphors to gloss over the more morally questionable parts, but I never lied. And I never will."

She looks away and catches the eye of the barman. She holds a hand up to signal she wants a drink, then points to her empty glass. The barman nods and sets about preparing another for her. He walks over and places a full glass of red wine in front of her, with a small napkin beneath it. She picks it up and empties it in another, quite impressive, gulp. She slams it down again and pushes it away.

Man, this woman can drink! Josh would love her.

Goddammit. There I go again!

I silently curse myself for the observation and refocus on Kaitlyn. She's staring at the surface of the bar, and I can see her trying to control her breathing. After a few moments, she finally looks back at me. "Okay. So, what's our next move?"

I smile. "As much as I hate to admit it, I could do with getting to a hospital. I'm worried about my hand, and I haven't even thought about the state my back's probably in from all that glass. Plus, it'll be somewhere we can rest and be relatively safe, at least for a little while. It'll give us chance to get you up to speed and think about what comes next."

She stands and looks across at the barman again. He smiles and moves over to us. "Yes, ma'am?"

He's a well-dressed, well-groomed man with impeccable English.

Kaitlyn smiles. "Can you please call us a cab?"

He nods. "But of course."

He disappears around a corner that leads into the back, presumably where the kitchen is.

Kaitlyn looks back at me and nods to my beer. "C'mon, drink up."

I raise an eyebrow and smile.

June 4, 2017 — 01:09 AST

One of the benefits of unlimited wealth is that you rarely have to wait around for anything. Money will always buy priority.

The cab dropped us at the main entrance to Rumailah Hospital, which is a short walk from the semicircular bay that makes up the coastline of Qatar, overlooking Old Palm Tree Island. It's a large, low building made of clean, beige brick, and it reminds me of something from the seventies.

However, despite its humble exterior, inside tells a different story. It's actually a state-of-the-art facility, clinically immaculate and mostly white throughout. The front desk that faces the entrance looks as if it belongs on the deck of the Starship Enterprise. There's a large screen hanging behind it, displaying information about the hospital. On the desk, there's an array of monitors and touchscreen equipment.

To the left of the entrance is a waiting area, which was mostly deserted, given the time we got here. Opposite, on the right, the area was blocked off. I think this place has undergone some major transformations in the last six months, and a lot of the work seems to be still ongoing.

Another shining example of what can be done by the governments of the world that found themselves thriving in the aftermath of 4/17. Over here in the East, they've invested heavily in transportation and healthcare, which is creating jobs and, ultimately, a better way of life for not only the people who already live here but also the people seeking refuge.

I acted out the part of a victim a little. I figured my injuries were of the extent that, if I looked as if there was nothing wrong with me, it would probably raise more questions than I would like. But I soon realized any acting was unnecessary. I'm actually in a *lot* of pain! The act had been me ignoring it all night, but getting to the hospital allowed me to relax a little, and the agony had quickly taken over.

The woman behind the counter took one look at me as Kaitlyn and I approached and immediately called for two orderlies to come and assist. I refused the wheelchair they offered, and they walked me through the facility and straight into my own room, which was one of many lining both sides of a wide hallway.

I sat down on the edge of the bed and asked Kaitlyn to take the cover off the bottom pillow. We were each carrying a handgun with two spare mags, so we stashed them in the pillowcase and hid it under the bed. About thirty seconds later, a doctor appeared. He was probably no more than a couple years my senior, but because his long beard was mostly gray, it made him look much older.

He had closed the door behind him and set about asking me a whole bunch of routine questions about how I sustained my injuries. Kaitlyn had taken a seat in one of the chairs facing the bed and remained quiet as I explained what had happened to me, using as many facts as I could without implicating myself in anything.

I then peeled my T-shirt off to show the doctor my back, which was an unpleasant experience. I just figured, with everything that had happened and the climate being what it was anyway, the fact my T-shirt was sticking to me was just sweat.

It wasn't.

Prior to getting here, I had no idea what the extent of the damage was after absorbing most of the RPG blast, but my first clue came when the doctor took one look at my injuries and muttered "Holy mother of God..." under his breath.

You don't need a medical degree to know *that's* never a good sign!

He patched up as many of the wounds as he could, carried out a full assessment to see if I had any other injuries, and then arranged an X-ray for my right hand. I was in and out and back in bed within thirty minutes, and he advised me a surgical consult would come and look at my right hand soon.

That was almost two hours ago, so I'm hoping they'll be here any time now.

The meds he gave me have kicked in. I'm sitting up in bed, enjoying the reprieve from the pain that's been coursing through my upper body for half the goddamn day.

Kaitlyn's asleep on the chair, curled up in a ball. I don't

think I'll be getting any rest anytime soon, despite being in dire need of a few hours' sleep. My mind's far too busy trying to figure out how to stop Lily without killing her.

I know, I know...

But I don't like being manipulated, and that's exactly what Horizon's doing, which makes me not want to kill her just to piss him off. That's not the only reason, obviously, but it helps.

Don't get me wrong. I get *why* The Order's pissed at Lily, and despite everything that's happened and everything I've done... I kind of agree with them, to a point. I mean, I've been doing the whole *killer for hire* thing for a long time. I know what it takes to survive in this world, and I know what it takes to be the best. There's no way I would've made the mistakes Lily did, and the fact she made them at all makes me wonder what she brought to the table in the first place that made The Order interested in her.

That said, mistakes do happen. Whether it's directly or indirectly, sometimes shit just goes sideways, and there's nothing you can do to stop it. Your only option is to react in the best way you see fit to try to rectify whatever the situation is. That's exactly what Lily's done. She knew she couldn't fail The Order, so she came to me and asked for help.

If I'm being completely honest, the cynic in me thinks this is nothing more than the excuse Horizon's been waiting for to justify getting rid of her. This seems to be a disproportionate response to Lily's mistake, especially given she didn't technically break any of The Order's precious little rules. This seems personal. I might be way off, but that's what my gut's telling me. I mean, I quite brazenly broke one of their rules, and all I got was a stern talking to and an opportunity to redeem myself.

On top of that, given my almost genetic reflex to rebel against authority, I'm not blind to the fact that I've been pissing Horizon off more and more each time we speak. Him giving me the contract on Lily's life is probably just his way of putting me in my place and exerting his authority over me. He most likely knows Lily and I were growing close, and he knows there's nothing I can *really* do about it because of the fucking bomb in my head...

I sigh heavily and lean back against the pillow.

I need to focus. I'm letting my mind run away with itself, worrying about too many worst-case scenarios. I need to make a list of my problems and tackle one at a time.

The first problem is Lily. From what I know about her, she's most likely panicking and reacting to a threat without thinking clearly. Again, it makes me wonder what set her apart from everyone else in our business in the first place, but that's a question for another day. There's no denying she's lethal, but she's also proving to be resourceful. She's managed to hack her way into The Order's computer network and hijack the tracking signals from the devices implanted in every operative's neck. She knows exactly where I am at all times, which explains how she found me at Kaitlyn's office. I have to assume she knows I'm here too, despite Pierce saying he has people working to block her access.

So, that's my first problem. My second problem is the bomb in my neck. Aside from the fact that it's giving my position away, it's a fucking bomb. I can literally have my head blown off my shoulders at any moment. It can't be removed because any contact with the atmosphere will detonate it.

But given my head is still attached to my shoulders, I think it's safe to assume that the network she's hacked into doesn't control both the GPS tracking signal *and* the signal linking the explosive to the detonator. This is good because, if I'm right and the detonator signal is isolated, that means the only people who can blow my head off are the people who physically have one of the detonators in their possession. At the moment, that's only Horizon and Pierce. That I know of.

I need to start—

Kaitlyn groans and stirs in her seat. I glance over as she slowly opens her eyes.

"What time is it?" she asks groggily.

I look up at the wall clock opposite. "A little after one. You all right?"

She stretches and sits up in the chair, then nods. "I'm fine, I think. How are you? Has the surgeon been to look at your hand yet?"

I shake my head. "No, nothing yet. But yeah, I'm okay. Pain meds are the best..."

She smiles weakly. "Okay. Well, seeing as I'm awake, start talking."

"What about?"

"Everything. What the hell happened to you that made you wind up here, ruining my life?"

"That's a complicated question, and the answer is long."

She shrugs. "Bullet point it for me. You owe me an explanation."

I sigh. I guess I do. But she's not going to like it...

"Okay... you remember 4/17, right?"

She nods. "Kinda hard to forget..."

"Right, well, I was there, in the room at the exact moment the button was pushed to launch the tactical nuclear missiles that ravaged the planet."

She leans forward, her eyes wide. "Bullshit..."

"I wish it were."

"What were you doing there?"

I smile humorlessly. "I've been asking myself that same question for months. I'd retired from being an assassin, but a terrorist organization tried to recruit me. I declined their offer, and they tried to kill me. Turns out, the government had been keeping an eye on this group for a while, so I agreed to help stop them."

"Oh my God... I can't believe this..."

I chuckle. "It gets better. You see, it turns out this terrorist group wasn't actually behind the attack. They were being used—set up to take the fall in the aftermath of the attack. I and a few others stumbled across a conspiracy within the U.S. government, and we found proof that people working inside the White House were the real ones responsible for it all. It was just the first step in a plan to unite the world and bring around a new era of peace. In a kind of Nazi, genocidal kinda way."

She frowns. I can see the cogs turning inside her head as she starts piecing together what I've told her. She looks into my eyes. "Was all this... was this, in any way, related to President Cunningham's assassination last month?"

I nod slowly but stay silent. I'll let her come to it on her own. It might make it easier to process.

She stands and puts a hand to her mouth. She paces back and forth for a moment, then stops to stare at me. "He was involved?"

I nod again. "He was the brains behind it all. But 4/17 was only the first part of his plan and was designed to hit the reset button on the world. The next part was supposed to unite everyone in fear, so we would all turn to him to save us. See, he had some friends in North Korea..."

She sits down again and rests her head in her hands.

"Oh my God. Oh my God. I can't believe what I'm hearing! Are you saying the president of the United States was working with North Korea when they tried to take over the world? That's just—"

"Fucking insane? Yes, it is. But sadly, that doesn't make it any less true. Luckily for us, Cunningham drastically underestimated GlobaTech's ability to kick ass, so we were all saved. But..."

She looks up at me. Her eyes are wide and welling with tears. "You. It was you, wasn't it?"

She catches on quick...

I nod silently.

She puts both hands over her mouth and gasps. "Oh my God! You killed the—"

I hold my good hand up to silence her. "Kaitlyn, will you keep your voice down! Jesus. Yes, I... I killed the president."

She gets up and starts pacing back and forth in front of me again. Tears are flowing freely down her face, and she's shaking her head, seemingly arguing with herself.

"But... how? They said you were dead. You *caused* all this... I can't—"

"Okay, just relax. The guy was a piece of shit and most definitely deserved it."

She looks at me like I have two heads. "How can anyone *deserve* to die?"

The anger is burning in her eyes. She's furious with me. The professional relationship we had is gone. I'm assuming the confidentiality we had between us has too.

I'm getting frustrated with her again and angry with myself for doing so. I clench my fist as a gesture to suppress—

Ah!

I wince. I just clenched my busted right hand. Goddammit!

I take a deep breath through the pain. "You know the missile that hit Texas, during the North Korean invasion?"

She takes some deep breaths of her own, like she's trying to calm herself. She nods but says nothing.

"Well, that missile was fired by Cunningham himself, as he stood behind his desk in the Oval Office. I know this because I was standing next to him with a gun to his head when he did it. And do you want to know *why* he did it? He did it to fuck with me. You see, the final stage of his plan was to attack the United States and frame North Korea for it. In his twisted wisdom, he had convinced himself that doing so would guarantee that every man, woman, and child on this planet would turn to him for protection. Protection from a war *he* started. He said it needed to be done, but because he wanted to fuck with me personally and make some kind of point, he actually aimed the missile at the small town of Devil's Spring, which was where I'd been living for the last two years or so. It was where my life away from all this was rooted. Where the woman I loved was. He put a hole in America just to make me suffer, so yes, I think he deserved to die."

I've just realized I'm breathing heavily, like I've been running, and I'm grinding my teeth hard enough to make my jaw ache. The anger in Kaitlyn's eyes has gone, replaced by what looks like sympathy and... understanding.

She walks over to me, stands at the side of the bed, and puts a hand on my shoulder. "I'm sorry. I... I had no idea. All this time, all our sessions together... you were trying to deal with this incredible burden and the pain it's been causing you, without actually telling me what you were going through."

I shrug. "It's not exactly something you can go into great detail about..."

She sits on the edge of the bed and smiles. "I'll make you a deal, Adrian. You get us both out of this in one piece, and I'll gladly continue being your therapist. And you'll be free to talk about anything, openly and honestly, in our sessions. Okay? I'm good at what I do, but I don't need to be to see when someone really needs help."

I take a deep breath and calm down. I smile back at her. "That... that would be great. Thank you."

Over her shoulder, I see the door to my room open. She looks around as a guy steps inside holding a tablet. I haven't seen him before. He's younger than the first doctor, maybe early forties. He stands at the foot of my bed and presses the screen of the device a few times, looking at it thoughtfully. He has a thick, dark beard, trimmed and styled, and thin-framed glasses resting low on his nose.

He looks up at me. "Mr. Foley?"

Again, the English is impeccable.

I wave at him with my bandaged right hand. "That's me."

Kaitlyn turns and smiles at me, then moves to sit in the chair she was sleeping in.

The new guy looks back at the tablet, taps the screen a few more times, and then looks up from it and holds it down by his side. "Mr. Foley, you have suffered some moderate damage to the flexor tendons in your right hand."

I frown. "That doesn't sound good..."

He shrugs. "It's not really a case of it being good or bad. It's just something that can happen. Obviously, the circumstances surrounding your injury are quite extreme. I understand you've also suffered some minor injuries to your back?"

"Yeah, cuts and bruises mostly, I think. Nothing to worry about."

"If you don't mind my saying so, you seem awfully calm and collected, considering you were recently in a building that was blown up."

I glance over at Kaitlyn, then back at him. "I'm just... It's over, and I'm alive. That's all that matters, y'know?"

He smiles professionally. "Of course. It's not really my place or area of expertise, but there are services available if you want to talk. Sometimes the onset of shock can come about after the events have transpired."

I nod. "I appreciate that. Thanks, but I'm okay."

"Okay, then. So, I've taken a look at your X-ray, and you're going to need surgery to repair the damaged tendons."

Surgery? Shit.

Shit, shit, shit!

He smiles, as if he's trying to offer some comfort. I'm guessing it's because of the look I undoubtedly have on my face. He'll have taken it as fear at the idea of surgery, but it's not. I'm not scared of the surgery. I'm not scared at all. I'm concerned about the fact I'm going to be incapacitated and completely defenseless when there's someone trying to kill me.

"It's a simple procedure and nothing at all to worry about," he says.

"Yeah... that's fine. Listen, is this surgery possible with a local or regional anesthetic by any chance?"

He shakes his head. "No, you will need to go fully under for the procedure. Recovery time, all told, is usually around three months, give or take, depending on the individual. Your hand will need to be fully splinted for the first few weeks. We can then start looking at rehabilitation. I see no reason why you won't be able to fully recover from this, but it will take time to regain the strength and movement in your hand that you had before this."

I lock eyes with Kaitlyn, and her expression mirrors how I'm feeling right now.

Like we're in deep shit.

20

I open my eyes slowly. My vision's blurry, obscured by a fog that only ever follows an unexpectedly deep sleep. I blink hard to clear it and wait for my surroundings to morph into focus. I'm lying on my side, staring at a wall. Sunlight is streaming in through the nearby window. I frown and squint as I try to remember where I am.

What—

I widen my eyes as everything comes flooding back.

Shit! I can't believe I fell asleep!

I turn and sit bolt upright, immediately alert. I instinctively scan the room for any hint of a threat. The door's still closed, which is a good sign. But I'm alone, which isn't so good...

Where's Kaitlyn?

Shit.

I look down at my right hand. The bandage is slightly discolored from the blood that's still seeping from the wound. I try to clench my fist but don't even get halfway. The pain is manageable. The thing I'm struggling with is that it feels like I'm making a fist when I'm not. Like, it's clenched as much as possible when, in fact, my palm is practically open.

Shit.

Shit!

I can't believe I need surgery on my shooting hand. I'm all right with my left, but I wouldn't say I'm proficient enough with it to confidently use it instead of my right. That's going to take some practice.

Not exactly the best time to handicap an assassin, either...

The door opens, and Kaitlyn walks in holding two cups of coffee. She smiles. "Morning."

I flick my head up. "Hey. You scared the shit outta me. Where've you been?"

She frowns, confused. "I only went for coffee, Adrian..."

I look away for a moment. I need to pull my head out of my ass, stop myself from turning into an over-protective parent, remember who I am, and start focusing on the goddamn problem at hand.

...

...

...

Okay—head's removed. Focus resumed.

I turn back to her. "Yeah... sorry. This whole thing with Lily has put me on edge, and now I'm basically one-handed. I'm worried about my ability to keep you safe."

She smiles again, warm and friendly. "And what about you? Who's keeping *you* safe?"

I frown. "Well... me, I guess. But I'm not really concerned about my own safety. I can handle myself. I need to protect you. You've already been affected by problems. I don't want you getting caught in the crossfire. I need to—"

She's raised both eyebrows and looks bemused.

"What?"

She shakes her head, walks over to me, and sets my coffee down on the table beside my bed. Then she moves over to her chair at the far end of the room. She sits down gracefully and crosses her legs, then blows her coffee to cool it and takes a sip. "You're doing it again."

"Doing what?"

"The big brother thing. You're putting more pressure on yourself, putting more weight on your already overworked shoulders. You need to focus on dealing with Lily, right?"

"Well, yeah... but—"

"Then focus on *her*." She leans forward, clasping her drink in both hands. "I spent a lot of last night sat in this chair, wide awake."

I absently scratch the back of my neck and smile sheepishly. "I... wasn't snoring, was I?"

She grins. "No. I was trying to process all the information you gave me last night. See, the problem is, I believe you. It would actually be *easier* to wrap my head around what you were saying if I knew it was a lie. But the fact you were telling the truth makes it more difficult to comprehend. But by the time the sun had risen, I had come to one conclusion."

I raise an eyebrow. "Which was?"

"The safest place I can be right now is with you. I've seen what you can do—how you handled yourself in my office when we were attacked. And I'm guessing I know better than most how your mind works. I'm not some stupid, scared little girl, all right? I'm actually very smart. And I've been on my own for a long time, which has made me independent. I've done plenty of self-defense classes, and I feel confident looking after myself. Now all that might not sound impressive to someone like you, and it might not make me some badass assassin, but what it *does* mean is that you don't have to worry about me. I'll do whatever you say without question. All I ask in return is that you focus on getting us out of this in one piece. Sound fair?"

I lean back and rest against the pillows in bed.

Huh. Talk about being put in your place...

I stare at her. She's relaxed back into her chair, holding my gaze in a practiced, professional way—approachable and open but respectfully distant. Right now, she's working. She's not Kaitlyn the target or Kaitlyn the victim. She's not even Kaitlyn my friend. She's Kaitlyn the therapist, and I'm simply one of her patients.

Under these extenuating circumstances, I'm impressed she still has the strength to try to fix me. To still work and forget everything else.

She reminds me of me.

I nod and smile. "That's fair. Thank you." I reach over and pick up my coffee. I move it toward my mouth to take a sip but stop as I catch a glimpse inside the cup. I frown and look back over at her. "You say you'll do whatever I say without question, right?"

She nods.

"Good." I hold the cup out to her. "Then take this away and get me a real drink! Seriously, what the fuck is this?"

She frowns, then laughs. "It's coffee!"

"All right, listen... *this* isn't coffee. For a start, it's not black. It looks like an old lady's diarrhea."

She was just taking a sip of her own coffee when I said that. She stops mid-mouthful and puts the drink down on the table beside her chair. "And I'm no longer thirsty..."

I set my drink back down next to me. "I'm just saying, if we're gonna be hanging out together, you need to learn what real coffee is. You see—"

The surgical consultant who came to see me last night just walked in. His eyes are red, and he looks tired. Poor bastard must be on a long-ass shift if he's been working through the night.

He smiles weakly at me. "Mr. Foley, how are you today?"

I shrug. "I'm okay."

"Good. We've got you booked in for surgery in a couple hours. I'll be performing the procedure myself. A nurse will be along in a few moments to fit the cannula. Do you have any questions?"

"How long am I gonna be out for?"

He thinks about it. "Hard to say exactly, but your X-ray suggests the damage is moderate at best, so barring any complications, I'd say the procedure shouldn't last any longer than an hour."

I let out a frustrated breath. I'm the target for a dangerous assassin, and I'm going to be completely defenseless. An hour's going to feel like a lifetime!

"Okay. Thanks, Doc." He nods and leaves. I look at Kaitlyn. "I need you to do me a favor. Get my cell from pocket and call Pierce. His number's programmed in. Explain what's happening and tell him I need either him personally or some of his men to get their asses down here and make sure I'm actually able to wake up from this goddamn operation. I know you can look after yourself, but if I'm out for an hour, there's nothing to stop Lily walking in here and getting you, and I can't have that."

She nods, gets the phone from my shorts, and steps outside the room. I lean back, resting my head in the palm of my left hand. I hate this. For the first time in... possibly my entire life, I feel like a victim. I know I need this surgery, and I know I'm lucky it's all I need after what we went through in Kaitlyn's office yesterday. But asking The Order for help... asking them to *protect* me... it doesn't feel right.

I don't feel like *me* anymore. I don't feel like Adrian Hell. I wanted him dead and gone, out of my life forever, but that plan went to shit a few months ago. So, now he's back, and I'm living that life again. But it's not the same. It's not how it used to be. *I'm* not how I used to be. It's as if I've been... neutered. I mean, look at me! My head's a goddamn mess.

I dread to think what I'd be like if I didn't have Kaitlyn. I'm nothing more than Horizon's pet. His wild animal, reluctantly tamed and kept on a leash for his amusement. I'm hiding from someone who's trying to kill me because I don't feel like I can defend myself...

I let out a long, heavy, tired sigh.

Maybe I should just let Lily get to me during my operation... put me out of my fucking misery.

21

Consciousness hits me like a lazy wave crashing over a shoreline. I keep my eyes closed as all my systems and senses fire up again, rebooting after a factory reset.

You have to be impressed with my computer metaphors there.

Instinctively, I try to move the fingers on my right hand.

Nothing.

Oh, man, I hope the surgery worked.

I concentrate on my arm. I can feel something on it... something heavy and tight. I slowly, cautiously, open one eye and glance down. There's a plastic cast molded to the outside of my forearm and held firmly in place by two black Velcro straps, which are fastened over the inside, partially covering my tattoo. The top of it fits like a fingerless glove. Another strap is fastened across my palm, which has bandages beneath it. There's a final strap across my wrist.

Well, that explains why I can't move my fingers. At least

it's secure. I'm guessing that's a sign the surgery went well, and it's been prepared for rehab.

I close my eye again and take some deep breaths. Since waking up, I've felt pretty nauseous. I don't think general anesthesia agrees with me.

In fact...

I sit bolt upright, turn to my left, and grab the cardboard bucket—you know, that thing that looks like an upside-down hat—and vomit.

Oh my God, that sucks...

I cough and spit the last bit out and sit back.

Well, I'm awake!

I look around the room. The sun is still bright outside, despite the blinds being closed at the window. I'm alone and the door is shut.

Kaitlyn!

No, wait.

She'll be fine. Don't get all wound up over nothing, Adrian. She's probably just gone for a drink.

I hope she brings me some real coffee this time.

Oh, man, I feel like I'm going to throw up again.

...

...

...

No, false alarm.

God, I hate this. I can't wait to get out of here. I need to head back to my place and grab a change of clothes and some more weapons. I have no idea where my car is. I parked it outside Kaitlyn's office yesterday, but given how most things have turned to shit since then, it could be anywhere.

Damn it. I liked that car. I mean, I know I can just go and buy a new one with my bottomless credit card, but that just seems wasteful. Plus, right now, I don't want to give The Order the satisfaction of seeing me taking advantage of everything they've given me.

I'm drifting in and out because I'm still feeling the effects of the surgery, but I can't help noticing how quiet it is. I haven't seen one person pass by my room since I came to. There's no equipment in here, which makes it easier to hear what's going on in the corridor outside. But there's nothing.

That's weird.

It's not even like it's the middle of the night. It's just after twelve, so you would expect any kind of medical facility to be busy.

Hmm.

I shake my head. No, Adrian, just… stop. You've just had surgery and you're not yourself. Stop overthinking things. Kaitlyn would shout at you for it.

I smile to myself for a moment, but it fades quickly.

Who am I kidding? I don't overthink anything. I worry and I plan ahead, but the only thing I do unnecessarily is feel guilty—or so Kaitlyn tells me. I think it's too quiet, and that's because my spider sense is telling me it's too goddamn quiet.

No rest for the wicked…

I swing my legs out of bed and place my feet tentatively down on the refreshingly cold floor. I stand slowly and remain still for a moment, allowing a fresh wave of nausea to pass. I quickly get dressed into my shorts, my torn and blood-stained T-shirt, and shoes. I shove my watch in my pocket because I can't fasten it around my left wrist with my busted right hand. I kneel to retrieve the pillowcase of guns and ammo from underneath the bed, then empty the contents out onto the bed. I tuck one inside my waistband at my back. The steel is cold against my body, and the weight provides me with a welcome reassurance. I put both spare mags in my other pockets.

I keep hold of the other gun and head for the door. I catch my reflection in the long mirror mounted on the wall just behind it as I pass by. Jesus... I look like an extra from *The Walking Dead*. I adjust my T-shirt to cover the gun at my back and carefully open the door. I look up and down the hallway and frown. It's like a ghost town out here. I'm seriously expecting a tumbleweed to roll past at any moment. I strain to listen for any sign of life, but I'm getting nothing. I edge out of the room, tightening my grip on the gun in anticipation.

I have a really bad feeling about this...

I head left and turn right at the end, toward the entrance. Another long corridor stretches out before me, well-lit and devoid of life. At the end, it veers toward the reception area. Halfway along, another corridor cuts across it. I walk on, trying to forget the constant nausea and the uneasiness of standing. I focus on running through every possible scenario I might come up against that will involve me squeezing the trigger.

I make it halfway and pause for a moment to check left and right.

It's clear.

I carry on but slow as I near the dogleg at the end. I can hear something approaching. It's faint, but it's getting louder with each step I take. I raise the gun slightly, preparing to fire if I need to. I'm maybe a hundred yards from the turn.

Oh, shit...

I recognize the low clacking of footsteps ahead of me. It sounds like there are two people coming this way, walking quickly together. I clench my jaw muscles until my teeth ache. My brow furrows as I strain to focus. Whoever this is better have some answers for me…

I raise the gun in front of me and rest my finger gently on the trigger. It feels weird leading with my left, but I'm good enough with it that it won't make a difference at this sort of distance.

Here we go…

Kaitlyn appears from around the corner, walking at an urgent pace. She sees me and slides to a stop, staring at me with a look of shock on her face. Lily appears a second later and stands beside her, sporting the same expression. Our eyes meet, but I don't react. I'm just as surprised to see either of them as they apparently are to see me.

I take a step toward them and snap my aim so that the barrel is pointing at the center of Lily's forehead. I glare at her with a ferocious and immediate fury. I'm willing the sudden rush of adrenaline and thirst for violence into my eyes, so I can release them in a controlled fashion, instead of rushing over to her and tearing her apart in a blind rage.

My gun doesn't waver. "Step away, Lily, or I swear to God, I'll fucking shoot you."

Our eyes are locked. Each of us watch the other's mind working, planning the next move … desperate to be the one who finds a way out of this standoff alive.

Lily nods without a word and steps to the side, putting some distance between them.

"Kaitlyn, are you all right?" I ask without looking at her.

"I—I'm fine. Listen, Adrian, this isn't what it looks like. You need to hear what Lily has to say…"

I narrow my eyes and shake my head. "I don't want to listen to her." I turn to Lily. "There's nothing you can say to make this better."

She shrugs but stays silent.

"Lose your weapon."

She sighs and takes out her gun. She holds it loose, and then crouches and places it on the floor. When she stands, she holds her hands out to the side. "Look, Adrian, we need to talk, but now isn't the time. You have to trust me. We need to—"

I scoff with disbelief. "*Trust* you? After everything you've done?"

Kaitlyn moves over to me. "Adrian, please. We need to get back to your room. It's not what you think."

I frown, confused. I look into her eyes. I see confidence... certainty. She knows something I don't. I need to focus on that, not the fact that Lily's here.

I sigh. "Okay, but then someone's telling me what the fuck is going on."

Lily scoops her gun up off the floor and moves alongside me as the three of us head back to my room. We file inside quickly, and I close the door gently behind us. Kaitlyn sits down in her usual chair. Lily moves around the bed and turns to face me.

I stay standing near the door and aim my gun at her again. "I know you were just protecting yourself, Lily, but dragging Kaitlyn into this was a real dick move."

Kaitlyn shifts in the chair and looks at me. "Adrian, this isn't about Lily. She's—"

Lily steps forward and gestures with her own gun. "You don't get it, do you? You can't see what's really going on here."

She sounds impatient... frustrated. It just makes me angrier. How can *she* be frustrated with *me*?

I shake my head, bewildered. "Lily, you blew up Kaitlyn's fucking office to get to me! *I've* been trying to think of a way out of this that doesn't involve me killing you. You know I won't ever take a contract without an explanation. I never intended to kill you. I wanted to talk, to find out what all this was about and figure a way out of it *together*. But you took it upon yourself to attack me first. You know how The Order works. You must have assumed Horizon would give me the contract on you, and you knew I couldn't say no to him on account of our explosive tracking devices. So, yet again, you acted like an amateur—reacting without thinking. You hacked the signal to find me and then you waited until I was with Kaitlyn before you tried to take me out."

I'm short of breath. My adrenaline-fueled rage increased my heart rate with every word.

She steps forward. "Have you finished?"

I shrug. "For the moment..."

She lets out an exaggerated sigh. "Thank *God* for that. Listen, you're right. I *do* know how The Order works—a lot better than you do. If Horizon wants an asset out of The Order, he plays mind games with them. He breaks them. He turns friends and other assets against them. He makes sure they die knowing he was *better* than they were."

I look at her. She's wearing the same outfit she had on yesterday morning, and she still looks incredible. Her body language is calm and confident. Her stance is relaxed and comfortable. Her eye contact is unwavering, and her tone is steady. I'm pretty sure she's not bullshitting me.

She throws her gun onto the bed. "Adrian, are you listening to what I'm saying? You need to get your head out of your ass and read between the lines. *I'm* not trying to kill you—The Order is!"

Kaitlyn stands and walks over to me. She places her hand on my shoulder. "Adrian, she's telling the truth. When they took you away for surgery, Pierce and his team showed up with a fleet of ambulances. They cleared the hospital of everyone except the bare minimum of staff and positioned themselves at all the entrances and exits. He said he was securing the place, and The Order was using its influence to move all the other patients and staff to another facility. I couldn't believe something like that was even possible, but he did it, and no one questioned anything."

I nod absently. "That explains why it's so quiet around here..."

"I was standing outside your room when Lily showed up. She didn't know who I was. She introduced herself and told me what she just told you—that Pierce was here to set a trap for her and to kill you and me. She wanted to hide me away until you woke up, and then the plan was for the three of us to get out of here."

I gesture toward Lily with a small nod. "Okay, let's say I believe you. Let's say Horizon actually wants *me* dead instead of you—or as well as you. Whichever. Why me? Why give *me* the job of killing you? What have I done wrong? He's only just recruited me."

She flicks an eyebrow up questioningly. "Are you being serious? The constant questioning of his orders... the complete and total lack of respect you show him... the fact you helped me and disregarded the only three rules they asked you to follow in the process. If I were you, I'd be wondering why he's not tried to kill you sooner."

I feel Kaitlyn's gaze next to me. I glance at her and smile sheepishly. She just rolls her eyes and smiles to herself.

I'm impressed she's managing to see the funny side...

I turn back to Lily. "I'm assuming Kaitlyn's told you what happened to us in Abu Dhabi?"

She nods.

"So, if that wasn't you, who was it?"

She shrugs. "If I had to guess, I'd say Pierce. He's Horizon's main guy for keeping everyone in line."

I shake my head. "No, Pierce was standing next to me inside the office when the RPG hit. He came to me with a team to warn me you were after me."

She sighs. "Look, Adrian... I don't know, all right? If it wasn't Pierce, it had to have been one of his team. If he were there, it was so he wouldn't look guilty. Horizon wants you to believe *I'm* the one coming after you, so you'll have the incentive to take me out. He would've known the moment he gave you the contract that you'd struggle to go through with it."

"So, if you're not coming after me... if you're not tracking me... how did you find me?"

She shakes her head. "I didn't. I was following Pierce, and he led me here."

"Wouldn't he have known you were tracking him?"

She shrugs. "Maybe. Maybe not. Sure, he can see where I am, but that doesn't mean he's always looking. I figured he was coming for you, so I gambled that he was tracking you, not me."

Shit.

What she's saying makes sense. But does that mean I should believe her?

I look at Kaitlyn, silently asking for advice. I see the switch in her eyes as she flicks into her professional mind-set. "You said you were trying to figure out how the two of you could survive this. Maybe this Horizon guy has noticed the connection you two have and anticipated your reaction. It makes sense that he would use Pierce to fabricate the story about Lily, to give you the push he felt you needed in order to do your job and kill her for him. Plus, the reasons Lily just surmised about why he would want you dead as well... they make sense too—especially given what we've discussed and what I know about your personality."

I slowly lower my gun. My gut says Kaitlyn is on the money, and the fact she's implying Lily is too is good enough for me.

I look over at Lily and nod. "Sorry."

She waves her hand. "I think we know each other well enough now to understand that either of us would have acted the way you just did, under the circumstances."

We exchange a subtle nod of forgiveness. "So, what's our move?"

She shakes her head. "We don't have one. If they want us terminated, we will be."

I smile. "Don't make me do the thing where I reintroduce myself to make the point that I am who I am, and people don't get to do shit like this to me."

She rolls her eyes and smiles back. "You're an asshole. *But*... if anyone can get us out of this... it's you."

"Damn right. I think the first thing to do is get the fuck outta *here*. How did you get in if Pierce has the place surrounded?"

She points to the ceiling. "I snuck past a couple of his team and climbed the fire escape around back. This is a big place, but it only has two floors. I got inside the ventilation ducts and dropped down inside the supply closet at the other end of the hall."

"Nice. No help here, though." I hold my right hand up and wave with it. "I'll never be able to climb with one hand, and I'm too heavy for you to pull me up. I think the only option is the front door."

"But Pierce has this place surrounded..."

I nod. "I know, but I'm hoping that, even if he knows you're here, he might not know we've spoken. He'll see we're close together and figure we're trying to kill each other. That means *he* won't know *I* know he's a piece of shit. Lily, if you sneak out the way you came in, Kaitlyn and I will head out the front door. When we link up with Pierce, I'll play along, say we scuffled and you ran away, and then get him away from here."

She shrugs. "Then what? You're still basically giving yourself up."

I shake my head. "I'll take him out before we get too far."

Kaitlyn raises her hand apprehensively. "I'm sorry if this is a dumb or even callous question, but what's to stop him from just blowing your heads off with those devices?"

Lily and I exchange a look, then I turn to Kaitlyn and shrug. "That's a good point and one I'm trying not to think about." I turn to Lily. "What do you think?"

She shrugs. "If you're right, and Pierce still thinks we're trying to take each other out, he won't feel the need to use the detonator. He's here to help you kill me before killing you himself, most likely. It makes no sense to simply pop our heads off. They've gone to so much trouble fucking with us to prove a point. Why undo all their hard work by simply pushing a button?"

I nod. "Agreed. Plus, from their point of view, it must be hard keeping a bunch of trained killers in check all the time, so I bet they use the threat of being able to remove our heads remotely, with no warning, to keep us in line."

Lily picks up her gun and heads for the door. "Okay, I'll head right. You two head for the main entrance. Watch your backs. Pierce might be just a trained grunt, but he's not stupid. If he suspects anything, you're dead."

I move next to Kaitlyn and hold out my gun. I look her in the eyes, my face softening with regret. "Take this."

She looks at it and shakes her head. Tears begin to well

in her eyes. "I... I'm not using that thing, Adrian. It was bad enough carrying it for you."

"Look, I know you don't like this, but with one hand, I'm only half an assassin. You need to have one."

She takes it from me apprehensively and wraps her own hand around the butt. She assesses the weight, steeling herself to the inevitable fact that she might need to use it.

Lily steps toward her. "Screw the safety, all right? Rest your index finger against the trigger guard—*that's* your safety. Only touch the trigger itself if you want to shoot someone."

I watch as she helps Kaitlyn adjust her grip to make it more comfortable. Yet again, things have taken a random U-turn on me. After yesterday, I never thought I'd see Lily and Kaitlyn working together...

I take out the other gun from my back and open the door. I glance over my shoulder at the women. "Come on. Time's a-wastin'."

I step out into the corridor, and the two of them follow a few steps behind me. We stand in a tight triangle, with me facing my room and Lily and Kaitlyn either side of me. We all check our weapons.

I look at Lily and hand her one of my spare mags. "Go on. Get out of here. I'll make contact when I've dealt with Pierce."

She nods and turns to leave but stops almost straight away. "Uh, Adrian..."

I look left. At the end of the corridor are two men, both wearing Kevlar body armor and carrying automatic rifles.

Shit.

Instinctively, I look right. Kaitlyn's already seen Pierce and two more men standing at the opposite end, dressed and armed the same as the others.

The two men on either side move closer and take aim, gesturing menacingly with the barrels of their rifles. Pierce pushes through and steps toward me. His own rifle is hanging loose from its shoulder strap.

He points to my left hand. "Put your gun down, Adrian."

There's no way I can talk my way out of this. There's no way he doesn't know Lily's told me everything. He has us surrounded, and there's enough distance between us and them that we can't do anything fast enough to be successful.

When in doubt...

I shake my head. "Fuck you."

He rolls his eyes. "See, *this* is why Horizon's decided to cut his losses with you. Your fucking attitude and your fucking arrogance."

I sidestep and put my body between him and Kaitlyn. I aim my gun at him but almost immediately feel my arm wavering slightly. I'm still not fully functioning after my surgery.

Behind me, I feel Kaitlyn place a hand on my arm. "Adrian, what do we do?"

She sounds terrified. I close my eyes for the briefest of moments, silently cursing my own uselessness.

I honestly have no idea.

22

I'm fighting to keep my arm raised, to keep my gun pointing at Pierce's head, but it's not happening. I lower it but still keep a firm grip of the weapon. The two guys behind Pierce are maybe fifty yards away, with Pierce a few steps in front of them. The other two at the opposite end of the corridor are easily a hundred yards behind us.

Too great a distance for anything effective.

My priority's Kaitlyn's safety. I need to get her out of here.

I stare into Pierce's dark eyes. "So, what happens now?"

He shrugs. "That's up to you. You can either kill Lily, like we've told you to, and put all this unpleasantness behind us, or you can continue down the path you're on and be killed in the next thirty seconds."

I take a small step backward, closing the gap between Lily and me. This is a pretty shit situation. Even if I did kill

Lily, that wouldn't be the end of it. He's insulting my intelligence if he genuinely believes I don't know he'll try to kill me before her body hits the floor.

Under the circumstances, I can only see one way out of this, and it's a long shot.

Pierce is directly in front of me, partially blocking the direct line of sight for the guys behind him. I need three accurate shots in quick succession. Normally, it wouldn't be an issue, but left-handed, not feeling a hundred percent... it's a big ask.

I just hope Lily's thinking the same thing I am, or this is going to be the shortest escape plan in history.

I nod. "Thirty seconds, eh? If I were you, I'd give me five. I'm too good to justify leaving it so long..."

He smirks. "Why? What are you gonna do? You're a washed-up cripple with an attitude problem. Nothing more. You're not even *half* the man we thought we were recruiting."

I frown.

Washed-up?

Does he know who I—

Nope... stopped myself from saying it. Don't want to look like a douche.

Anyway, fuck him. What does he know?

I'll show him *washed-up*...

I drop to one knee and fire three shots. The first hits Pierce in the center of his chest. He's protected, but the impact sends him sprawling to the floor anyway, as I'd hoped. The second and third are aimed at the heads of the men behind him. The first hits the mark, and the guy drops, leaving a faint spray of crimson on the wall behind him. The second misses, catching the guy in the shoulder. His body armor doesn't protect him, but it's not a fatal wound—just enough to make him drop his rifle and spin away.

At the same time as my final two shots, I heard two more behind me, which I take as a sign that Lily had indeed been thinking along the same lines as me. I snap my head around just as the second of the other two men is hitting the floor. Both are dead. I lock eyes with Lily for a brief moment, and we exchange a nod of thanks and understanding.

Three out of five dead and two distracted. Not bad.

I turn to Kaitlyn. "Come on. We're leaving."

The color has drained from her face. Her unblinking gaze is transfixed on the bloodstain spread across the wall in front of her.

Lily appears next to me and puts a hand on her arm. She jumps with shock and spins around to face her. Lily smiles sympathetically. "Kaitlyn, come on. I've got you." She looks at me. "Go on. We're right behind you."

I nod and set off down the corridor, heading away from the main entrance and toward the men Lily took out.

"Which way?" I call over my shoulder.

"Left, then right, then left," replies Lily.

I follow the network of corridors as per her instructions. It's not going to take long for Pierce to get back to his feet. Even though body armor will withstand a low caliber round at mid-distance, it still hurts like a bitch. It's like being punched in the sternum by a sledgehammer. It'll knock the wind out of you and leave a bruise the size of a watermelon. But Pierce is a tough sonofabitch. I can attest to that personally. He's probably organizing his men as we speak. I've no idea how many he has and have no wish to find out.

As I take the second left, we come to a dead end. There are two doors on the left—one has a plaque on it saying

SUPPLIES. Must be where Lily dropped in. Opposite that is a fire exit, which is closed and looks alarmed. I can see the shadow of a guy standing outside it through the frosted glass.

I stop and turn. Lily and Kaitlyn move next to me. I aim my gun at the corner. "What's the move, Lily?"

She lets out a short sigh, which I think is frustration. "We need to get outside. I can take the guy out who's standing there, but I don't know who else is nearby. Also, we're on the opposite side of the building to the front entrance and, more importantly, to the parking lot. There's no quick way out of here."

I stare at the corridor, focusing all my strength on keeping my arm raised. I wait a few moments to see if anyone appears.

...

...

...

Nothing.

Could be a good sign.

Probably isn't, but I feel optimism is the way forward right now.

I turn my head slightly. "I'll cover you. Do what you gotta do."

Behind me, Lily says, "Kaitlyn, stay low against the wall. Get your gun ready. Watch Adrian's back. Shoot anything you see that isn't him. Just point and squeeze like we talked about, okay? I'll call out when it's clear."

I take slow, deep breaths, concentrating on keeping my aim steady. I hear Lily kick the door open. The guy outside grunts, then shouts out in pain. It's cut short. I hear the thud of a body hitting the ground outside.

"We're clear," announces Lily.

I walk backward until I'm level with the fire exit. Kaitlyn's already moved outside. Still no sign of anyone following us. My guess is they regrouped out front.

I force myself to lower my gun and step through the fire exit. The heat is intense, and a faint wave of nausea hits me. I stand still for a moment while it passes...

I hate this.

I stride over the dead guy. I can tell he's dead because his eyes are open and blank, looking up at me. From the position of his head, I'm guessing Lily snapped his neck.

Nice.

There's a small, grassy area ahead of us, with trees planted sporadically around the perimeter. A high wall surrounds the miniature garden ahead of us and to the right, with benches positioned in front of them. The graveled courtyard stretches left around the corner.

Lily takes point, with Kaitlyn close behind. I'm bringing up the rear, moving backward as fast as I dare, aiming at the fire exit. I round the corner and turn, quickly catching up to them. It's a wide passage that seems to lead around the back of the facility. There's a set of double doors about halfway along on the left.

Lily's pressed against the wall at the end, peering around the corner. Kaitlyn's next to her, holding her gun awkwardly and staring ahead with a *what the fuck am I doing here?* look on her face.

I smile to myself. I know that feeling.

I rest against the wall next to her and catch my breath. "What are we looking at, Lily?"

"It's a parking lot, maybe half-full. It runs all the way around the side and links up to the front, which is the good news."

"I'm assuming there's bad news too?"

"Yeah... I can see eight men at the far side. They're spread out but in an obvious formation. There's a chance they won't see us back here, but there's no way past them."

"Shit. Okay, let me take a look."

We swap positions, and I peer carefully around the corner.

She's right. The formation is spaced but tight. There's no way we can get past them unseen. I can't make out facial features from this distance, but I can tell by how they're all standing that Pierce isn't among them.

As of right now, we're against the clock. Realistically, I have to assume it's only a matter of time before someone decides enough is enough, and the button's pushed to remove both mine and Lily's heads. There are only two people I know of who can do that, so the safest option is to kill them both. Unfortunately, one of them, as best as I can tell, pretty much runs The Order and is surrounded at all times by a sizeable security detail. The other is somewhere on the other side of this parking lot, also surrounded by a sizeable security detail.

Shit.

I turn back to Lily. "What do you know about The Order's network?"

She frowns. "What do you mean?"

"Well, when Pierce was feeding me his bullshit, he said you'd hacked into their network and hijacked the signal from the tracking devices, giving you visibility of everyone's location. I assumed, because I wasn't dead, that viewing the tracking signal wasn't the same thing as having control over the detonator. That might still be the case. I don't know. But is anything like that remotely possible?"

She thinks for a moment, then shrugs. "It's possible, I guess. But I wouldn't know how to do it."

"Do you know anyone in The Order who could? Who do you trust enough to ask?"

She shakes her head. "No. You?"

I return the gesture. "Nope. Only person I know could do that shit, I'm not allowed to contact."

"Your GlobaTech friend?"

I nod.

"Listen, Adrian. Whatever happens from this point on, you have to accept that you're done with The Order. If reaching out to him is our only way out of this, maybe you should consider it."

I think about it for a moment but quickly dismiss it. "No. He believes I'm dead. Regardless of what Horizon told me I can and can't do, I can't just announce to him out of the blue that I'm alive and immediately ask him to risk his life for me. We need another way."

Kaitlyn stands up straight and steps away from the wall. She turns to face us both. "I... I might know someone."

Lily and I exchange a glance, both equally surprised. I look at Kaitlyn. Her face is contorted with the familiar struggle of an internal debate. I'm guessing she's trying to decide if she wants to involve whoever it is in this mess. Can't say I blame her, and under any other circumstances, I would try to talk her out of it.

I move toward her. "Who is it?"

She stares at the ground for a moment, fidgeting with the gun in her hand. "It's... my neighbor. He's a sweet kid, nineteen. It's just him and his mom. He's studying at Zayed University in... I.T. and Cyber Security, I think it is. He's off-the-scale intelligent. If you want a computer system hacked, I bet he'll be able to do it."

I raise an eyebrow. "Kaitlyn, this is brilliant. Do you have a good relationship with him? Can we approach him with this?"

"More importantly, do you trust him?" adds Lily.

She looks flustered. "I... yes, I think so. We can trust him, I mean. I speak with both Yaz and his mother when I see them. I think he might have a small crush on me, actually..."

Lily giggles. "That's perfect. Just show a little of what God gave you, and he'll do anything!"

Kaitlyn goes bright red and looks away.

I roll my eyes and look back around the corner. The men are still fanned out across the parking lot. I glance around the area directly across from me. There aren't many cars nearby, but one does catch my eye. It's a white Range Rover Sport. A big, sturdy 4×4 with a grill on the front and large rims on the tires.

We might be able to get to it unseen.

I look back at Lily. "I've got an idea."

"Oh, no..."

I smile. "You're gonna love it." I look at them both in turn. "You see that Range Rover behind me? We're going to steal it and plow straight through Pierce's team. Lily, you can drive. I'll shoot whomever I can. Kaitlyn, I want you lie flat on the back seat, out of sight. It's a strong vehicle, and I'm hoping the surprise means we won't take too much fire on the way out."

The women exchange a look, then Lily stares at me. "Adrian, that's fucking stupid."

I nod. "Correct."

"I mean, the chances of that working and us getting out of here are... next to nothing."

"I agree."

"And yet, you're still standing by your plan?"

I shrug. "Unless you can think of a better one..."

Kaitlyn clears her throat. "Ah... I know I'm not, like... y'know... one of *you* or anything, but would it not make sense to cause a distraction first? Get them looking somewhere else and then hit them with the Range Rover from behind."

I look at Lily and smile. That's a good idea, and I concede I didn't think about that. I was too focused on what's right in front of me.

I wink at Kaitlyn. "You sure you're not secretly an assassin?"

She smiles awkwardly.

Lily moves back along the wall, toward the fire exit. I look over at her. "Hey, where are you going?"

She glances back and shrugs. "To cause a distraction. Kaitlyn will be fine driving. You shoot whomever you can. I'll meet you out front."

"Lily, that's... you talk about *my* plans being stupid! Pierce and God knows how many more men are still in there."

"I'll be fine. Just make sure you're waiting for me out front."

"Okay. Well, at least take this." I throw her my remaining spare mag.

She catches it and nods. "Thanks."

Before I can say anything else, she disappears around the corner, heading back inside the hospital.

Shit.

I tuck my gun behind me and move next to Kaitlyn. I grab her arm in my left hand and turn to her. I take a deep breath. She does the same, knowing that the time for action has come. I look into her eyes and see her searching for every ounce of courage she can find, steeling herself for what lies ahead. She's about to walk into a life-or-death situation and charge headfirst toward the threat. That's never an easy thing to do, but I imagine that up until yesterday, it had never even crossed her mind that she would be here.

And she wouldn't be if it weren't for me.

I'm a real piece of shit sometimes, aren't I?

I'm like a cancer to the people around me, bringing danger and death to their doorsteps.

Well, I promise when all this is over, I'm going to remove myself from the rest of the world. I'm going to find a quiet little corner where no one knows me and stay there, so I never endanger anyone again.

But first...

"Are you ready?"

She nods. "I think so."

I smile, trying to reassure her. "You're gonna be fine. I've got your back, okay? Don't worry. This is what I do."

We stand, poised just out of sight, behind the corner. After a moment, I can feel her staring at me. "Adrian, what are we waiting for?"

I hold up my right arm and listen...

...

...

...

I hear a small explosion somewhere behind us, followed by muted bursts of gunfire.

I turn to her. "That! Come on!"

We run toward the Range Rover. I quickly try the door, but it's locked. I take Kaitlyn's gun from her, hold it by the barrel, and smash the butt into the bottom corner of the driver's window. I quickly hand it back, yank the door open, and lean in and down to hotwire the car and disable the alarm before it goes off.

It's... ah... it's not that easy... with... one... hand...

And...

The engine splutters and surges into life.

Got it!

I stand up and take her gun from her one more time. "Get in!"

I aim at the far end of the parking lot as I move around the hood of the Range Rover. The team of men is disappearing toward the main entrance, which is good, but we need to be quick. Otherwise, Lily will be overwhelmed.

I jump into the passenger seat. "Go! Go!"

Kaitlyn hammers the gas, the tires screech, and we speed forward. There are two stragglers, who both stop and turn to look at us, moving to raise their rifles.

"Kaitlyn, don't stop!"

She locks her arms and grips the wheel until her knuckles turn white. She grimaces and looks away as she lets out a scream, venting against every natural instinct she has to hit the brakes. "Oh my God!"

The men don't get a shot off. She bulldozes straight through the pair of them. One was sucked beneath the vehicle, and we bounced over his body. The other ricocheted off the hood and disappeared out of sight.

She slams on the brake and makes a hard left, sliding out of the parking lot to the ambulance approach at the front. The six other men from the team are hustling inside, but the back three guys stop and turn to face us.

"Stop here!"

We come to an abrupt halt. I throw the door open, put one foot down on the ground, and rest my left arm in the angle between the chassis and the open door. I empty the full mag of Kaitlyn's gun into the three guys. I see numerous small splashes of blood from the impact of each bullet finding its mark.

I quickly look inside the car. "You okay?"

She doesn't reply but nods hurriedly. Her lips are pursed together, and I think she's fighting against the onset of shock and tears.

"You've done well. Just wait here a sec. I'm gonna go—"

"Let's go! Let's go!"

I turn and see Lily running toward us, firing blindly behind her.

I lean back and open the rear door, then jump back inside and slam mine shut. I look at the main entrance as she reaches the car and see at least ten more men filing through, shooting from the hip, desperate to hit her.

Shots pepper the hood, though none of them are accurate enough to hit anything important.

"Kaitlyn, go!"

Lily closes her door, lying flat on the back seat. Kaitlyn shifts the car into reverse, floors the gas pedal, and kicks up smoke as we speed out onto the main road. She slams it in gear, makes a U-turn as fast as she dares, and we speed away. The hospital quickly fades away in the rearview.

I shift in my seat and look behind me. "Are you okay? What happened?"

Lily's laughing to herself, gasping for breath. "That... was... fun!"

I raise an eyebrow. She looks at me and smiles. "Sorry. I headed for the supply closet and found lots of cleaning products. I made a small explosive cocktail and threw it down the corridor, past your room. It got their attention. I took a few of them out and muscled my way through in the confusion." She lifts her head slightly and turns to Kaitlyn. "Nice driving, sister!"

Kaitlyn doesn't respond.

I look over at her and place a hand on her shoulder. "We're clear. You can ease up off the gas a little. We don't want to attract any attention, all right?"

She slows down a little, and after a moment, I see her visibly relax. Her shoulders drop, and her grip on the wheel loosens.

She'll be fine.

I look back at Lily. "What about Pierce? Did you see him?"

"See him? I *shot* him!"

"Really? Is he dead?"

She shakes her head. "No, but he's really pissed."

I frown. "Where did you shoot him?"

"In the shoulder. I couldn't really stop to aim, but at least he's having as bad a day as we are, which is something."

I smile and turn back around, settling into my seat and staring at the road ahead. We have maybe a six-hour drive ahead of us. We need to get back to Abu Dhabi, find Kaitlyn's neighbor, and convince him to help us hack The Order's network. Then we'll see if we can deactivate the signal that controls the bombs in Lily's neck and mine.

I just hope we can make it before it's too—

"Oh my God..."

I snap back into the moment and turn to Kaitlyn. "What's wrong?"

"Behind us."

I glance over my shoulder, out the rear window, and see a fleet of Suburbans following us. There are five identical vehicles, all with tinted windows. Just like the one Pierce gave Kaitlyn and I yesterday, back when he was on my side. Or at least, back when I didn't know he *wasn't* on my side.

"Shit. Okay, Kaitlyn, you have this. Just focus on driving

and not crashing, all right? Let Lily and me worry about them."

I throw the empty gun in the foot well and take out mine from behind me. Lily's crouching low on the back seat, reloading hers.

This is going to be a long ride.

23

The sun is bright, and its glare reflects off the windows of the cars around us. Now that the adrenaline's subsided, I'm starting to feel a little nauseous and groggy again. The after-effects of anesthesia, I'm guessing. I'm struggling to focus my mind because it's desperately trying to shut off.

No time for that, though.

I look across at Kaitlyn. She's squinting as she stares ahead, trying to position the visor to shield herself from the sun, but it doesn't seem to be working. I open the glove box. This is Qatar; there's no way people don't keep sunglasses in their cars. I rummage through the papers and the CDs inside and... I think... bingo! There's a pair right at the back. I take them out and hand them to her. She glances sideways and smiles, takes off her own glasses, fumbles for the shades without taking her eyes off the road, and slides them onto her face.

She takes a deep breath. "Better... thanks."

"No problem."

I watch her for a moment. She's doing a great job of driving under pressure. I can't imagine how hard all this is for her. She weaves in and out of the slow-moving traffic. It'll be difficult for Pierce and his men to follow us effectively and get close, which is good. But if they decide to stop playing nice and open fire anyway, we're screwed.

I look down and rest my gun against my cast as I check the mag. It's half-full, which isn't ideal, but it's the only one I have. Kaitlyn's gun is empty now too.

I glance over my shoulder at Lily. "How much ammo you got?"

She quickly checks her gun. "A few rounds. No spare mags left, either. Why?"

"Because I'm starting to get tired of running." I turn in my seat. "What about you?"

She's sitting low in the seat. "I thought my days of running from anyone were over. But there are too many people around. This is a busy road. We can't engage them here."

I nod. "Agreed. But it's unlikely to stop *them* from engaging *us*. Besides, I don't want to lead them all the way to Kaitlyn's place. I know they can track us, but if they're watching remotely, it at least buys us some time to get away from there afterward. I don't want them to know what our plans are. I need them to think we're just running *from* them, not *to* somewhere else."

"Maybe we can lead them away from the city, out into the desert?"

"No, it's too far. But a wide-open space is a good idea. Nowhere to hide or get boxed in. We need—"

We're heading south along Al Matar Street, and we've just passed a sign that flicked on my light bulb. I turn to

Kaitlyn. "Take the next left up ahead."

She doesn't respond. She just positions herself so that she's ready to turn as we approach the exit.

"Where are we going?" asks Lily.

I look back at her. "To the nearest wide-open space there is."

The road ahead leads all the way to Al Wakrah, which is roughly ten miles from Doha and sits on the shores of the Persian Gulf. We could try losing them there, or try outrunning them through the city, all the way back to Abu Dhabi. But the chances of either of those things happening are slim at best. So, our only real option is to fight. Worst case, there's twenty of the bastards following us. I've been in similar situations before on my own but not against men of this caliber. I have Lily, which evens things up a little, but it's still not ideal.

Which is why we're heading left... toward Hamad International Airport.

Kaitlyn accelerates and makes the turn just as the lights change. I look behind me and see the five Suburbans frantically trying to navigate through the long line of stationary vehicles and jump the red light to follow us.

We speed along the F Ring Road and exit left onto the Ras Abu Abboud Expressway. Pierce and his men are still behind us but farther back than before. Kaitlyn's driving has bought us some time.

Lily leans forward and looks through the windshield. The outline of the airport takes shape in the distance to the right of us, just beyond a large construction site. "I don't know if this is genius or insanity..."

I smile. "Story of my life. Way I see it, we get them out of their vehicles, we can pick them off on foot among the crowds in there."

"Yeah, if we can get in there," Lily says.

I frown. "What do you mean?"

"Adrian, there's no way Horizon didn't start putting another seven contingency plans in place the moment we left the hospital. That's what he does. And I can guarantee his first thought will be that we'll run. He would've locked down every airport in this time zone the minute he tracked us leaving Doha."

I shrug. "Maybe you're right, but staying visible is the only chance we've got of surviving long enough to get back to Abu Dhabi."

She gestures to the tracking device in her neck. "We're nothing but visible. How does that help?"

"The Order's existed for as long as it has because the people in charge have ensured it's stayed hidden, right? It's like society's guilty secret. They're not going to risk everything they've built just to kill the three of us. I doubt we're the only people who ever went rogue on them. They'll have their ways of handling shit like this quietly. What they *won't* do is remotely blow our heads off in front of thousands of witnesses."

Lily looks at me and smiles. I see a flicker of life in her eyes, as if, for the first time since all this started, we might finally have a plan that gets us all out of this. "It's still a little insane..."

I smile back. "The best plans always are. If people think something's too stupid to do, they're less likely to be prepared when you actually do it."

Kaitlyn chuckles. "My God, I've created a monster!"

I laugh. "My mind's always worked this way. It's who I am. It's what makes me as good as I am at shit like this. I just forgot for a while. That's all. All the loss and guilt distracted me. I mean, it's still there, and it's still hard, but remembering who I am—finding my own identity again... it's helped. So, it's not that you created a monster, Kaitlyn. You simply helped remind the monster how fucking scary he is, and for that, I'm forever grateful."

Kaitlyn smiles. "You're welcome."

Lily rolls her eyes. "Oh, would you listen to yourself..."

I hold my hands up. "What? I'm just saying, what makes me a good assassin is the fact that I don't think like other people do."

"Such modesty..."

"I'm not modest. I'm... complex. Tell her, Kaitlyn."

Kaitlyn glances over her shoulder at Lily. "Oh, he's complex, all right. I can vouch for that."

She scoffs. "Complex? He's the simplest man I've ever met!"

I frown. "Hey! Simple?"

"Hell yeah! Just like every other man. Seriously, Kaitlyn, you should've seen him trying to flirt with these two young blondes the other night..."

Kaitlyn giggles, and her eyes go wide, feigning shock.

I shake my head. "I was *not* flirting with them! They were flirting with *me*. I was trying to put them off!"

"Oh, whatever. You were—"

Lily slumps forward heavily as a thick splash of blood explodes across the windshield.

Fuck me!

Time reduces to a crawl. I look behind us. There's a small, neat hole in the rear window, with thin cracks branching out from it. Beyond that, I see the Suburbans. I see Pierce standing up through the sunroof of the one in front, holding a sniper rifle. Well, it clearly wasn't a serious gunshot to his shoulder...

I turn back and stare down at Lily, dumbstruck. Her

body has sagged against the center console. Half her head is missing, and her lifeless, empty eyes are wide and unblinking, staring up at me.

For what feels like a lifetime, I'm gone. I'm wandering through my own purgatory somewhere far away from here. Every moment I've shared with Lily flashes before my eyes. From meeting her for the first time in Kuala Lumpur, when she hit me with the door, to how relaxed she made me feel after my first contract in the restaurant, to drinking together in the bar, to when she kissed me in front of those blondes. I think about the attraction I felt that I couldn't explain, vehemently denied, and still feel guilty for. I think about my heartache and anger when I thought she was trying to kill me and the relief I felt when I realized she wasn't. Now I'm staring at the inside of her head as she's slumped beside me.

That's a lot to absorb in about three seconds.

I snap back to the here and now and look over at Kaitlyn. She's just beginning to register what's happened, flicking her gaze between the road and Lily's corpse. The blood on the windshield has obscured the view in front of her. She's shaken, panicking. She frantically turning the wheel to her left. I reach over to her, but I'm too late. We're doing nearly sixty as we approach the exit for the airport's security checkpoint. The Range Rover doesn't even slide. It just flips.

Holy shit!

The world barrel rolls outside. I push my left hand against the dash, bracing against the inevitable impact. Kaitlyn brings both hands up to cover her head, but as time resumes its usual speed, she's thrown against the wheel and ricochets back hard against her seat.

Ah!

Shit!

Uh!

Fuck!

The size of the vehicle has helped limit the roll. We slide across the road on our side as it doglegs right, branching off toward the main entrance of the construction site. Kaitlyn's fallen down into me, pressing me against my door as it grinds and screeches along the ground like nails on a chalkboard.

I bring my right arm around Kaitlyn and hold her as tight as I can to my body. I'm trying to protect her as much as possible, but I can already see a thin trickle of blood coming from a head wound. Must've banged herself when she—

Shit!

The hood just hit something. The sound of metal twisting and warping from the impact feels as if it's making my ears bleed. We've spun around, so I'm now facing right instead of left. I can feel us slowing down, which is something.

We screech to a gradual halt.

I can't hear much of anything, and I'm too disoriented to check if anything's hurting. My only instinct right now is to get Kaitlyn and run. Pierce and his men will be on us any second, and...

What's that smell?

I sniff hard. I'm trying to focus my mind long enough to identify the odor.

What the hell is—

Shit.

That smell... it's gas. The fuel tank must be damaged. If we're leaking gas everywhere, we need to get out of here now, before—

FWUMP!

That sounded suspiciously like a fire starting somewhere outside...

Kaitlyn's laying on her side against my chest. She stirs. "W-what... happened?"

My eyes dart in every direction, desperately searching for a way out. I'm pinned against my door, between my seat and the dash. The window's cracked but still intact. The driver's side door is above us. Lily's body is sagging over the edge of my seat. I can't see her legs, but her torso and head is resting on Kaitlyn, which is adding more weight on me. My left arm's trapped beneath me, and my right arm hurts like hell.

Oh, not good... not good...

Pierce and his merry band of assholes will be here any moment. Or maybe not, thinking about it. Our crash would have caught the attention of anyone nearby at the time, so emergency services are bound to be en route. He might want to save himself some time and avoid going through the motions of dealing with the authorities.

Either way, we have to go. Right now.

I lift my head. "Kaitlyn, are you okay?"

She groans. "Yeah, I... I think so."

"Okay, good. Now... listen to me carefully. You need to push Lily's body off you and... kick the windshield out."

I see her move her head to look at Lily. She screams.

Shit.

"Kaitlyn, did you hear me? You need to move Lily and... kick the glass out of the windshield right now, or... we're gonna die. I can't move until you do. Please... I know it's hard, but... I need you to focus."

She nods frantically, like she's trying to convince herself it's a good idea, despite every natural urge she has saying otherwise. "Okay."

She lets out a low grunt of effort as she pushes Lily's body up. She guides it back onto the rear seat and uses the edge of my seat to heave herself up. I hear the unceremonious thud as the body lands hard against the rear door, level with me on the other side of the seat, out of sight.

I'm sorry, Lily. You deserved better than this.

Kaitlyn shifts awkwardly, trying to move her legs behind her, so she's essentially standing over me. I move my right arm up and rest it over my face to free up some space at the side of me, so she can—

Ah!

She just stood on my chest...

She looks down and sucks air apologetically through her teeth. "Sorry!"

I shake my head. "It's fine. Just... get us outta here."

She leans to the right and rests both hands on the windshield. She pushes a couple of times, and I hear a creak as the entire pane of glass opens out like a door.

Huh... that was easier than I thought it would be.

Not that I'm complaining!

She looks down and carefully steps around me, then ducks as she shuffles herself out and onto the road. Once she's clear, I push against the seat, first with my hand and then with my legs. I slide out on my back and shimmy along on my elbows as quickly as I can.

I... hate... only... having... one... hand...

My body's clear. I feel Kaitlyn tuck her hands under my arms and drag me out the rest of the way. The second my feet are clear, I'm on them. I grab her hand and we run.

What the...

My face feels warm and wet.

Oh, shit...

Head wound.

Fuck it. I'll bleed later.

We keep moving. There's a barrier running along the outside of the road. We climb over it and set off as fast as we can across the sun-scorched wasteland that sits between the expressway and the large construction site, which is maybe five hundred yards ahead of us.

I'm counting in my head how long we've been sprinting. Five seconds… ten…

An explosion erupts behind us, and we both drop to a crouch as a wave of heat rushes over us. We glance over our shoulders and see what's left of the Range Rover's metal frame engulfed in a hungry fire, blackened and torn from the initial blast. One of the wheels lands a few feet to my right and rolls for a moment before falling on its side.

Fuck, that was close!

The smoke is thick and dark, and the slight breeze is blowing it left, which is good. It'll obscure Pierce's view if he's kept his distance, at least for a minute or so. Every second counts right now.

I look across at Kaitlyn. "You okay?"

Her eyes are wide, staring with horrified disbelief at the burning wreck we were trapped in less than thirty seconds ago. She doesn't answer me.

I reach for her arm again. "Okay, I'll take that as a yes. Look, we gotta move, but I need you to check my head first. I think I took a blow to it in the crash, and I'm a little spaced out. Kaitlyn? Kaitlyn, are you with me?"

She doesn't react for a few moments. Then she frowns. "What do you mean you're a little…" She turns to look at me, and her eyes go wide again. "Oh my God!"

"What? Is it bad?"

"*Is it bad?* Adrian, it's like you're wearing a red mask! Let me look at you."

She kneels up beside me and sits back on her legs, renewed focus and concern etched on her face. She puts her hands on either side of my head, forcing me to look down. I hear a gasp.

I roll my eyes. "What?"

"Uh... you've got a nasty-looking cut on your head."

"Define *nasty*..."

"Well, it's about two inches long, running down the center of your head. It's pretty deep. You'll need stitches. We should get you to a hospital."

I shake my head, and a few drops of blood splash on her top. She glances down, then at me. I shrug. "Sorry. But no... no more hospitals. We deal with Pierce and then we get to your neighbor to see if he can disable this thing in my neck. That's got to be our priority. Especially now that Lily's..."

I let my words trail off. I'm not saying it out loud. If I do, it means I'm acknowledging it's happened, and I'm not ready for that. Not yet. Before I start with all that, I have more important things to sort.

I put my left hand under my T-shirt and use it to wipe the blood from my face. I look down at it.

Man, that's a *lot* of red...

I go to stand. I push myself vertical with one hand. I'm a little light-headed actually...

Whoa!

Kaitlyn jumps to her feet and puts a hand on my shoulder, propping me upright. "You're losing a lot of blood, which is bad. You only woke up from surgery a couple hours ago. You're far from a hundred percent, Adrian. Plus, you only have one useful hand. This isn't a fight you're going to win. We need to get out of here, get you patched up, and then, *maybe*, we think about this psychotic gang of hitmen you work for."

I don't know if this is the blood loss talking, but she's making sense. Damn it. I hate it when people who aren't me make a good point.

I let out a tired sigh. "Fine. Come on."

We hadn't gotten far when the car blew up. We set off jogging again, with Kaitlyn leading me by the hand. After a minute or so, we're well over halfway there. I risk a glance back at the road. No one's following us, but the Suburbans have split up. Two have carried on along the slip road where we crashed, which will bring them through the security gates and into the construction site ahead. The other three have gone back the other way. They're probably heading for the airport, thinking that's where we're trying to reach. They'll want to be prepared for when we get there.

Well, I can't go to the airport looking like this, so that's irrelevant. The immediate problem is what's waiting in front of us.

We reach the fence. It's chain link, maybe ten feet high, with the last foot being four strips of barbed wire running horizontally along it.

I look at Kaitlyn. "You first."

She shakes her head. "Adrian, I... I... I can't climb it. I'm useless with heights. I—"

I shrug. "Me too."

She rolls her eyes. "You're just saying that to make me feel better."

"No, I really do hate heights. But this is about ten feet, if that."

"Adrian, this is *really* high. And I was never any good at climbing as a kid..."

She's scared. I get it. I'm trying to be sympathetic and understanding and patient, et cetera. But we don't have time.

I let out a long, painful breath. "Look, about a month

ago, I was pushed out of an airplane twenty thousand feet over Vietnam. I woke up in the back of it, already in the air. Two guys fastened a 'chute to me, opened the door, and threw me out. *That* I have a problem with. *That* was a height and a situation worth worrying about. *This*... really isn't."

She stares into my eyes for a long moment, reading me. I can see it in her expression, searching me for any hint that I'm bullshitting her. We all know she won't find one.

"Are you... being serious?"

I nod. "That was The Order's initiation, I guess."

"And them throwing you from a plane didn't make you think that maybe they're not the kind of people you want to get involved with?"

I shrug. "It's not like I had much choice. At that stage, they had just rescued me from my own execution. I figured I owed it to them to jump through a few hoops."

"Adrian, has anyone ever told you that your life just... sucks?"

I smile. "Is that your professional opinion?"

"That's my personal opinion. We don't have time for my professional one."

"Fair enough. Now get your ass over the fence. Please."

She huffs at me and grabs hold of it. She finds her footing and slowly starts to climb. I can hear her grunting from the exertion.

"You're doing great, Kaitlyn. Aim for the thick metal pole that separates each section of fence, okay? When you reach it, put one hand on it to brace yourself and one foot on the top, underneath the bottom line of barbed wire."

She glances down, which I can tell from her expression that she instantly regretted. "And then what?"

"Then you push with your hand and foot, swing your

body out slightly, then vault over the top and drop down the other side."

"*What!*"

"Land in a crouch and let yourself roll naturally to the side. You'll be fine."

"You couldn't have mentioned that was the plan *before* I started climbing?"

I have to squint as I look up at her because the sun's shining right in my eyes. I shrug. "What difference would it have made? You'd still have to do it."

She huffs again. "I hate you..."

I nod. "Yeah, I get that a lot."

She reaches the top and, to her credit, does exactly what I said. She lands a little awkwardly on the other side and sits in the dust and sand for a moment to compose herself. I wave at her through the fence. She gives me the finger.

I smile and grab the fence with my hand. I place one foot on it and...

Shit.

I only have one good hand.

I can't climb up like this.

Shit!

"What's the problem?" she asks.

I shake my head. "I can't scale the fence with my arm in a cast."

She sighs loudly. "And you didn't think about this beforehand?"

"Nope."

"So, now what?"

"I'm thinking..."

I walk along the length of the fence, searching for anything that might help, but I don't really know what I'm looking for. I guess I'll know it when I see it, but...

Hang on.

I crouch maybe a hundred yards from where Kaitlyn is. The section of fencing is slightly curled toward me in one corner. I slide the fingers of my left hand through the links and get a firm grip. I plant my feet as best I can in the dust, and I pull hard on it.

The fence moves a little, coming away from the post just a fraction.

The whole thing was most likely erected hurriedly when they first started building here. Each section of fencing is attached to the posts separately by cable ties. Where I'm pulling, it's come free near the bottom. The pole is a little unstable, and the ties themselves look pretty weak.

I think with enough force, I might be able to...

I give it another strong pull, shuffling to my right and teasing it back a tiny bit at a time. I stop after a couple of minutes. The metal has left deep, red imprints in my palm. I flex it to get the blood flowing again.

I wish I could do this with both hands...

I've managed to make a decent-sized gap near the ground, but I don't think it's enough for me to fit through.

Kaitlyn walks over and stares at the fence. "I can't believe you made me climb over the damn thing when we could've just done this. Unbelievable."

I smile. "Let's not dwell on the past, eh? Give me a hand with it, would you? I need you to push as I pull."

"Whatever..." she mutters, not quite under her breath.

She crouches opposite me and grips the fence with both hands. I grab it again with my left.

"Okay, on three. You push. I'll pull. Ready?"

She nods.

"Go."

We manage to make a gap twice the size of the one I

made on my own, which is perfect for me to fit through. She holds it up as much as she can, and I crouch as low as my legs will allow. I scuttle through the gap and get to my feet, standing beside her as I brush the dust off my shorts.

Kaitlyn looks at me. "I really hate you."

I smile. "I can live with that."

We turn and look over at the site before us. This must be the planned extension to the airport they've been talking about. It seems to be split into three distinct parts. An assortment of construction vehicles are parked together over on the left, with some portable offices stacked two high next to them. Behind them, stretching almost the entire width of the site, is the half-built skeletal structure of what I imagine will one day be a seriously big building. Huge concrete blocks, lying both vertically and horizontally, form the meat, with wide metal girders and cabling acting as the bones. I read somewhere not so long ago that this was going to be a new terminal for the airport. It's been in the pipeline for a couple of years. Some people were against the idea initially, but in the current climate, I think the fact that it's created so many jobs has made people embrace it.

We set off walking toward the new building. The crunch of our footsteps on the gravel echoes around the deserted site. The next work shift won't start for a couple of hours, so we're alone here for now.

Kaitlyn turns to me. "We can search these cabins for a first aid kit. It might be worth regrouping here for a short while to see if we can patch you up a little."

I nod. "Yeah, that's—"

I hear more crunching away to the left. Tires this time. I look over, beyond the parked vehicles, away to the left of the site. I can see two Suburbans speeding through the entrance. They disappear out of sight, rounding a bend that will lead them to the far side of the new building.

"Shit."

24

I point to the office cabins, which are less than fifty yards away. "Come on. Stay low and quiet."

There are four of them in total, positioned in a tight U-shape. Two are sitting roughly side by side in front of us, with one jutting out at either end. They're dark blue and covered in dust and dirt. A metal staircase has been fitted to the end of each one, running up to the second door above. We move along the front of the one on the right until we reach the door. I try the handle.

Locked.

"Damn it."

I take a couple steps back and then kick out, pushing my right leg forward as hard and fast as I can. My foot connects with the door just below the handle. The thin wood splinters and cracks, and the door flies open. It bangs against something behind it. I gesture Kaitlyn inside. She doesn't

275

hesitate, and I follow her in and push the door closed again behind me.

Oh my God, it's hot in here! It's like I've just stepped inside the sun!

There's a large desk on the left, with a few chairs standing around it. One of them has been knocked over—must've been the door. There's a whiteboard on the wall facing the entrance, filled with writing and diagrams in blue marker. To the right is a large metal shelving unit, like lockers without doors. There's a small compartment running along the top and bottom, with safety helmets and work boots resting haphazardly in each one respectively. The middle section is long and has safety apparel hanging there—reflective vests and coveralls, mostly.

I point to the corner of the room behind the table. "I want you to crouch there. Stay quiet and stay hidden. I'll be back soon."

She takes a step toward me, looking panicked. "Wh-where are you going?"

I gesture outside. "Worst case, there are eight guys just arriving, armed to the teeth and looking to kill us. I'm gonna go ask them real nice not to."

"Adrian, you can't. You'll—"

I smile and shake my head. "No, I won't. This is what I do. Back when it was twenty-on-one, yeah, that was stupid. But eight-on-one, I can handle. Trust me."

She holds my gaze for a moment and then nods. She moves to the corner and crouches down behind the table. I walk back over to the lockers and search quickly through each section. I strike gold in the middle one. Behind the clothing that's hanging down, on a small shelf, is a rusted, black metal toolbox. I open it up and immediately grab the claw hammer resting on top. It has a flat, circular part on one side for getting the nails in and a curved, two-pronged hook on the other for getting them back out again.

Perfect.

I look back at Kaitlyn and smile, trying my best to look reassuring. I don't think it's working, though, because she looks terrified. I just nod to her and step outside before she starts trying to talk me out of this again.

I move along the front of the cabin and press my body against it as I reach the end. I stare ahead and see the smoke billowing into the sky in the mid-distance. A sea of flashing lights has surrounded the crash already.

Let's hope no one comes looking for the survivors...

Holding the hammer low and close, I peer around the corner to my left. Straight ahead is a large, brick archway, which looks as if it might be the future entrance. Beyond that, the majority of the walls are no more than waist-high, with taller pillars and girders sticking up periodically. There are at least two different levels of scaffolding, which forms a roof of sorts, lined with walkways and ladders. There are plenty of opportunities for cover, but I'll have to stay low and move quickly between them.

I strain to listen for any movement. I can't hear the tires of the Suburbans anymore, so they've stopped somewhere. My guess is they'll fan out and sweep through the site quickly. Orders will undoubtedly be to shoot on sight.

Eight highly trained operatives, employed by an organization of elite assassins, all armed with assault rifles. And me... holding a hammer, with my good hand in a cast and a head wound that's bleeding so badly, I can barely stand or see.

I'll be fine.

Oh, which reminds me...

I crouch, rest the hammer on its head, and use my T-shirt to wipe more blood off my face and away from my eyes.

That's helped a little.

I retrieve the hammer and make my way around the corner. I jog under the archway and into the main building site.

Dude, this is fucking nuts. You know that, right?

I do, which is why you're going to help me, old friend. *Fucking nuts* is your specialty.

I duck to the left and press myself against one of the wide pillars. I go to move along the low wall to the pillar on the opposite side, but the crunching of boots on gravel freezes me to the spot. There's a guy heading right for me, just around the corner over my left shoulder. I glance to the ground to make sure I'm hidden from his line of sight. I rest my head back against the wall. The warmth of the new concrete is pleasant on the back of my head. I tighten my grip on the hammer, turning it in my hand so that the flat surface is facing out.

I look left and right, but I can't see any signs of anyone else immediately near him.

I need to time this right and hit hard and fast to minimize any exposure so early on.

I close my eyes and bring the hammer up to my chest, counting the steps, picturing where the guy is in my head.

Three...

Two...

One...

I lean left and whip the hammer out as hard as I can. The flat, circular metal head smashes into the kneecap of the guy as he draws level with me. The impact sends his leg flying out from under him, and he drops heavily to the ground beside me. His face ricochets off the dirt. He's dressed in a lightweight black outfit, with a thin Kevlar vest over the top. He's wearing an earpiece linked to a comms unit sitting in his back pocket.

Any hesitation now will get me killed. Time and luck are running out. I don't have long before Horizon decides I'm not worth the hassle and just blows my head off.

I'd like to avoid that ...

So, I don't pause for a second. I smash the hammer down onto the side of the guy's head. Once... twice... three times in quick succession. Momentum makes each blow heavier than the last. His body jerked after the first. I heard bone crack after the second. The third one was like splitting a watermelon. Thick blood erupts in a fountain from the gaping hole I've created in his head, just above the ear, level with his temple.

I put the hammer down beside me and shuffle to my feet. Using only my left hand, I drag the guy's body around the corner and rest it against where I was just sitting. I unhook the assault rifle from around his neck. It looks like a modified AK-12, with an ACOG scope and a long, thin suppressor over the barrel.

Nice.

I hook the strap over my right shoulder and let it hang loose at my side. I stay in a low crouch and pick up the hammer again. It's good that I have a weapon, but the hammer's quieter. No sense in announcing I'm here until I need to.

Right, seven left...

I take some deep breaths, trying to keep my heart rate down. I'm listening for any more footsteps.

I think I heard something to my left.

I turn and make my way along the low wall, all the way to the opposite end. I peek around the corner, but I don't see anyone. I quickly use the back of my hand to wipe some excess blood from around my eyes.

Across the walkway is a ramp that leads up to another level, which starts a little farther forward from where I am. The additional height would be an advantage...

I scurry across the gap and step slowly and carefully up the ramp, desperate to keep any noise to a minimum. The floor above drops level with my eye line as I climb. I hear some more footsteps—sounds like they're away to my right...

I glance around, taking in the details of my new surroundings. There's a large group of crates sitting on a wooden pallet in the middle of the floor. There's a high concrete ledge ahead of me and some makeshift barriers made from metal poles running along the left edge.

I make it over to the crates and drop down behind them. I can hear another guy approaching from the far side. There must be another ramp over there that leads down to the other side of the site. I peek between the crates. After a moment, the guy walks into view. He's dressed the same as his recently deceased colleague.

Which way's he going?

He's walking straight toward me. I need to know which way he's going to move around these crates.

Come on... come on...

Make a move, asshole...

...

His footsteps are getting louder.

...

He's four feet from me, on the other side of these boxes. I hear him adjusting his grip on his AK-12.

...

He steps to his right.

Got you!

I move right myself, counterclockwise around the crates. I come up behind him, stand up straight, and bring my arm up. The hammer is turned around so that the curved hook is exposed.

I strike him with brutal accuracy, burying the claws in the base of his skull. The squelch as they pierce his flesh sounds loud in the ghostly silence of the construction site. He drops with a thud, pulling the hammer from my grip as he goes down. I crouch beside him to retrieve it from his—

"Hey!"

Oh, shit...

I snap my head right to see another guy standing at the top of the ramp, frozen for a split-second, staring at me.

I spin my body around to face him. The momentum swings the rifle forward, and I move my left hand to catch it. Instinctively, I grab the handle and squeeze the trigger, letting out a short burst of suppressed fire. He's close enough that I don't need to worry about aiming, even with my weaker hand. The bullets punch into his stomach and chest. He flails backward and slumps against the low wall behind him.

Two more down... five left.

"He's over here!"

Uh-oh.

Gun still in hand, I move over the wall in front of me, which runs almost the full width of this floor, separating both ramps. I peer over and see the five remaining guys regrouping just below me.

If they have any sense—which I'm assuming they do—they'll split up and approach up both ramps. I can't shoot in both directions at the same time, so that's the logical approach if they intend to try to kill me.

They'll either split into a three and a two, or they'll split into two teams of two and leave the last guy in the middle on his own, to give them an additional level of cover. I know what I'd tell them to do, and I'm conscious of giving them either too little or too much credit here...

My gut says a three and a two.

I peer over the edge again. Two men are just disappearing out of sight, running for the ramp behind me. The other three are heading to the one nearest to me.

Damn, I'm good!

Now which group am I most likely to beat to their respective ramp?

I jump up and sprint to the ramp on the right. I stand next to the dead guy and use my foot to push him down. He hits the bottom at the exact moment the three guys appear.

I drop to one knee and empty the mag at them. My field of vision is narrow and focused. Their dead colleague dropping on them took them by surprise. They're standing like rabbits in the headlights as I shoot them like fish in a barrel.

Not that I condone animal cruelty in any way...

The strain on my left arm is intense, holding the rifle steady and absorbing the recoil while trying to remain even remotely accurate. I hear the wet impact over the staccato scream as bullets tear into them. They never stood a chance.

I wait for the last body to hit the ground before turning to look over at the other ramp.

"Oh, fuck!"

The remaining two men are already standing by the crates, their rifles leveled at me. Gunfire sounds out as they—

Ah!

Ow!

Shit!

I fell sideways and rolled down the ramp. Those bullets must've missed me by a hair's breadth.

Jesus Christ, that was close!

The blood on my face is stinging my eyes, and I'm running out of clean T-shirt to wipe it with. This head wound is pissing me off.

I landed heavily, but the dead bodies cushioned my fall. My cast is definitely durable, although my right hand is hurting like hell. I look back up the ramp. I'm squinting in an effort to stop the blood flowing into my eyes. It looks like...

Yeah, both guys are standing at the top, looking down at me. Their rifles are aimed at me, and their stances are relaxed and confident. They've got me dead to rights. I'm lying flat on my back. My gun's God-knows-where. I'm really starting to feel dizzy from all the blood coming out of my head, although that's probably the least of my problems right now...

Time stops as a hail of bullets sounds out without warning. I screw my eyes tightly shut and grit my teeth, bracing for the inevitable onslaught I have no chance to prepare for. This is it. I'm about to—

...

...

...

Huh?

What happened?

The shooting's stopped, but I'm still breathing. I'm not that lucky, and it's unlikely they're that bad at shooting...

I use my left hand to wipe the blood from my face and slowly open my eyes. I raise my head slightly and stare up at the top of the ramp. The two men aren't there anymore.

Instead, I see Kaitlyn, breathing heavily, holding an assault rifle.

What the...

"Oh my God, Adrian! Are you all right?" she shouts down.

I relax my head again and let out a heavy sigh. Then I smile. Then I start laughing.

Sonofabitch!

I hold my left arm up long enough to make the universal OK signal with my thumb and trigger finger. Then I close my eyes.

It's been a long fucking day.

25

The sounds of the city drift in through the open windows on a lazy breeze as we navigate through the bustling metropolis of Abu Dhabi. The burnt-orange sun is a beacon in the evening sky, dominating the landscape as it begins its descent.

After Kaitlyn saved my ass in Qatar, we found the first aid station on the construction site. It was fully stocked, and there was even a change of clothes in one of the lockers. I grabbed a new T-shirt, given how torn and bloodstained my old one was.

She patched me up pretty well, but I still look like shit. I have a bandage wrapped around my head, stained dark with blood from the cut I sustained in the crash. She's right—I'm going to need stitches in that bastard. My right hand is pulsing with agony too. It's taken a real beating, despite the sturdy plastic cast protecting it. I've taken some painkillers, which helped for a while, but now it's at the stage where only a few beers will do.

Not much chance of respite and refreshment, though.

We requisitioned one of the spare Suburbans, left behind by the corpses we created. It's packed full of weapons and tech, so we're well armed now. We headed straight here, keeping to the speed limit to avoid attracting any unwanted attention. There's no hiding from The Order —not yet, anyway—but there's no sense in putting ourselves on anyone else's radar unless we have to.

Kaitlyn's been managing really well, all things considered. Her clothes are filthy, her hair's all out of sorts, and I think our crash broke her glasses, but given she killed two people with an assault rifle this afternoon, she looks surprisingly composed. I don't know how much of that composure is genuine and how much of it is the result of a strong, focused mind trained to remain neutral when faced with extraordinary emotional trauma. Either way, it's working for her, so I'm not about to question it.

I've said the best thing to do is stop in a public place and call her neighbor, explain as much as we can without going into too much detail, and ask him to meet us. Given The Order can see where I am at all times, I don't want to lead them straight to Kaitlyn's house and endanger the lives of the people around her. The more public I stay, the less chance there is of them blowing my head off. I'm putting a lot of faith in this kid being able to help us.

And God help Horizon if he can.

We've not spoken much on the ride here. She insisted on driving, and we haven't stopped once. I think I fell asleep for a little while, which I felt bad about. The way I see it, the driver can't rest, so out of respect, neither should the passengers. I felt the same way when it was just Josh and me, back in the day. She didn't seem to mind, though. And to be fair, given I woke up from surgery a little over eight hours ago, I reckon a bit of sleep was probably long overdue.

We stop at a red light.

"Any ideas where you want to go?" asks Kaitlyn.

I think for a moment. "We need somewhere busy. Maybe not too far from your house."

The lights change and we set off again. She takes the first left. "I know the perfect place."

We drive for another ten minutes before she pulls over outside a plaza, spitting distance from the coast. It's a circular park with a fountain in the middle, illuminated for the evening by multicolored lights beneath the water. There are sizeable areas of grass around the edges, with a café and a restaurant covering the area, both with seating outside. There are steps leading up from the sidewalk at regular intervals around the park. Across the street is Abu Dhabi beach. The lapping of the waves is audible over the traffic. The area is busy but not overcrowded.

I turn to her. "This is perfect. I'm going to stretch my legs. You wanna make the call?"

Kaitlyn nods. "Yeah." She takes the cell phone from the center console and types in a number. "My house is maybe fifteen minutes from here, so it won't take him long."

"What are you gonna say to him?"

She sighs. "I'll need to give him enough information about what's really happening, so he brings everything he needs, but I'll skim over the finer details."

I nod. "What if he's reluctant?"

She shrugs. "Then I guess I'll take Lily's advice and use what God gave me..."

She gestures casually to her chest and smiles. I look,

which is unavoidable, and then smile. We both laugh, but after a moment, we fall silent.

She puts a hand on my arm. "Are you all right?"

"Yeah. What about you? This is a lot for a normal person to take in."

"It is, but I'm doing okay. I feel better knowing you're here."

I smile but only for a moment. "Listen, I know you're the expert on the mind, but I'm the expert when it comes to this special kind of shit that we're in. I know what you're probably going through, whether you know yourself yet or not. What you did for me back on that construction site... You saved my life, Kaitlyn. I'm grateful beyond words, but I know what you did isn't normal to people like you. Killing someone shouldn't be *normal* to anybody. What I'm trying to say is, at some point, the gravity of what you did is going to hit you, okay? I just want you to know when it does..." I return the gesture and put my hand on hers. "You can talk to me."

She holds my gaze. I can see tears forming in her eyes, but she holds them back. "I'm fine, honestly. Besides, it's normal for *you*, isn't it? You manage okay, and I know how much of an emotional train wreck *you* are!"

She smiles at me.

I shake my head. "Are these insults included in the service I pay three hundred dollars an hour for?"

She laughs. "No, they're extra. I'm going to invoice you when all this is over."

"I can't wait. But to answer your question, Kaitlyn—no, it's not normal for me. It's just all I know. It's all I'm good at. It's the only thing I was ever going to do with my life. But that doesn't make it normal."

We look at each other silently for a moment. She nods. "Thank you. Now let me make the call."

I reach inside the glove box and take the handgun I stashed there. It's a GlobaTech weapon and kind of looks like the old SIG Sauer P226 from the mid-nineties. The grip is a little longer than most semi-automatics to accommodate the twenty-four-round mag. It's dark gray with a matte finish. There's a small laser pointer built into the underside of the barrel, in front of the trigger guard. As always with GlobaTech's creations, it's a really nice piece.

I tuck it behind me and pull my T-shirt down over it. I climb out of the car, stand up straight, and push my shoulders back gently. I take in a deep breath of humid air and look around. I assess the customers outside the restaurant and café ahead of me and the groups of people milling around the plaza. I don't see anything that sets my spider sense off. If anyone from The Order has tracked us here, they're good at hiding in plain sight.

I walk up the steps to the left of me and stroll over to the fountain. I keep my pace intentionally slow and idle. I sit down on the edge and look back at the car. I can see Kaitlyn talking on the phone.

Man, I hope this works. If it doesn't, the only other option is Josh, and I really don't want to involve him in this shit. He's probably the only person alive actually mourning me. I can't put his life on the line. I don't have the right.

Kaitlyn gets out of the car and walks over to me. I stand to meet her. "Everything okay?"

She nods. "Yes, he's on his way."

"Amazing. What did you tell him?"

"I said I think one of my clients has bugged my laptop, and I was wondering if he'd be able to check for me. He was skeptical at first, but I told him this client was a bad person and that I'm scared and feel safer in a public place. He said he'd be here as soon as he could."

"That's good work, Kaitlyn."

She glances around. "Nice, isn't it?"

"Yeah, I've never been here."

"I come down here sometimes at the weekend, just for a bite to eat or to meet up with a girlfriend for lunch." She sighs. "So, what now?"

I shrug. "How long do you think this kid will be?"

"I dunno... twenty minutes, maybe?"

"Okay." I gesture to the café over my shoulder. "Drink?"

21:14 AST

We're sitting on separate tables adjacent to one another outside the café. We have our backs to each other and our chairs pushed out a little, so we're almost sitting next to each other but facing opposite directions. We're close enough that we can talk but far enough away that, to the casual passerby, we don't look together. I told Kaitlyn to try her best not to move her lips when she talks to me too.

She lets out a taut breath. "Here he comes."

He's approaching from her side, so I can't see him. I nonchalantly lean forward on my forearms and take a sip of my coffee, then glance absently around. I catch a glimpse over my right shoulder as the kid reaches her table.

He's almost as tall as me but thin, with long limbs. He has the beginnings of a dark beard forming on his pock-marked face. His hair is thick and short, and he's dressed casually in shorts and a thin sweater. He has a bag over his shoulder.

I look back at my table. He didn't see me staring.

"Yaz, thanks for coming," says Kaitlyn. "Can I get you anything?"

"N-no... thank you. Are... you all right?"

His English is pretty good, but his voice is cracking with nerves.

"I'm fine, I think. Please, sit down."

I hear the chair scrape along the ground as he joins her at the table.

"Yaz, I really do need your help with something, okay?"

He clears his throat. "Ah... yeah... I mean, sure. I'm happy to. That's if I can. You think your computer's bugged? That's crazy..."

Kaitlyn sighs. "Yes, it is a little strange. It's... also a lie. I'm sorry, but that's not why I asked you here. I just thought if I told you the real reason, you wouldn't come."

"I... I don't understand. Is everything okay? I can get my mom to come, and maybe she can help, or—"

"No, it's fine. It's you I need. I know you're, like, a computer genius. I figured if anyone could help, it'd be you."

Feeding his ego... nice. But she needs to hurry this along.

"I wouldn't say I'm a *genius*... but—"

"Yaz, this is the situation. A friend of mine—"

I get up and walk around to their table. I stand between them, facing the café. The kid looks up at me, frowning with uncertainty and maybe a little fear. I bet I look pretty weird with my head all wrapped up and my hand in a cast...

I smile. "It's Yaz, right?"

He nods tentatively.

I extend my left hand, turned outward. "I'm Adrian. Kaitlyn's friend."

He shakes it weakly. His palm's a little sweaty. I casually wipe my hand on my shorts. "Look, what I'm about to say is gonna be a little difficult to take in, all right? But I need your help. See, I have a tracking device implanted in my neck, and I need you to disable its signal. Can you do that?"

He hasn't blinked in a while. He's just... staring at me.

"Y-you look... r-really scary... sir."

I glance at Kaitlyn, who smiles. I nod at Yaz. "I can be pretty scary when I need to be. I won't lie. But I promise I'm a nice guy. I'm just in a bad situation. Can you help?"

He looks over at Kaitlyn, presumably for reassurance. When he gets some, he takes a deep breath and seems to relax a little. He reaches into his bag and takes out a laptop, which he sets up on the table. "Can't you just... y'know... take the device out?"

I shake my head. "If only it were that easy. See, it's a pretty sophisticated piece of tech. If it's removed, it kinda... explodes."

His eyes grow wide. Kaitlyn leans forward and puts her hand on his. "Yaz, it's okay. You're not in any danger. We just know that some bad people can use this tracking signal to find Adrian and me, and we'd rather they didn't."

He shakes his head. "What are you mixed up in, Miss Moss?"

The kid clearly has a crush on her. I can see it in his eyes. His gaze softens when he looks at her. And like any other kid in the later stages of puberty, he keeps staring at her breasts, thinking no one is noticing.

I put my hand on his shoulder to offer some additional reassurance. "Nothing too bad, I promise. And Yaz... I'll keep her safe, okay?"

He nods, as if he's resigning himself to the fact that this is happening and he needs to accept it. He takes a breath and starts tapping away on the laptop. "Okay, uh, Adrian... take a seat."

I pull the chair out in front of me and sit down.

Yaz reaches back inside his bag and pulls out what looks like a small walkie-talkie. It's a small black box with two antennae sticking out the end. He plugs it into a USB slot and resumes his key tapping. "Right, this is going to scan for the frequency your implant is transmitting on. Once we find its signal, I can identify the coding of it and, hopefully, disable it remotely."

I raise an eyebrow. "I'm impressed. You remind me of an old friend."

He ignores me. He's focused on the screen. I exchange a glance with Kaitlyn, who smiles.

"Oh... oh my..."

That doesn't sound good.

I look at the laptop, then at Yaz. "What is it?"

"Well, I've located the signal, but it's got some sick encryption on it. Like, military-grade stuff. This is... insane!"

"But you can still block it, right?"

He shakes his head. "Honestly, I don't know, sir. Wait..."

I roll my eyes. "What now?"

"There's... It looks like there's a second signal coming from the device. It's a different frequency but has the same encryption."

I sigh. "Yeah, I'm gonna need you to disable both."

"Wh-what's the second one for?"

"That's... ah... that's the one that can remotely detonate the device and blow my head off."

His eyes go wide again. I genuinely think he's about to throw up.

"So, thinking about it, if you could go ahead and disable that one *first*, I'd really appreciate it."

"I... I can't... I..."

Kaitlyn stands and moves around the table to his side.

She crouches next to him and puts her hand on his arm. "Yaz, please... We need you."

He stares at her for a moment, a mixture of fear and longing dancing in his eyes. Then he snaps his gaze back to the laptop and sits up straight. "Okay... wait a second..."

This looks encouraging. Josh used to do the same thing when he thought of something.

I lean forward. "What have you got for me, Yaz?"

"I'm gonna be honest. I don't think I can hack either signal to disable it. But I might be able to redirect it..."

I nod. "Keep talking... and pretend I'm an idiot and don't understand a word you're saying. Because... y'know... I don't."

He points to the screen, which shows a busy display with lots of wavy lines. "Okay, so your device has a unique signature, right? Something that identifies it on the bandwidth that allows it to be found and tracked by the system on the other end of the connection. I might be able to alter that signature, so the system thinks it's connected to something else, even though it's not."

I frown. "Okay, I kinda understand that..."

"So, the signal from your device will still be there, and it'll still be sending information, but the connected system won't see it. All it'll receive is the information coming from the new signature I assign to the device, which will essentially mask the original signal by sitting on top of it."

"And you can do that for both signals?" asks Kaitlyn.

Yaz nods. "I think so, yeah. There's no way I can stop the signal altogether, but I should be able to disguise it."

I nod. "Okay, I think that makes sense. But what information will they actually be receiving?"

He shrugs. "It could be anything. I'll extract from a

random cell phone signal, so they'll just receive a bunch of basic binary commands from the cell network. That's all."

I laugh. "Man, that's fucking brilliant! How long will that take?"

He's still tapping away on the laptop. After a few moments of silence, he looks up at me. "Done."

"Huh? Are you serious?"

He nods. "Yeah, it was pretty simple. There's a lot of network traffic because we're in a public place. Didn't take long at all."

"So, that's it? The tracking device is no longer visible to anyone, and it can't be remotely detonated?"

He shakes his head. "No, sir."

"Holy shit! Yaz, you really are a genius!"

He looks away, awkward and uncomfortable. Kaitlyn and I stand.

"What now?" she asks.

"Well, now we're free... kinda... I'm gonna drop you at your place and leave for Dubai."

She frowns. "Leave? What do you mean?"

"If they can't find me anymore, then you're in no danger. This is my last known location, so once we leave here, we disappear. You can go back to your life, safe and sound."

"But..." She stops herself, knowing there's no logical argument. "What are you going to do?"

I take a deep breath, steeling myself for what I know comes next. "I'm going to pay Horizon a visit and finish this once and for all."

26

It made sense to offer Yaz a ride home, which he gratefully accepted. Kaitlyn's driving, and we've just turned onto her street now. The traffic was light on the way here, given the time. The sidewalks were busier, filled with people going about their normal lives, drinking, laughing, socializing...

Ignorance is bliss.

We pull over outside a low apartment building about halfway along on the right. I step out and look around. It's a quiet neighborhood. I can't hear any of the bustle from the city center. I look up and down the street, instinctively cautious. It looks clear. The moon is full and bright. The last slivers of daylight are disappearing in the dark sky. Street-lights create shadows as their beams illuminate the sidewalk at spaced intervals.

Kaitlyn and Yaz walk down the path toward the building. I follow a few steps behind. It's only two stories, and given the size of the place, I reckon there's maybe eight or nine apartments contained within. The ones facing the street have sliding doors serving as a main window, with a barrier just in front of them, as a kind of balcony for the living room.

The main entrance is under cover, with mailboxes built into the wall to the left. Yaz reaches into his pocket and takes out a key. He opens the door and steps through, then holds it open for Kaitlyn and myself. Inside is cool—the air conditioning must be on constantly. There's a wide hallway with an elevator lobby on the left, just before a flight of stairs.

As we draw level with it, Yaz gestures down the hall. "This is me."

Kaitlyn gives him a hug. "Thank you for everything you did tonight, Yaz. I can't tell you how grateful we both are."

I step forward and pat his shoulder. "Yeah, you saved my life tonight, kid. I owe you one."

He shrugs bashfully. "I'm... I'm glad I could help." He looks at me. "So, are you, like, a spy?"

Kaitlyn laughs. I guess I do owe him an explanation. Plus, I can have a little fun with him.

I nod, keeping my expression solemn. "I used to be, yeah. I'm just trying to enjoy retirement, and my old boss won't leave me alone. Listen, you need to keep this between us, okay? No one's supposed to know I'm here."

He shakes his head enthusiastically. "Oh my God, no way, man! I won't say anything to anyone, I swear. Man, this is awesome!"

I smile. "You're a good kid, Yaz. Are you going to look after Miss Moss after I'm gone?"

He nods. "Yes, sir."

"Good man."

I look at Kaitlyn, who rolls her eyes at me. She turns to Yaz. "Say hi to your mom for me, okay?"

"I will."

He disappears down the hall. I watch him go, then turn to Kaitlyn. "Listen, I promise I'll come back to check in on you when all this is over, okay?"

She frowns. "What? You're going right now?"

I shrug. "Yeah. No sense in waiting. I have to finish this. I have to make them pay for what they did to Lily..."

"I know you do. I never thought I'd be accepting of what you do for a living, but I think I know *you* pretty well. Regardless of what's right or wrong—or legal—I know you need revenge on that Pierce guy for killing Lily. But... look, you're here now. At least let me change your bandages. Maybe get a drink and something to eat? They can't find you here, and they'll still be there tomorrow. You need to rest. You look like crap."

"Gee, thanks..."

Ah, damn it. She's right, isn't she?

I nod. "Okay. I'd appreciate that. Thanks."

"Come on. My apartment's upstairs."

I follow her up, and we take a left at the top. Hers is the first door on the left—number four. She opens the door and holds it for me. I step past her and inside. There's a small foyer with four doors around it, two ahead of me and one either side. There's an old-fashioned coat stand to the left of the door and a small table against the strip of wall between the two doors in front of me.

She shuts the door and puts the chain on, then moves past me. She points to the first door on the left. "That's the kitchen. Next to it is the living room." She turns her body slightly, so she's facing the other side. "Then we've got my bedroom and, finally, the bathroom. It's not much, but it's home."

I look around. "No, this place is nice. Modest. Fit for purpose... I like it."

She smiles at me and points to the living room. "Make yourself at home. I'll just grab the first aid kit."

I push the door open and step inside. It's a decent-sized room, dominated by a large, L-shape sofa in the middle of it. Mounted on the far wall is a big TV screen. On either side of it, large windows look out over a large, well-maintained communal garden. There's a bookshelf running along the left wall. I move over to it. She has a variety of classics on here—*Pride and Prejudice, The Complete Works of William Shakespeare*... even some *Sherlock Holmes*. Next to them are books about psychology and therapy, including some works by Carl Jung.

I hear her come in behind me. I turn and smile. "Just admiring your collection."

She shrugs. "I work long hours and don't really watch much television. Reading is how I shut my mind off from my job."

She walks over to me holding a box containing a roll of bandages, some scissors, Band-Aids, painkillers... everything a beaten-up old man needs. We sit down on the sofa, and she begins peeling my bandage away. I wince a little as she does.

"How's it looking, Doc?"

She screws her face up as she stares at it. "Like you need stitches. Like I keep telling you..."

"I know... I'll go to a hospital after I've dealt with The Order, all right?"

She leans back a little and stares at me.

Shit. I was a little off with her then, wasn't I?

"Ah, damn it. I'm sorry. I didn't mean to... I'm just—"

She holds her hand up. "You don't have to apologize. I

can't imagine what you're going through right now. I know you didn't mean to take anything out on me. I'm sorry for hassling you about it."

I go to speak, but I can't think of anything else to say. It's been a really long day, and as I sit here, I'm realizing I'm more tired than I thought. I just don't have the energy for all this anymore.

Kaitlyn patches my head up again. "We might as well take a look at your hand while we're here."

I hold out my cast, and she unfastens the straps securing it in place. She slides it off and starts gently unwrapping the bandages across my palm. I wince as she pulls the last of it away. There's a dark incision across my hand, neatly stitched together. Keeping my palm flat, I try to flex just my fingers and thumb.

"Ah! Shit..."

Kaitlyn shakes her head and pulls a face. "Yeah... maybe don't try clenching your fist just yet, eh?"

I smile but say nothing.

She rebandages my hand and wrist, like a coach would a boxer, wrapping it around multiple times, weaving it between and around each finger until it's thick and tight. She tapes it all down and slides the cast back in place. She fastens it and checks that the straps are as tight as they can be without cutting off the flow of blood.

I move my hand around, admiring her work. "Damn... thanks. This is great."

She smiles as she packs everything away. "Well, just don't get carried away, okay? I'm running out of medical supplies because of you." She stands. "I'm gonna grab a shower. I think there's a beer in the refrigerator. Help yourself, okay?"

I nod. "Thanks."

Kaitlyn leaves, and I sit back on the sofa and stare up at the ceiling.

So, now what?

I'm working on the assumption that Horizon's still in his fancy penthouse in Dubai. I'm figuring that, after Qatar and the fact that I didn't head for the airport, Pierce will have gone to see him. When my tracking device disappeared off their systems, they'll have started to panic, and it makes sense that they would assume I'll be coming after them. That means, knowing Horizon, the hotel is going to be locked up tight and surrounded by security. Heading there is stupid.

Which is exactly why I'm going to do it.

Given everything he's told me, I doubt The Order ends with him, but if I can do enough to get them off my back, I'll happily disappear, never to be heard of again. I've been thinking about it. The world thinks I'm dead. This could be my opportunity to truly start over and put Adrian Hell behind me. I know it didn't work out so well the last time I did that, but I've learned from my mistakes. See, last time, I tried to properly retire and be happy. For a while, it was fine, sure. But I was too visible. Too normal. Too happy.

This time would be different. I don't want to find peace. After all the shit I've done, whatever the reasons, I probably deserved that lethal injection for real. If I get the chance to start over again, I'll just stay under the radar. I'll be alone. I won't allow myself to get close to anyone. That way, no one will ever get hurt again because of me.

I sit up straight and let out a long, tired sigh. That's the plan. Do what I have to, so I can get free of The Order and then vanish forever. I'll crash on Kaitlyn's sofa tonight—this is actually pretty comfy—and head out at first light.

Right, I need a drink.

I walk out and into the kitchen. It's small and narrow but functional. The fridge is on the immediate left as you walk in, and a worktop runs along the left wall and across the end, beneath another window. There's a stove fitted in there and a sink and garbage disposal at the end.

I open the fridge door. I can't see any beers, but there's some orange juice in a plastic jug, so I find a glass and pour myself a glass. I take a sip and walk back out into the foyer.

I frown.

What's that?

I listen carefully. It's coming from the bathroom. I can hear the shower running, but it's something else. It's...

Kaitlyn.

She's crying. She sounds hysterical, but it's as if she's trying to mute the heavy sobbing as she stands under the water.

I feel a pang of guilt as I think about everything she's been through and everything she's done for me in the last forty-eight hours. She went from being my therapist to having her office destroyed, going on the run from a team of killers, and becoming a killer herself. She's just a normal person and doesn't deserve to be exposed to any of the shit I accept as being part of my everyday life.

Should I say something?

I don't know... I mean, I *should*. No sense in waiting until she feels she's dealt with it and moved on. Then I'll just be making her think about something she doesn't want to. But I can't exactly walk in there while she's in the shower...

I put my glass down on the small table and walk over to the door. I tap on it gently. "Kaitlyn... is everything all right?"

The sobbing stops. I hear her sniffing and taking some deep breaths. "Yeah, I'm fine."

The water stops a moment later. I step away from the

door. After a minute, she steps out with a towel wrapped around her, covering her chest and down to just below her knees. She's leaving wet footprints on the carpet. Her hair is wet, clinging to her shoulders. She looks completely different. I'm used to seeing her with her hair up, her glasses on, and simple make-up applied—ready for her day job. I haven't really noticed how run-down she's looked over the last two days because we've both been a little preoccupied. Now that she's standing in front of me, completely natural, she looks... different. She looks amazing if I'm honest.

Shit, I think I've been staring...

"I'm sorry. I didn't mean to intrude. I got up for a drink and... well, I heard you crying, and I just wanted to make sure you were okay."

She's hugging her chest, maybe feeling a little vulnerable and probably paranoid about her towel dropping. She smiles. "I'm fine, honestly. I just... I had a moment, and everything got to me. But I feel better after a good cry." She shrugs. "It's a chick thing."

I laugh. "Yeah, okay. Well, as I said, I'm here if you need to talk. Not many people can even comprehend the shit you've been through in the last couple of days, let alone take it in their stride."

"Thank you. But I'll be okay. How are you doing?"

"I'm all right. Tired, but I'll be fine. I think I'm gonna take off after Dubai. I don't know what's gonna happen, but if I get the chance to start over again, I'm going to find a little corner of the world somewhere and hide in it."

"That sounds... lonely."

I shrug. "It's for the best. I have a habit of endangering the lives of people I care for. You can attest to that. It's a consequence of the life I've led, and I can't change that. Best thing for me to do is stay out of people's way."

"So, are you saying you care for me?"

I scratch absently at the back of my head. I suddenly feel a little awkward. "Well, I mean, we've been through a lot together. I don't want to see you hurt, obviously. And you've lost so much because of me. I just..."

She takes a deep breath and steps closer to me. She looks up at me. She has blue eyes... I've never noticed that before. "Adrian, my job requires me to stay detached from my clients and not become personally involved. But that went out the window, literally, when my office was destroyed by... an RGP? Is that right?"

I smile. "RPG. It stands for rocket-propelled grenade."

"Ah, right. Well, one of those. From that moment on, my life was in your hands. And I was scared. I was angry that you had come into my life and turned it on its head. Then I realized it wasn't your fault. Not directly. It was... fate, I suppose. You needed me, and when I found myself exposed to this... this whole other world that you live in, I quickly realized I needed you too.

"I've been watching you. How you deal with things. How you think about things. Having already had some insight into your mind, watching you face the things we've faced—head on, without question or hesitation— our sessions made a lot more sense to me. I saw you, the real you, for the first time. I know you've done some terrible things. And I'm sure you've done much more that I don't know about, but... deep down, Adrian, when you strip away this exterior, this uniform of an assassin that you wear... you're a hero. You're... my hero."

She steps in closer, so her body's resting against mine. She steps up on her tiptoes and kisses me softly, tentatively, on the lips. I can smell her natural scent, mixed in with the fruity essence of her shampoo. I don't kiss her back. I remain upright and tense, scared out of my mind.

She moves away again and looks at me. Her mouth is slightly open, and she's breathing a little heavier.

Me too, actually.

"Look, Kaitlyn, I... Everything you said, it means a lot to me, honestly. But I can't open up to you if I'm involved with you. I know I won't be able to because I won't want to expose you to that side of me."

She shrugs. "You said you're leaving after you deal with The Order. It's unlikely we'll have another session."

Huh... fair point.

She turns and paces idly toward her bedroom door. "I don't know what it is. Maybe it's the adrenaline... maybe I'm not thinking straight, trying to deal with trauma I don't understand. I just know that..." She turns back around and stares at me. I see a fire in her eyes that I haven't seen all that often in anyone. "I want you."

She moves her hands and allows her towel to drop to the floor, revealing her still-wet body.

Holy crap...

Her work clothes really didn't do her any justice. She has a pretty well-defined frame. Her stomach is flat and toned. Her breasts are modest and firm. Her hips are narrow, and her legs are long and shapely.

Goddamn. What do I do now? I mean, I—

She walks back over to me, puts both hands on the bottom of my T-shirt, and starts to pull it up over my head.

I don't think there's anything I can do to change what's about to happen.

I lift my arms, and she peels it up and over my head, discarding it on the floor. She takes my hand and leads me into the bedroom. She doesn't turn on the light, so I have no idea what the room looks like. We stand by the edge of the bed, and she turns to face me again. She snakes both hands around my neck, pulls my head down, and kisses me with much more passion and ferocity than before.

All doubts and fears quickly leave me. I wrap my left arm around her waist, and she jumps up, wrapping her legs around me. I hold her in front of me as we lose ourselves in the moment. We put all the shit we've been through in the last two days behind us. We forget the world... forget everything. Right now, it's just her and me.

I walk around the bed and lay her gently down on it.

I'm suddenly not feeling all that tired...

27

I feel consciousness washing lazily over me. The bright morning sun shines in through the vertical blinds and hits my face. I roll onto my back and let out a long, slow breath, allowing myself to embrace just how relaxed I feel right now.

What a night. I feel like I've slept for days.

Kaitlyn and I... we, ah... we had a nice evening together. I barely felt all the cuts on my back as she...

Y'know what? Never mind.

I look to my left.

I'm alone.

She must be awake already, making coffee or breakfast. That would be nice. I smile to myself for a moment, but it soon fades. I get flashbacks of Devil's Spring... of Tori making me coffee and breakfast... of me lying in bed, happy...

I put my hand on my face and rub my eyes.

Leave it, Adrian. Don't ruin something great by thinking too much.

I swing my legs out of bed and step into my shorts. I stand tall and stretch. Man, even my usual aches and pains aren't bothering me today. Maybe I should get...

I smile to myself and look down at my tattoo.

WWJD.

What would Josh do?

Josh would say there's no maybes about it. I should *definitely* get laid more often!

I pad out of the room and into the kitchen. She's not here. There's no sign of any coffee or breakfast, either. I frown and walk into the living room. She's not here, either.

"Kaitlyn, are you all right?"

I feel myself starting to worry. My mind instantly defaults to the paranoia I've been trained to live with. But I stop myself, take a deep breath... and another... and relax. That's something Kaitlyn taught me. A technique for dealing with the onset of my spider sense. Or what she initially referred to as an anxiety attack, although that was before she knew the real me. But even so, the technique helps. Just stopping for a few seconds and taking a breath helps me calm down and see what's really happening, not what my anxious mind is telling me.

I take another breath...

She's probably just gone out to get some breakfast. That's all. Bottom line is that she's safe now. I need to stop thinking she's not just because I'm here. Neither of us is on The Order's radar anymore. I have time to figure out how to deal with them.

I wander into the bathroom and stare into the mirror. I run my hand up and down my throat, assessing how desperately I need a shave. Yeah, it'll be fine for another day. Maybe two.

I lean over the basin and splash some cold water on my face to help wake me up. I pause for a moment, staring absently at nothing in particular as the water drips off me.

Wait.

Something's caught my eye. I must have registered it subconsciously at first because I wasn't immediately aware of it, but it must be important because it's been fast-tracked to my conscious brain.

Kaitlyn would be so proud of me.

There's a small bruise on my right arm, in the crook near the elbow. It's no larger than a dime, with a tiny red dot in the middle.

I frown and examine it more closely.

Yeah... that's a puncture wound. I've been injected with something. Recently.

All the deep breaths in the world aren't going to stop my spider sense now.

"Kaitlyn?"

I've missed something. I don't know what's happened, but I know she's not out getting breakfast. I've had a needle stuck in my arm at some point between me and Kaitlyn... y'know... and me waking up just now. Which means...

"Oh, fuck!"

I dash back into the bedroom and look around. I don't see anything.

Goddammit! Come on, Adrian...

I close my eyes, take one deep breath, and subdue the mixture of panic and anger that I'm feeling right now. I open my eyes again. This time, I look around the room properly, calmly, like I've been trained to.

Her underwear drawer, just inside the door on the right,

is slightly open. It wasn't last night. I open the closet next to it. A hanger falls out. It mustn't have been put on the rail properly. That means she got dressed quickly, like she was in a hurry.

I look at the bed. The cover is messed up on her side, hanging off one edge more than the other. It doesn't look natural, like when it's moved around during the throes of passion or sleep. It's more like she was dragged out of bed by her feet, and she was holding onto the duvet in an effort to resist.

Sonofabitch. They've taken her.

I throw my T-shirt on and step into my shoes. No sign of my gun. I definitely left it on the bedside table last night. I screw my face up with frustration.

Shit.

I quickly walk out into the small foyer and look at the front door. The chain is still in the latch, but it's been cut, presumably through the narrow gap between the door and the frame. I move over to inspect it. The edges are smooth. It's a pretty thick metal chain, so maybe some kind of laser cutting tool was used. That's some high-end tech.

Double shit.

I hear a beep in my pocket.

Huh?

I take out my cell phone. There's a message from Horizon. I open it.

It doesn't have to be like this, Adrian. We should meet to discuss your future. I'm in my suite when you're ready to talk. No rush...

Triple shit!

Goddamn... fucking... sonofa... asshole... bastard!

I don't hesitate. Hell, I don't even *think*. I yank open the door and run out, down the hall and down the stairs. At the bottom, I head straight for the entrance but skid to a halt as I reach the door.

I've just had a thought. A really unpleasant thought.

If they found me and Kaitlyn here, maybe they...

I glance over my shoulder, down the hall, to where Yaz disappeared last night.

Oh, please don't tell me...

I spin around and run along the hall. I turn right at the end. There are two apartments down here. I'm assuming Yaz lives in the one on the right because the door's standing open, and there's a pool of blood slowly expanding out into the hall.

"No... no... no..."

I step toward the doorway cautiously. I press myself against the wall and peer inside.

"Oh, fuck me..."

There's a woman lying in the middle of the floor, face-down, surrounded by blood. I'm guessing that's Yaz's mom.

I move in, careful not to step in anything and leave a print. "Yaz? It's Adrian. Are you in here?"

Nothing.

Don't tell me they've taken him too.

Bastards.

I sprint back down the hall, out the main entrance, and onto the street. The Suburban's still parked out front, seemingly untouched. I look inside. The key's in the ignition. I check the trunk.

Empty.

All the weapons are gone.

I slam my hand on the roof.

"Fuck!"

That's it.

I climb in and start the engine. Thankfully, it's an automatic. It'll be hard enough driving with one hand all the way to Dubai, without having to try working a stick too.

I step on the gas, spin it around, and speed away, leaving tire marks on the road behind me.

I have no idea what I'm going to do when I get there, but one thing I know for sure... this ends today.

10:10 AST

I'm doing sixty along the stretch of road that takes you out over the water and onto the island home of the Burj Al Arab Hotel. I circle around the huge water feature and slam on the brakes, screeching to a halt outside the entrance. I grip the wheel tightly in my hand. I've worked myself up into such a fury on the ride here, I can barely see straight now that I've arrived.

I do a quick mental assessment. My back's fine. Kaitlyn removed all the Band-Aids last night, and despite the sheer number of lacerations I sustained, they were mostly superficial and have already begun to heal.

I glance down at my right hand. After the amazing job Kaitlyn did changing the bandages and tightening the cast last night, my hand is as protected as it's ever going to be. It's still mostly useless—I have no grip and no strength—but I guess I can use the cast as a weapon if I need to. It'll probably hurt like hell, but without a gun, I'll take what I can get.

I pull the sun visor down and slide back the cover on the mirror. The little light flicks on automatically, and I examine my head wound. Again, Kaitlyn did a good job of taping me up, and a lot of the bleeding has stopped now. But that doesn't take away from how bad the cut was to begin with, and without stitches, the slightest knock is going to open it up again, which I could really do without.

So, I'm far from a hundred percent, but I could be worse, I guess. I'm not armed, but I'm really pissed off, and with one good hand and two good legs, I'm three times the fighter most men are—armed or otherwise.

Don't forget you've got me, you crazy bastard!

Oh, yeah... and my Inner Satan is going to be putting in a shift today. I can promise you that.

I step out of the car and look up to the heavens, squinting against the glare of the scorching sun. I stare at the helipad jutting out from the roof of the hotel. Damn... that's a whole lot of real estate standing between me and Horizon.

I grind my teeth, clenching my jaw muscles as I feel the rage building inside me. Violence seethes through my veins. I don't care how many floors there are... how many men... how many guns... I'll burn this whole fucking place to the ground if I have to. I'm going to—

"Adrian Hell?"

Huh?

I lower my gaze and see four men standing maybe ten feet from me, forming a neat line in front of the extravagantly decorated glass doors. They're all wearing fitted white shirts, suit pants, and shoulder holsters. They're all big guys, with tanned complexions and various styles of facial hair. Their weapons aren't drawn. They're standing with their hands clasped in front of them.

The guy second from the left steps forward. "Horizon's been expecting you. Come with us, and we'll take you to him. There's no need to cause a scene."

I move my left leg back slightly, dropping into a loose

southpaw stance. I bring my right hand up, ready to use it as a weapon if I need to.

The guy holds a hand up. "The Order has no desire for any further conflict. Don't make this hard on yourself."

I shrug. "If they didn't want more conflict, they shouldn't have killed my friend. Or kidnapped my... Kaitlyn."

"Look, I don't know about all that, all right? Nor do I care about it. I'm not one of their assets. I work for Pierce. My only job right now is to take you to see the man upstairs. If you wanna make that a problem, fine. They just said you have to be alive... not conscious."

He moves his hand to rest on the butt of his gun.

I raise an eyebrow.

Cocky little prick, isn't he?

Ah, well. Fuck him.

I breathe in heavily, embracing the flow of adrenaline, and glare at each of these guys in turn. I'm going to take them out, steal their guns, walk in through the front door, and kill anyone who gets in my way. Then I'm going to—

Adrian, listen to the man, all right? I want to go in there and rip everyone's head off just as much as you do, but this guy's giving you a free pass right to the big man's door. Take the easy option, save your strength, and you avoid having to fight hundreds of guys one-handed and unarmed. I'm just saying...

I sigh.

It's coming to something when I'm so angry, even the voice in my head that represents all of my uncontrollable rage and fury starts making more sense than I do.

Fine. You win.

I nod to the guy. "All right, ass-wipe. Lead the way."

I walk toward them, push through the line, and walk casually through the doors.

Holy crap!

This place is incredible!

The entrance is spacious, and the décor is lavish beyond words. Just to the right, there's a line of men and women, dressed formally and ready to offer me a hot towel... some hand oil, I think... some tea... chocolate... fruit...

Jesus.

Behind them is the front desk. There are two people standing behind it, ready to serve. The whole thing looks as if it's made out of gold. To be fair, knowing this place, it probably is!

The men quickly follow me inside and move to surround me, forming a loose square. We walk across the lobby and past a huge, star-shaped fountain, which is periodically shooting jets of water into the air. We head over to the elevators. The whole wall looks like a weird, golden honeycomb, with marble pillars running up between the plethora of windows.

One of the guys in front of me steps forward and pushes the button. A moment later, the doors slide open with a quiet hiss. Inside is a hotel employee dressed in a red velvet tunic with a gold trim and a matching hat. He looks young and fresh-faced, and he can't be older than twenty. He smiles and nods eagerly to us.

The two guys in front of me drag him out unceremoniously, then walk inside the elevator. I feel a hand on my shoulder, urging me forward. I stand my ground, turn my head slightly to look at the hand, then more to address the guy behind me. "Move it, or I'll break it."

He shakes his head. "Whatever."

He moves it.

I step inside slowly. I'm not thrilled about being in an enclosed space with these guys, but I don't really have much choice. They follow me in and press the button. Another moment passes, then the doors glide shut. The elevator surges gently, and we begin our climb.

I glance casually around, noting the positioning of each guy.

"So, are we going straight to see your boss? Or is this, like, the first of three elevators we need to take?"

"What's it to you?" replies the guy in front of me on the right.

I shrug. "I'm just not crazy about heights. I like to know how far off the ground I am, y'know..."

Silence.

"Yeah, this takes us straight to his suite."

"Ah, excellent."

I glance at the console of buttons on the left side. We've got thirty floors left to climb. Twenty-nine... Twenty-eight...

I don't like the fact that I'm surrounded before I even get up there. I know that Horizon's suite is well protected. I need the freedom to fight, should things go south up there, and I can't do that with these four asshats standing around me.

I look around the carriage idly. It's pretty spacious for an elevator. The doors are lined on the inside with a red velvet padding, like a cushion. There's a gold handrail on each of the other three sides, roughly level with my hips. Every side is decorated the same way, with a mirror above the handrail and the same padding as the doors below it.

Like on the way in, I'm standing in the middle, with a guy in each corner. All guns are still holstered.

Amateurs.

I close my eyes for a moment, planning each move in my head, seeing what works and what doesn't. I need to hit Bottom Left and Bottom Right first. They can grab me with minimal effort, so they're more dangerous in this situation. Top Left and

Top Right need to think, turn, and then act, which takes valuable seconds. I'll be ready for them by the time they're looking, so whatever they're thinking of will be ineffective.

I open my eyes again, feeling a renewed focus. I take another look at the console.

Twenty-two... Twenty-one...

All right. Showtime.

Time slows down as my Inner Satan gets to work. He knows what he needs to do.

I take a small step back and swing my right arm clockwise, hard and fast. No one's expecting anything, and my cast makes clean contact with Bottom Right's face. The second I see him start to drop, I jump backward, elbow first, and connect with Bottom Left's jaw. I force my body into him, pinning him to the side, stunned. I quickly grab the rail on my left, lean back harder against the guy, and whip my right leg up, like I'm kicking a field goal. I time it perfectly. Just as Top Left's turning around, my foot buries itself into his balls. I watch for a split-second as his eyes bulge from the impact.

I spin around, grab Bottom Left's collar, and fling him across the carriage, turning as I do for extra momentum. I see him collide with Top Right, who was reaching for his gun. I look over at Bottom Right, who's sitting on the floor with a vacant expression. I take one step toward him and thrust my knee into his left temple. He was just the right height. His head slams against the side of the elevator, and I see his eyes roll back in his head.

He's done.

I turn to look at Top Left. He's still upright but bent over, clutching his balls. Poor guy. No matter what the situation, I always feel a sliver of remorse after delivering a good kick to the nuts. Unfortunately, his day's not about to get any better...

I step to meet him and swing my cast down at his head. It arcs with refined accuracy and hits him on his jaw. He slumps sideways, landing heavily on the floor.

The last two guys are still fumbling against each other, stunned by the attack. Bottom Left still has his back to me. I snake my left arm around his throat and squeeze as I drag him away from the corner. I move him out to the left slightly, freeing up just enough space for me to launch another kick. This one catches Top Right in his gut. He doubles over as the wind is knocked out of him, and I throw another kick, meeting his head with my foot. It connects with his face, and I hear the squelch as the impact crushes the cartilage in his nose.

He's done.

I refocus on Bottom Left. He's struggling against my grip, but he doesn't stand a chance. I squeeze tighter and move my right hand behind his head. I grab the crook of my elbow with my left hand and push forward as hard as I can on the base of his skull. I push my chest into him and count.

One...

Two...

I feel him sag unconsciously against me. I let go of the chokehold, and he falls to the floor.

I'm breathing heavily. I feel like my heart's about to break through my ribcage. I look at the console.

Six... Five... Four...

Not bad.

I reach down and take the gun from the nearest body. It's another P226 look-a-like. Full mag—I can tell by the weight.

Two... One...

I stand in the middle of the carriage and aim the gun at the doors.

DING!

The doors slide smoothly open.

Oh.

There's a semicircle of... eight men, armed with either assault rifles or shotguns, all aiming them right at me.

I stare into the eyes of each and every one of them. No one speaks. Their aim doesn't falter for a second. There's no hesitation. No doubt. If I so much as sneeze, they'll shoot me.

Shit.

I lower my gun and nod a curt greeting. "Hey, fellas..."

28

One of the guys standing in the middle steps forward and gestures to my gun with the barrel of his. "Drop it, asshole."

I do. Not as if I have much choice, is it?

I hold my hands out to the sides. "Am I that predictable?"

The guy doesn't say anything. He just points at something behind me. I look over my shoulder. In the top corner of the carriage is a security camera.

I look back at him. "Sneaky bastards... I didn't see that. Good job I wasn't trying to be discreet, eh?"

He smiles humorlessly. "Come on... nice and easy. Horizon's waiting for you."

I step over the bodies and out of the elevator. The group quickly moves to surround me, revealing the hallway ahead of me. I recognize it from when I was here a couple of days ago. Nothing's changed. We walk halfway along and stop outside the door to Horizon's suite.

One of the guys knocks on it, then opens it without waiting for a response. He gestures me inside. I take a deep breath and step over the threshold, into the belly of the beast. I don't know what to expect or what's going to happen, but I do know, however this plays out, I'm done with The Order.

I look around the room. It's pretty much as I remember it, except, thankfully, Horizon's not naked in a hot tub this time. He's sitting calmly on one of the sofas in front of me. He's wearing his usual white suit, and he's sipping what I assume is some kind of tea from a cup, while holding a matching saucer delicately beneath it.

He nods courteously as I walk into the room. "Hello, Adrian."

I wave dismissively. "Whatever. Where is she?"

He frowns. "Where's who?"

I roll my eyes. "Don't bullshit me, Colonel Sanders."

He sets the cup and saucer down on the small table beside him. He stands, straightens his suit, and walks toward me. "Oh, you mean Kaitlyn? Your... therapist? I must say, in all my years, I've never known an asset to seek therapy before."

I shrug. "Yeah, well, in all my years, I've never given less of a fuck about what someone thinks. Where is she?"

He holds my gaze for a moment, then half-turns and glances over his shoulder, toward his bedroom door at the far end of the suite. "Bring them out, Mr. Pierce."

I look over as the door opens. Kaitlyn and Yaz are ushered out by Pierce, who's walking casually behind them, holding a pistol.

I take a step toward them. "Kaitlyn... kid... are you both okay?"

They each nod nervously.

I look at Horizon. "Let them go, you piece of shit. It's me you're pissed at. Deal with *me*."

He strokes the loose, mottled skin around his throat, then gestures to the sofa. "Take a seat."

I shake my head. "Not until you let them go."

His expression hardens, and his eyes narrow. "They won't be going anywhere until you and I have had a nice little chat. So, sit... down."

He sits down farther along from where he was before. He leans back, crosses his legs, and waits.

I glance over at Kaitlyn. She looks terrified, but she doesn't seem hurt, which is the important thing. Same with the kid. I move over to the sofa and sit beside him. I lean forward and rest my arms on my knees. "Okay, let's talk."

Horizon smiles. "Thank you. Now, first of all, I want to clear something up. I'm not angry with you. I'm disappointed, sure. You have a lot of potential and could've one day played an important role within The Order. But... I underestimated how difficult you would find letting go of your old life and your old ways. I knew it would be a problem with you from the beginning, and it's my mistake for giving you too much credit."

I sigh. "Look, I've got no problem with the idea of leaving my old life behind me. Yeah, it's definitely been hard, but there was little left of my old life anyway. The issue I've had is that you expect me to risk my life to kill people for you, without any reason, and I won't work like that."

He nods. "Okay. Tell me why. Explain to me what your big problem is with the way I run my assets."

"I'm incredibly good at what I do, but I won't kill someone if I don't believe they have it coming."

"And who are you to decide what someone's life is

worth, Adrian? What makes your moral compass such an authority on whether someone should live or die?"

"I could ask you the same thing."

He smiles like he feels bad for me all of a sudden. "Adrian, I'm far better informed to make such decisions than you will ever be. The Order of Sabbah has existed for centuries and has systems and infrastructures in place that help us see when people's actions are not suited to the greater good of our society. I am Horizon. It's not a name. It's a title, and I am not the only person to have it bestowed upon them. The title is earned by proving to a committee of superiors that you have the skills to plan ahead, to accurately predict the outcome of situations other people aren't even aware of yet. Once you can do that, you can see where someone's path is leading them. If that path shows they're working toward a goal in direct conflict with our own, they're eliminated."

I raise an eyebrow. "Okay, hold up. So, you're not the only *Horizon*? There are more people out there with the same stupid-ass name?"

He nods. "There are a number of us, yes. Each are charged with directing a different division of The Order."

"So, I was recruited to one... what? One small part of a larger organization?"

He nods again.

"Jeez... okay. This is good. We're sharing. So, these goals you keep mentioning—whose goals are they, exactly? And what makes them so damn important?"

Horizon stands and begins pacing idly back and forth in front of me. "Our committee is made up of many influential people around the world. High-ranking members of governments, board members of large companies, police officers... even pilots. Our reach encompasses the globe, and between us, we have a good idea about what's best for people. And if something threatens that, we use our assets to rectify things."

I rub my eyes. All this time, I've been after some kind of straight answer, and he's said nothing. Now I can't shut him up! This is information overload, and I don't even know if I believe it. I mean, I know The Order's big, but... could they really be so well established in the world?

"Okay, if all that's true—and I'm not saying I completely believe it is—then what about Cunningham? Surely, his delusional plan for world domination didn't conform to your ideal path for humanity. Where were you when he was blowing up half the goddamn planet?"

Horizon laughs. "We were monitoring the situation, but we believed you had it handled."

I shake my head with disbelief. "*That I had it...* Are you fucking kidding me? I sat there and watched 4/17 happen! How did *that* fit in with your grand plans?"

"Oh, it didn't. That was a tragedy, obviously. But... we knew that in the aftermath, the world would adjust and start us all on a new path—one that we felt was actually more beneficial than our original objective. There's always light after the dark, Adrian."

I stand and take a step toward him, stretching to my full width and height. I look him right in the eye. "You're just as fucking twisted as Cunningham was. And what about Lily? Huh? Was killing her a part of your big picture?"

Horizon, to his credit, doesn't back down. He doesn't even flinch. He's either mighty brave or mighty stupid. He just stands his ground and stares right back at me with his dark, unblinking eyes.

"No. That was necessary, albeit regrettable. She was one of my most capable assets. But she made a mistake and she lied to me. I can't have that. I need to be able to trust our assets as much as I expect them to put their trust in me. Involving you in her faux pas was unfortunate..."

"No fucking shit, it was unfortunate! Why play all those games? Why make me believe she was after me? If you were so disappointed, if you wanted her gone, why not just pull your little trigger and take her head off? Why make us both suffer?"

He chuckles. "You think that was suffering? Adrian... that was an *education*. That was for your benefit. Her fate was already sealed, but you... you still had a chance to redeem yourself. I've given you every opportunity to commit to our cause, but nothing was working. I didn't want to lose someone of your ability, and I knew all it needed was the right push. I've been trying to find the best way to convince you that working for us is a positive thing for you."

"Tricking me into killing Lily was meant to convince me you guys are actually all right? Are you being serious?"

He smiles and shakes his head. "No, Adrian. The situation with Lily was a lesson, designed to show you that fucking with me isn't an option. I am *better* than you. I am your superior in every sense of the goddamn word, and you *will* conform, or you will die!"

I clench my fist repeatedly. My jaw's aching from tensing it this hard. I'm glaring at him, angry beyond words.

He paces away from me. "But... that didn't work either, so I simply had her eliminated. You should be grateful. I asked Mr. Pierce to shoot her, so she didn't suffer. Had I activated her tracking device, the pain she felt before her head was removed would have been quite excruciating. A sensation I believe you're familiar with?"

"Yeah, you're all heart... you sonofabitch."

He turns and looks at me, clasping his hands behind

him. "Anyway, enough about the past. Let's look at how we move forward."

I shake my head. "That's easy. We don't. It's great that you finally told me how you work, but it doesn't change a damn thing. I'm done. I'm out. If you have a problem with that, we settle it now." I point behind me to Kaitlyn and Yaz. "But you leave them out of it. Understand?"

He chuckles again, a smug little giggle to himself. Prick.

"Adrian, I'm... I'm sorry. I think you misunderstand me. I relented and explained our organization's workings as a gesture. To extend the olive branch, as it were, and to make you feel more comfortable with your life in The Order. I will admit, despite the shortcomings with your attitude, you are still one of the best operatives we have. As I've explained, I have invested considerable amounts of time and money to both bring you in and to try convincing you this is a good thing. But I see now that trying to explain how this benefits you simply isn't working, so let me put it another way. There is no getting out. I wanted to make your time with us more bearable for you, but you ultimately don't have a choice. You will do what we ask of you whether you like it or not, or you... and the people you care for... will suffer the consequences."

Shit.

He's moved far enough away from me that I'll never reach him before Pierce gets a shot off. Similarly, I'll never reach Pierce in time either. I don't actually have any moves. I don't know what to do.

Screw it.

I flip Horizon the finger. "Fuck you, Colonel Sanders. I'm leaving, and I'm taking those two with me. Anyone tries to stop me, I'll beat them to death."

He sighs. "Very well... have it your way."

He takes out a remote detonator, identical to the one Pierce had the other day.

It's my turn to smile. I can't help it. Arrogant bastard thinks he still controls me. He's in for a real—

"Argh!"

I clamp my hands to my head and drop to my knees.

"Fuck!"

Oh my God!

Ah!

I fall on my side, still clutching my head. It feels like someone's taking a blowtorch to the back of my eyes!

I hear Kaitlyn scream, but I can't do anything about it.

I feel like my head's about to—

It's stopped.

What... the... hell?

I roll onto my back and spread my arms out. There's a slight ringing in my ears, and I have a headache like you wouldn't believe. I need to catch my breath...

...

...

...

Oh, man, that sucked.

I don't understand. How did he activate the device?

I push myself up onto one knee, still breathing hard. "How... how did you..."

Horizon smiles. "How did I what? Activate your device after you blocked the signal?"

Shit.

Of course, he knows...

He walks over and crouches just in front of me. "There is nothing you do that The Order doesn't know about. We were monitoring the signal when your little friend here tried to hack it. We reversed his tampering the second he disconnected. You were never safe, Adrian, and I'd like to think that *now*... we're on the same page. That we... understand one another." He stands. "Now get up."

Fuck.

I'm trapped. There's no way of removing or disabling the device, which means they know where I am at all times, and they can kill me whenever they want.

I slowly get to my feet.

"So, can we finally put all this silliness behind us? Do you accept the fact that you belong to The Order?"

I stare at the floor for a moment, angry at myself for being so naïve all this time. I'm not giving him the satisfaction of hearing me say it.

I look at him and nod.

"Good. And just for my own peace of mind, are we going to have any more problems with the level of detail I provide you with your contracts?"

I sigh and shake my head.

He smiles. "Excellent. I'm glad we finally got all this straightened out. I'm excited about finally seeing you put to good use for us. But... there is one more thing..."

He looks at Pierce and gives him an almost imperceptible nod.

I turn and see Pierce take out another gun from behind his back. He puts one against the back of Yaz's head and one against the back of Kaitlyn's. "Both of you, on your knees."

They both let out a terrified whimper as they kneel down. Kaitlyn's eyes are filling with tears. Yaz looks like he's just woken up from a bad dream, and he's trying to process if it was real.

I instinctively take a step toward Pierce. "No!"

"Ah, ah..." says Horizon.

It takes every ounce of willpower and intelligence to stop

myself, but I do. I look over my shoulder at him. He's staring at me, holding the detonator in his hand.

He shakes his head. "Don't ruin our new working relationship so soon, Adrian."

Goddammit!

I take a step back and turn to face Horizon. "What do you want?"

"Even though we're embarking on a new chapter of your life in The Order, I can't let your previous misdemeanors go unpunished."

"Then punish *me*! Don't hurt innocent people to make another sick point."

"Adrian, you have to understand the position I'm in. I run my division of The Order well. I consider myself hard but fair. If any of my assets had done half of what you have, they would be dead. I've granted you an audience. I've given you answers you're not entitled to, and I'm letting you live. What more do you want from me? You have to be punished. An example still needs to be made."

I look over at Kaitlyn and Yaz. "It's going to be okay. Do you hear me? I'm going to get you out of this, I promise."

Horizon moves next to me, his hands casually in his pockets. "I wouldn't make promises I can't keep if I were you." He gestures to them both with his head. "You have to decide, right now, which one of them will live and which one will die. If you refuse to make that decision, Mr. Pierce will shoot both of them." He pats my shoulder. "I'll give you a moment."

Oh my God...

29

I feel numb. I feel hollow, like I'm not in my own body... like I'm looking on, watching an episode of someone else's twisted life. I stare blankly at Kaitlyn and Yaz. I see the fear in their eyes.

I don't know what to do.

I can't choose... I can't fight back. But I can't say nothing because I'll lose them both.

I feel myself defaulting to my instincts. When I see no reason or clear answer, I get angry. I look over at Horizon. "You sick bastard!"

He looks at me impassively. "You need to accept the fact that there's nothing you can do, Adrian. You make the choice, and whoever lives, I promise they will be left in peace. The Order won't go near them as long as you don't, either. We are your life. Nothing else. That's how this works."

I turn back to them. "I'm... I'm sorry. Both of you. I am.

I'm sorry I got either of you caught up in this shit, and I'm sorry I can't get you out of it. But I can't choose. I don't know how..."

Kaitlyn sniffs back her tears and clears her throat. "Adrian, look at me."

I do. It's hard looking into her eyes, but I do.

She smiles. "It's gonna be okay, but you need to listen to me. I want you to remember everything we've talked about. It's not... it's not your job to protect everyone. And the guilt you carry around with you is unnecessary. 4/17 didn't happen because of something you did or didn't do. Tori dying wasn't your fault. Right now, whatever happens, you can't blame yourself. All you've ever done is what you believed to be right. Even when you worked as an assassin. This isn't your fault. I don't want to die. I'm *terrified*. But I have to. We all know it. And I want you to promise me you won't punish yourself for this when I'm gone."

I feel my jaw hanging loose with disbelief. I'm in awe of the strength she's showing. I hate myself for not having the courage she does right now. I can't find the words...

"Adrian, you promise me! Do you hear me? You promise me, right now!"

I slowly start to nod my head. "I... I... I prom—"

"Kill me."

Huh? What?

All eyes in the room turn to Yaz. He's standing up, staring at Horizon. His jaw is set, though his arms and legs are shaking. His face is covered in a thin film of sweat. "Kill me. I c-can't let you hurt Miss Moss. You've... you've already killed my mom... so k-kill me."

I feel myself rushing back into the moment. My instincts and training kick in again. I'm in Horizon's suite. I know what needs to be done. I take a step forward. "Yaz, no. Don't be stupid. Just sit—"

BANG!

The gunshot startles me. I stare, stunned silent and horrified, as Yaz's body falls slowly forward to the floor. The exit wound has removed most of his forehead. He thuds against the thick carpet. I hear Kaitlyn's screams, but they sound distant. I'm not zoning out again. I'm not feeling lost. I'm feeling... really... really... angry. The reason she sounds distant is because I'm stripping away everything I don't need —every sight, every sound, every emotion—so that my mind is focused on one single thing.

Pierce.

I clench my fist.

I set my jaw.

Adrian, I got this. This piece of shit is—

No.

I don't need my Inner Satan. This asshole is mine.

"You sonofa*bitch*!"

I run toward Pierce, accelerating without warning. I side-step Kaitlyn without breaking stride and launch myself at him, bringing my cast up and down, like a club. He doesn't have time to react. I hit him across the face as I crash into him, and we both fall to the floor. His guns fly off in different directions.

He pushes me off him and scrambles to his feet, but I'm right back on him before he gets upright. I jab him in his side, under the arm where the ribcage is thin. The bones are easier to break there. I don't get enough power behind the punch, but it's enough to stop him.

I launch my cast again, aiming for his throat.

Shit!

He catches it in both hands and—

Uh!

—throws a short elbow at my face. He hits me below my right eye, and I stagger back.

He stands up straight and lifts his hands into an orthodox fighting stance.

I can't let him get comfortable. I can't give him time to prepare and start fighting *his* fight. I'm not strong enough. I need to stop him from building any momentum.

"No!"

I lunge forward, dropping my head at the last second and burying my shoulder into his gut. I force him backward and use my legs to lift him as much as I can.

It's not much but...

...

...

I roll him over the back of one of the sofas and allow my momentum to carry me over with him. I land heavily on his chest. He bounces back to his feet almost immediately and grabs a vase from the nearby table. He swings it and—

Uh!

Ah!

"Fuck!"

I drop to one knee as he smashes it over my head. I feel an instant warmth pulsing over my face. I'm guessing he's just reopened my head wound. Great...

I stand to meet him as he marches over, hands high, ready to swing. I bend my arms to cover and manage to deflect his first few shots.

Ah!

He tagged me in the ribs.

Uh!

And again. Shit!

I see a big right coming for my head. I try to get my hand to it and—

...

...

...

What the hell?

I'm lying on the floor between the two sofas, facing the door. He must have hit me and knocked me out. I'm guessing my head hitting the floor woke me up again.

I shake away the cobwebs and look over to where I last remember being. Pierce is striding toward me. Horizon has stepped away to the right and is standing over by the hot tub, watching intently. Kaitlyn's standing over by the Ganesha statue, crying, holding her hands to her mouth. I need to get—

Whoa!

Pierce hoists me to my feet with a handful of my T-shirt and winds up another shot. We're too close for him to get any real power behind it, thankfully. I duck under it as he swings, which sends him off-balance. I lash out with my foot and kick the side of his leg as he moves away from me. He stumbles, buying me some time.

I move toward one of the guns and manage three steps before I hear him behind me. I glance over my shoulder and see him running for me, albeit it with a slight limp in his step from the kick.

I'm standing only a couple of feet away from the small table Horizon rested his drink on earlier.

That'll do.

I reach over, grab it with my good hand, and then swing it around like I'm throwing the hammer in the Olympics. Despite being thin, the mahogany table's sturdy. It smashes over Pierce's arm and shoulder, knocking him off-balance again.

I take another step toward the gun, but I feel him grab my ankle, pulling my leg out from under me. As I start to fall face-first, I put my left hand out and turn, landing heavily on my arm. I allow my own momentum to carry me and roll onto my back, over again, and eventually back to my feet.

I see the gun in my peripheral vision. I lean down, grab it, then stand and spin around to face Pierce.

Shit.

He's standing, aiming his other gun at me.

Neither of us move an inch. We're both breathing hard. I can feel the blood trickling down my face. He has blood flowing freely down his arm, presumably from the table breaking over it.

Stalemate.

"Okay, that's enough." Horizon steps between us. "Mr. Pierce, lower your weapon."

He does, albeit reluctantly.

Horizon then turns to me. "You too, Adrian."

I shake my head. "Not until I've put a bullet in that bastard!"

He sighs and reaches into his pocket.

I watch his hand disappear.

Oh, sh—

"Argh!"

I drop the gun and desperately clutch at my head as he activates the device again. I sink to my knees and grit my teeth, trying to stifle a scream of agony.

Oh... my... God!

It stops.

I'm panting. The pain left in my head by that is

spreading like wildfire. It's like a million migraines all at once.

Horizon tuts. "It's like training an animal. You'll learn eventually." He looks at Pierce. "Take Miss Moss home. See that she's compensated for the loss of her business."

Pierce walks over to her and grabs her arm. She struggles at first, but it doesn't get her anywhere. He frog-marches her to the door. They pause for a moment, and she looks over at me. I see sadness in her eyes.

Horizon walks in front of her, blocking her view of me. "Oh, and Miss Moss... if you attempt to make any contact with my asset from this moment on, you will be killed without any further warning. Do you understand?"

"Y-yes."

He steps aside, and I watch as she's ushered out of the suite. The door slams shut behind them.

I slowly get to my feet. I haven't felt this broken in a long time. Mentally or physically.

Horizon is over by the hot tub again. He looks back at me. "You should freshen up. You look like shit." He points to his bedroom. "Use my shower. I'll have fresh clothes waiting for you."

I don't say anything. I don't have the energy to antagonize him further. I turn and stagger over to his bedroom. As I walk past the windows, I glance outside. The bay surrounding the island glistens below me in the sun. The water is a deep blue and crystal clear, even from up here. Beyond that, the city of Abu Dhabi bustles away, oblivious to the shit I've just gone through.

Lucky bastards.

11:29 AST

. . .

I'm standing under the showerhead, watching as a steady flow of pale, watered-down blood swirls around my feet, then vanishes down the drain. There isn't much that doesn't hurt right now. I have a small swelling under my eye from Pierce's elbow. My head wound reopened, so that's stinging like a bitch under the hot water. My hand's throbbing too. I shouldn't have used the cast as a weapon.

But the physical damage I can deal with. It's what's running through my head that I'm struggling to handle. I keep seeing Yaz falling, dead, at my feet over and over again. It's my fault the kid's dead.

Or is it?

Yeah... it is. I involved him in all this. When Kaitlyn suggested asking him for help, I should have said no. He's dead because of me.

So is Lily.

So is Tori.

So are nearly one billion people who died as a result of 4/17.

That's all on me. I should have done more. I should have...

"Fuck!"

I lash out and slam my fist into the tiles in front of me. I hold my hand there for a moment, absorbing the pain from the impact, glaring down at the wet floor of the cubicle.

An image of Kaitlyn flashes into my mind.

I liked her.

I didn't, y'know... *like* her, but I respected her and I admired her. And hell, the sex was great. I wonder if she hates me for all this. I wonder if she blames me for everything she's lost.

I smile to myself.

No, she wouldn't hate me.

What would she say to me if she were here now?

Yeah, I know...

She'd say I shouldn't feel guilty because all those things weren't my fault. She'd say I should stop punishing myself for simply trying to do the right thing.

I don't know... maybe she's right. I mean, she was a lot smarter than I am, and she was a damn good therapist. I still owe her three hundred bucks, thinking about it...

Well, I can't make any promises because I feel pretty shitty right now, but I'll try not to continue punishing myself over what's happened these last few days. I've been in a pretty impossible situation. Hell, I still am. But I reckon I've done the best I can with what I've had.

Now I just have to figure out how to adjust to my new life. I'm definitely not one to give up or back down from a fight, but even I can see I have no move to make here. I step out of line, Kaitlyn dies, and I die. I ask too many questions, we die. I do anything except what Horizon tells me to, we die.

I made my bed, and now I have to lie in it. I chose this. Well, actually, I didn't. Horizon gave me a choice, but he didn't give me the chance to answer. He made the decision for me, so regardless of what I would've done, this is my life now. I'm a killer. An assassin. *The* assassin. There's not really much difference between my life now and my life for the past God knows how many years.

Maybe it won't be so bad after all...

I shut off the shower and step out, wiping the excess water from my face and eyes. I reach out for the towel and—

It's not there.

I hear a giggle.

Huh?

I open my eyes and see two naked women standing in front of me, both holding towels.

I raise an eyebrow. "Hello..."

They smile and nod but don't reply. They step toward me and begin drying me by gently patting my skin.

Well... this is awkward.

I grab one of the towels from the woman on my left and take a step back, quickly wrapping it around my waist. "I'm... ah... I'm fine. Thanks."

They look disheartened but nod courteously and walk out of the room.

Jesus...

The bathroom is pretty big, considering it's an en suite. There's no door, just an archway made of marble leading into the wet room. There's a basin built into a marble surface a few feet from the shower, with a large mirror running the full width of the wall. I wipe away the condensation and stare at my reflection. I still need a shave, but I look a helluva lot better than I did ten minutes ago, which is something.

I walk back out into Horizon's main bedroom. A four-poster bed dominates the room, with closets lining the wall behind it. There's a balcony opposite, with the doors standing slightly open. I walk over to it and step outside. The warm breeze feels nice against my body. It's not as humid as in the city because I'm looking out over the ocean. It's almost refreshing—a feeling I've yet to experience in this climate.

I take a deep breath and step back inside. Fresh clothes are laid out across the bed. A plain, white short-sleeved shirt, dark blue jeans, and a pair of light brown shoes on the floor. I quickly get dressed, leaving two buttons of the shirt unfastened.

I walk out into the massive lounge. Horizon is sitting at a desk in the far-left corner, just to the left of the doors. He looks over as I enter. "Feeling better?"

I shrug. "Yeah, I guess. Thanks for the outfit."

He waves his hand dismissively. "The least I can do. Now, if you're feeling up to it, I have a job for you."

I make my way across the room. "You don't waste any time, do you?"

He stands and walks over to meet me. "Not when there isn't any to waste. I've had a new contract handed to me by the committee. One of the utmost importance."

I nod. "Fine. Who's the target?"

"I'll send the details to your phone in a moment. He is an influential and public figure who has recently ascended to a position of power we would rather he wasn't in. We consider his approach to things... problematic. He does not have a place in our future plans for this world."

I frown.

Wait a minute.

My mind's racing, putting the pieces together in my head.

Influential public figure?

New position of power?

...

...

...

Oh, no!

Ryan Schultz!

I close my eyes for a moment, processing the fresh batch of bad luck I've just been handed.

He's going to ask me to kill the new president!

"Getting to him won't be easy. I figure you're the perfect asset for the job, considering your talent for difficult assassinations."

Shit! He really is!

"Also, as the target is well protected, Mr. Pierce and his team will be on hand to offer any support you need."

I try to remain calm and stop panicking. I shake my head. "I see that prick again, I'm gonna kill him."

"Now, now, Adrian, we're all on the same side. The Order is more than willing to move forward in our relationship, and it would be in your best interest to do the same. I understand you might still harbor some... animosity toward Mr. Pierce, but you shouldn't. He was simply doing his job. Just like you will be. He's here to support you, should you need it, or to keep you in line, should I deem it necessary."

"Then why not just send him to do your contracts, if he's so good?"

Horizon smiles. "Mr. Pierce is a loyal employee and an excellent soldier. But he's not an assassin. He lacks the mindset... the finesse required to plan and execute a world-class hit. You do not."

I'm trying to figure a way around this, or a way I can at least warn him before I leave for Washington, but I'm drawing a blank. There's no way I'm going after the new president. Unlike his predecessor, Schultz doesn't deserve it. Sure, he can be an asshole sometimes... and yes, he did authorize my execution, but I don't hold it against him. He had no choice, and I bear no grudge for that.

Shit.

I need to calm down, accept this is happening, and try to figure out a way to actually pull this off. If I don't, I'm dead.

I roll my eyes. "Okay, quit stroking my ego. We both

know I'm only going along with this because I have no other choice, so let's get on with it."

He regards me for a moment, then nods. "Very well." He takes out his own phone and begins typing. "You will be sent details of your target's schedule. This information will be sufficient to carry out the mission. There will be no more details provided."

My phone beeps in my pocket. I roll my eyes as I reach for it. "Yeah, yeah... whatever."

"All I will say is, his recent actions are in direct conflict of our committee's vision for the future, and he must be eliminated. I'm sure I don't need to remind you of your mandatory compliance and what will happen, should you fail."

I type in the security code to unlock my phone. "No, you don't. I know what I have to do, all right? Just let me—"

My words catch in my throat as the file flashes up on my screen. My heart begins to hammer against my chest as the gravity of how much shit I'm in finally hits home.

I was wrong. My target isn't President Schultz...

...it's Josh.

THE END

Dear Reader,

Thank you for purchasing my book. I hope you enjoyed reading it as much as I enjoyed writing it!

If you did, it would mean a lot to me if you could spare thirty seconds to leave an honest review on your preferred online store. For independent authors like me, one review makes a world of difference.

If you want to get in touch, please visit my website, where you can contact me directly, either via e-mail or social media.

Until next time...

James P. Sumner

CLAIM YOUR FREE GIFT!

By subscribing to James P. Sumner's mailing list, you can get your hands on a free and exclusive reading companion, not available anywhere else.

It contains an extended preview of Book 1 in each thriller series from the author, as well as character bios, and official reading orders that will enhance your overall experience.

If you wish to claim your free gift, just visit the website below:

linktr.ee/jamespsumner

*You will receive infrequent, spam-free emails from the author, containing exclusive news about his books. You can unsubscribe at any time.

Made in the USA
Columbia, SC
15 August 2023

21693019R00212